RSVIP SERVICES, LLC

This book is a work of fiction. Names, characters, places and incidents either are products of the author's imagination or are used fictitiously. Any resemblance to actual events or locales or persons, living or dead is entirely coincidental.

Copyright © 2011 by Tanisha Janice Beecher

Synopsis

Lexi, has the type of body that attracts any man she wishes to have. Her sexy curves, topped with her Jamaican accent makes her the perfect man magnet. However, her own personal appearance means very little, if anything at all to her. As a matter of fact, it's her audacious and unrestrained personality that rocks the lives of nearly everyone with whom she comes in contact. The burden of a childhood secret, combined with her ambition to execute revenge, gradually transforms her into everyone's worst nightmare. Lexi contemplates her life to this point, from being a young Jamaican girl, growing up in the country sides of Manchester, Jamaica, to being a grown woman, living as an immigrant in the US.

Her best friend, JT, who is also Jamaican, suddenly finds his life spiraling out of control, after a strange woman appears out of the blue, and sets her gaze upon him. The riveting tale of his experiences will shock you, as twists are unveiled and the unexpected unfolds.

Readers, I dare you to fasten your seatbelts and prepare yourselves for an adventurous ride that will allow you to explore luscious Jamaica, and the rich culture and flavors of its people. The story is double the fun as it's blended with a hint of the American dream. You will be able to identify with the highs and lows of these dynamic characters, while being entertained beyond your expectations!

The CHRONICLES Of LEXI

What a Girl Would Do to Survive in America

Second Edition

Tanisha Beecher Bell

This book is dedicated to Rosemarie. I
appreciate your love, support, and the
wonderful mother that you are to me. You
are God's gift to me.
Love you,
Tanisha

ADVISORY

If you are a prude, please do not read any further. Close this book and walk away. Though this story may appeal to many types of readers, I do believe that it should be read with an open mind. Parental discretion is advised for readers under the age of eighteen.

If you are over eighteen years of age, and a prude, but still decide to go through with reading the following pages, then you have made the right decision.
Enjoy!

CHAPTER ONE
LEXI

I am an 'only child', and by right, I should be spoiled rotten. There is an unwritten law, somewhere out there in limbo, that governs the well-being of children who grow up being the only child for their parents. In fact, that law states that children who grow up without siblings are supposed to be spoiled rotten by their parents, and are entitled to get whatever they want, whenever, however possible, and if not, the parents of these children should be punished. Puleez! That shit ain't true! If it was, I guess my peeps never got the freaking memo. As a matter of fact, my daddy should be listed as one of the greatest magicians that ever walked this planet. He pulled the disappearing act on my mother and me when I was barely eight years old. What real man would just up and leave his woman and young child to fend for themselves? That punk ran off with some old ass, sugar momma, but now I hope he's paying the price - both of them with their old, shriveled up asses. People may think I'm angry, but I don't give a rat's tail about what people think. All I know is that my father had better not let me catch him wandering around somewhere by himself.

Over the years, I'd grown to love and trust my mother, at least until she'd taken up with a Rastaman who called himself, Everhard. My mother threw me out of the house when I was only fifteen years old, because of this lock-wearing, pig. She had to throw me out of the house because Everhard raped me. Now I know what you're asking yourself. You want to know why my mother threw me out of the house and continued to live with that pedophile. That's exactly why I mentioned earlier, that I'd grown to love and trust mother, up until then. My mother threw me out of the house for lying on her boyfriend, and hating on her happiness. So my grandparents took me in with open arms. Since then, I have been planning on executing my revenge against the bastard who stole my innocence. And I will, at least before these pages are through. I will change his name from Everhard to So-soft, and that right there is real talk.

Months after living with my grandparents, I began receiving letters from my sperm-donor. My mother had somehow informed him that I was living with my grandparents, and he was writing me to find out why. As to why my father had chosen now, out of all times to be concerned about me, I haven't a clue. All I know is, he was eight years too late. As a matter of fact, his last letter informed me that he had now relocated to the US, and married the old heifer for whom he'd left my mother and me. Good for them both. They suited each other. Like I gave a rat's ass that he was living in America. All these certified letters from him, all of a sudden, with no money enclosed, and no offer for me to come and live with him in America. Worthless animal!

Like I said, my Father better not let me catch him on the streets somewhere.

A year after I moved in with my grandparents,

Uncle Desmond visited us with good news. My US visa would soon be ready, and I'd be able to migrate to the States and live there with him and his wife. That was good news indeed. I'd always loved Uncle Desmond. He'd been my favorite uncle since I knew myself. Matter of fact, Uncle Desmond assured Grandma and Grandpops that he and his wife would take very good care of me, and that they shouldn't worry. "Don't worry, mon. Me and my wife will take very good care of Lexi," he told us. And we all believed him. After all, he was Uncle Desmond! And so my story began.

"Lexi, if I knew you were this rotten, I would have left you in Jamaica to suffer!"

Those were the nasty words of Uncle Desmond, five months after he'd filed for me to come and live with him in the States. What made those words even nastier was the fact that they were meant for me, his precious niece, whom he'd promised to take care of. He'd even started calling me Lexi. He used to, so fondly, call me Princess. I do not believe I'd done anything to deserve my Uncle's constant verbal attacks. However, it seemed as if America had its way of changing people. And it had done a number on my favorite uncle, turning him into something or someone that was alien to me. He'd now become a mad man. This wasn't the uncle whom I'd known as a kid growing up. This could never be the uncle who, five months prior, had promised my grandparents that he'd take very good care of me. Standing before me, was a stranger - a mad man who had a likeness to my uncle; who even claimed to be my uncle, but actually wasn't. The person who stood before me was a monster.

"Get out of my way," I instructed him, as I pushed past him to get to my room. He stood towering over me, barring the way with his body, as if to intimidate me into doing his will. So I pushed him away and stormed towards my bedroom. I could hear his heavy footsteps tramping closely behind, so I purposefully stepped inside of my bedroom and slammed the door shut.

"So you slammed the door in my face?" he asked in his heaviest Jamaican accent. I meant to ask him if he really needed the clarity, but I immediately dismissed the thought. I knew better than to waste time arguing with him. It wouldn't do any good, and it wouldn't be moral. I was taught better than that by my grandparents.

My grandparents always taught me to respect those who were my elders, and to always honor my parents.

"Honor your parents so your days may be long on this earth…", my grandmother would quote from the Bible. But somehow, she'd forgotten the verse that followed:

"Parents, provoke not your children to wrath," which is exactly what my mother and father had done.

They had both provoked me to wrath, and I no longer saw them as parents. I guess Grandma had forgotten that I did not have any parents. I was appalled to think that my mother would call me an ungrateful liar. To even fathom how she could think I was jealous of her relationship with Everhard was beyond me.

She'd called me a disgraceful pickney, meaning 'child', in Jamaican Patois, and forced me to live with my Gramps. It's a good thing she'd done that though, because if she hadn't, I would have killed Everhard. So far, I'd been successful in keeping the step-dad thing out of the way because I knew that one day he would leave my mother, and then I could have his ass kicked decently. I often fantasized about killing

him, but I would rather see him suffer, than die.
I have a lot of bitterness in my heart. Bitterness
against my mother's weakness and bitterness
against an animal like the aforementioned rapist.

"Did you hear me, Lexi?" my crazy uncle
shouted outside my bedroom door.

"The next time you get paid, I need you to put
that paycheck on the dining table. If not, I'll be
forced to drive you out of this house!"

All this shit, because he'd found out I'd gotten
my first paycheck, and had sent half of the
money to my grandparents back home in
Jamaica. I'd only been working in Florida for two
weeks, and this was my first paycheck. I got up
from my cheap bed, shocked at the crap that
spewed from my uncle's lips. I wished there was
a toilet on his face so I could flush it.

I slowly opened the door and snapped back,
"Repeat that!"

"I said, Miss Rotten, put your paycheck on the
table the next time you get paid."

"Why would I do that?"

"So that when it's cashed, I can give you how
much I think is suitable for you to get."

"Did you help me work for it?"

"Say what?" he asked, shocked. "Are you

back-answering me?"

"Uncle, I'm simply stating the obvious here. You weren't at Alejandro's Farmer's Market, helping me sell goods. So why should I give you my money? Will you give me yours?"

"Say what?" he repeated.

"I'm asking you if you will give me your paycheck when I give you mine. Are we exchanging?"

"You see why I should have left your little ass in Jamaica?"

"No. I don't see why, Desmond."

So my Uncle and I made a bet. His bet was that in two weeks, when I got paid again, I'd have to give him my paycheck. My bet was that, I wasn't gonna do that shit.

Two weeks later, I was on a bus going to the Pembroke Lakes Mall, in Pembroke Pines. I needed to do some shopping, right after I sent half of the pay I'd just received, to my grandparents. Furthermore, there was this "thing" I needed to get at the mall. Not sure how handy it would be in the future, but I knew I needed it, just in case.

As I treaded outside of the money transfer facility, I reflected on how brutally unreasonable Uncle Desmond had been. His deal was quite unacceptable. I'd only been in America for five and a half months and he was already threatening to throw me out of the house. He'd even broken his promise to take me shopping and support me throughout my college career. I never saw the car he'd promised to buy for me once I got to the U.S. His promises to me while I was in Jamaica were all lies to get me to migrate to live with him, so he could extort money from me. Extortion is a pretty strong word, but call a spade a spade.

When I arrived home that night, Uncle Desmond greeted me at the door. Who the hell did he think he was, trying to step to me? He obviously didn't know me very well.

"I was just stepping out, Lexi," he said in his deep Jamaican accent.

"Ok," I replied nonchalantly as I walked past him.

"Do you have the thing?" he questioned, still standing there looking dumb.

"What thing?" I asked him without altering my steps towards my bedroom.

"It seems as if you think I'm playing games with you," his tone became cold.

"I don't know what you're talking about," I said, entered my bedroom, and slammed my door shut. What the hell did this man want from me? Was he possessed by the devil? He was acting as if he did me a favor by getting me a green card and now I was supposed to wash his feet in return for doing his rightful duty as a close relative. He had neglected me since my arrival at his home. But how could I blame him when my own father had done the same?

"Lexi, I expect to see that paycheck on the living room table by tomorrow morning. If it's not there, I'll need you to leave my house immediately!"

I heard him stomping away. Shortly after, the door to the living room slammed shut, indicating his departure. He'd left. Thank God! There was finally silence in the house. I had won the bet.

About an hour later my disturbed, tormented uncle returned. Didn't he give me until morning? He just had to come back to the house to start some more shit with me. My door was still locked. My TV was turned down low, and I heard every nasty word he uttered.

"Lexi, first of all let me say this. You cannot stay here..."

For me, that was the icing on the cake. I

didn't need to listen to anymore of this nonsense. I got up and grabbed the only suitcase I owned. I heard him outside my door, still bitching about how I was just like my mother, and that I was a disappointment to him. He also mentioned some things along the line of wanting me to leave his house before he had to call the police on me. So I packed my shit and left. As I made my exit, he stood at the door with eyes and mouth wide open in shock, but I no longer cared. I had my mind made up, even though I had no idea where I was headed.

At that point, it was me against the world. I stopped at a bus stop to think for a minute. I prayed for guidance, and braced myself to thug it out.

CHAPTER 2
LEXI

Hours had gone by as I just sat at the bus stop blinded by rage and frustration. Buses had come and gone. If there had been anyone else at that bus stop with me that night, I wouldn't have noticed. I didn't see them. My mind was miles and miles away.

Even though I didn't know what the exact time was, I figured it had to have been very late. I did the rough work in my head, trying to calculate what time it was, starting from when I had left work that day. My boss handed me my check at 4:30 pm that evening after my shift ended. I left work and decided to take the bus directly to the mall where I cashed my check, and shopped for a few things. When I arrived home it was 7:40 pm. I knew because I remembered checking the time. I had to check the time because my uncle had greeted me at the door as if he was awaiting my arrival, and I wondered how long he had been waiting. He'd begun pestering me right away and then he had left shortly thereafter. When he returned and resumed his pestering, I checked the time again and wondered why the hell he was back so soon. It was 8:55 pm. It didn't take me very long to pack the few things I owned into the only suitcase that I had. So, when I left the house that night, it was about 9:20 pm.

Hours had passed since I'd been at the bus stop - at least three hours. Therefore, it was safe to assume that the time was a little after midnight. I began to observe that the flow of traffic had dwindled. It felt so damn lonely just sitting there all by myself, not knowing where to turn or what move to make next. The last bus had already left and that's when I definitely knew for sure my ass was SOL. For a moment I thought about checking into a Women's Social Care Center, but dismissed the idea with swiftness, since it just didn't appeal to me. Hell, nothing had appealed to me -- except for revenge. I opened my pocket book and retrieved a small package I had carefully tucked away. I stared at the envelope which contained the last letter I'd received from my father. There was a return address, but it was a PO Box address. I shook my head in absolute disgust. I placed the envelope back into my bag, stood up and began pacing without realizing I was potentially drawing unnecessary attention to myself. The moment I thought about it, someone honked his car horn at me. After that car had passed, I watched as another car slowed down. A few Hispanic men shouted,

"Muchacha, tu eres muy sexi!"

If I had a gun I would have certainly used it, but I didn't, so I sat my ass back down. How the hell had things gotten this far? Where the hell did I go wrong in my life? I watched again as a white Escalade made a u-turn. I had an eerie feeling that I was the reason behind that turn. I had a gutsy feeling, that whoever was driving that Escalade had seen me standing there by myself as he drove by, and was now on his way to join me. I was furious. Over the years, out of all the emotions I had experienced, anger was the one I was most familiar with, and it seemed as if my anger had begun to intensify with each passing day. I sat there motionless, as the huge, white vehicle approached me.

The vehicle veered into the lane which was nearest the bus stop. As it got closer, I noticed that its windows were so darkly tinted, it was frightful. I couldn't see who was behind the wheel. My adrenaline kicked in and I held my purse closer to me. It contained my butcher knife which, I had no idea, I would probably end up using so soon. I remained motionless, but my mind was prepared. I was ready for anything, and I meant it. The vehicle pulled up right in front of me and stopped. The windows were still up, and I still couldn't see who was driving. Instead of fear, I felt disgust. I was disgusted at both my parents, especially my greedy-ass sperm-donor-wanna-be-father. I didn't care about the impending danger.

Whoever was in that car could go jump off a bridge, or even kiss my ass for all I cared. I just knew that if and when I had a child, I would do for her what my parents didn't do for me. I would never put her out on the streets in the middle of the night or at all. Neither would I allow any man to put his filthy hands on her. I regretted having the parents I had, but you can't choose your parents. Such a pity! I continued to stare at the windows of that SUV, wondering who could be behind the wheel. As much as I focused I still couldn't see inside, and no one had gotten out of the vehicle.

My chest heaved up and down as my breathing intensified. Then slowly all the windows facing me slowly opened, revealing the stunning faces of three light skin 'brothas'. They all had dreads. For some unknown reason, I was drawn to them first. There was something peculiar about them; I couldn't stop myself from staring at their faces. They smiled at me, and thoughts of my butcher knife disappeared instantaneously.

"What's up beautiful?" a baritone voice resonated from the front of the car.

I shifted my focus towards the driver's seat and that's when I saw the fourth occupant. His face was strikingly handsome; untamed muscles protruded through a dark colored silk shirt, and the ray from a street-light kissed his rich, mocha skin.

Even though I was seated and he still hadn't gotten out of the car, I could easily tell that he was great in bed— if you know what I mean. Either I had died and gone to heaven, or had fallen asleep at the bus stop and was dreaming. When I didn't reply, one of the dreadlocked guys in the back said, "Aren't you scared?" The other two busted out laughing.
Still, I did not respond.

"Whatchu doing at the bus stop this time a night?" another one of them questioned, while the other two laughed and continued to stare at me. I remained silent and purposefully appeared emotionless as I observed how their idiocy defied their good looks. I stared into deep, green eyes. Green eyes stared back at me. I shifted my focus back to the front of the vehicle to gaze upon the mocha glory. Though they remained seated in the car, even the blind could see that they were all very gorgeous.

"What's up shorty?" the dark chocolate, brotha asked me.

"Do I look short to you?" I asked. My mind suddenly had no room for thoughts.

"Aww shit!" another instigated,

"Vaughnn, I think you should be scared of this chick!" The others started laughing again.

"He is scared," someone else chimed in, "and she's as fearless as a mofo!"

Their looks were breath-taking. I didn't know what the hell was going on, but I sure was about to find out. Something about these men kept pulling me in. I felt so drawn to them. I kept thinking that they were angels. Maybe my head was all screwed up from all the mess I had been going through, and none of this was real. I really didn't know what to think.

I stared at the mocha brother, the eye candy who sat behind the steering wheel. The three men in the back had referred to him as Vaughnn. I really like that name.

"Stand up so Vaughnn can see if you're short," one of the idiots in the back goofed. I stood boldly and shrugged. They all busted out laughing, "Naw, you definitely ain't short."

I was tempted to smile but I didn't. I'd now gotten myself into some serious shit. I knew if these men wanted to hurt me they could have easily done so in a heartbeat. I observed as they enjoyed themselves at my expense. I suddenly realized what was so peculiar about the three passengers sitting in the backseat. They were triplets. I knew I still needed to be cautious. Vaughnn remained calm and collected, while he smiled at me with perfect teeth. It was obvious these men took proper care of themselves.

"Spin around!" one of them continued to joke, while the others laughed.

"All of you just shut up," Vaughnn demanded, cutting them off.

"So now you mouthing off at us because of a chick?" they continued to goof.

"So, where are you headed?" he asked me, ignoring them. His expression was cool and easy, letting me know he was unfazed by their antics. Though they joked around like teenagers, their facial features indicated otherwise. I could tell that they were possibly in their early thirties.

"I'm headed the same place you are," was the best I could come up with. If this was going to cost me more than I could afford, I was ready and willing to go bankrupt. The risk was worth taking.

"Can we go together?" Mocha offered.

"Can you help me with my suitcase?" I smirked.

CHAPTER THREE
LEXI

"What about our stop?" one of the triplets asked Vaughnn. They'd stopped joking around all of a sudden, and smiles were now replaced by apprehension.

"So, you want me to abandon a damsel in distress?" Vaughnn asked coolly.

"Naw, Baldy," he defended, "I'm just saying that we should come back for her."

"And leave her here?"

"We'll come back for her."

Vaughnn thought for a moment then replied, "I think that makes sense. You're not as dumb as you look." He got out of his car and walked over to where I was standing, while his three friends in the back muttered curses amidst chuckles at Vaughnn's response. He ignored them and extended an arm towards me, "My name is Vaughnn," He smiled at me again exposing neon white teeth.

"I'm Lexi." I shook his hand. "Nice to meet you," I said, and I meant it.

It was very nice to have met Vaughnn. He was the highlight of my night. Matter-of-fact, he was the highlight of my entire life. Once he had gotten out of the car, I was able to admire every inch of his God given beauty. His body was a masterpiece, chiseled to perfection. He was fine from head to toe. They called him, Baldy as he had shaved his head. However, it went well with his good looks and charm.

"Listen, Beautiful Lexi," he said, still holding my hand in the palm of his, "I have some business to take care of less than a mile away. It'll only take a few minutes," he paused and looked me dead in the eyes.

"I'm listening," I said, subtly encouraging him to get to the point.

"It would be more appropriate for us to come back for you," he paused again and looked around, then spoke again, "If I had more time, I'd drop you off somewhere safer."

"No problem," I replied, acting as if it was all good; pretending that things were okay when they clearly weren't; giving the impression that it was normal to be stranded at a bus stop after midnight with a suitcase and nowhere to go, and accepting a promise from a random stranger who said that he'd return to help me. Vaughnn let go of my hand and returned to his vehicle.

"See you soon, Lexi," the triplets teased. "Can't wait to see you again- right Vaughnn?"

My lips parted a little, giving way to a minute smile. The car windows rolled back up, and the car drove away into the distance. I sat back down and longed for the emptiness in my heart to go away. I hoped that Vaughnn would keep his word and return for me. For all I knew he could be a serial killer, but I had my mind made up. I was desperate, and desperate situations required desperate measures.

It had to have been after 1 am. My butt began to burn from sitting down so long. My stomach growled.   I felt tired, sleepy, hungry and homeless. I felt like a loser. My parents had truly screwed me up. I wasn't about to have a pity party though. I wasn't about to allow myself to be swallowed by grief. I thought that if I'd survived the night I'd be a day closer to making a woman of myself. When that was done, I'd have to personally teach that rapist a lesson - the man whom I believed deserved to die for taking my innocence by force. My thoughts of hurting him had always motivated me to never give up. If I were to give up, then he would have won. I needed to stay focused.

As for my parents, I concluded I had no parents. They had failed miserably at parenthood, and were therefore officially disowned and renounced by me, Lexi Jones. My stomach suddenly stopped growling. My hunger was replaced by anger. I should have been fearful sitting there by myself at a bus stop, but I wasn't. I looked around and observed that traffic had substantially decreased which made being out on the streets that late at night, even more dangerous.

I watched as a bright purple Cadillac on 22's slowly rolled by. Like the Escalade, its windows were tinted and I knew whoever was behind the wheel had spotted me. Once again, my adrenaline kicked in and I held my purse real tight. The driver got into the turn lane and made a u-turn. It was the same u-turn previously made by Vaughnn. Deep inside, I knew that the purple machine was headed in my direction. What on earth did these people want from me? Why couldn't everyone just leave me alone?

I watched as the car completed its u-turn onto the other side of the street and proceeded to the next light, to make a second u-turn to get back on the side of the street on which I sat. I quickly slid out of my sneakers, removed my socks from my feet and used them to cover my hands, like mittens. I slid my sockless feet back into my shoes, and then retrieved my butcher knife from my pocket-book and tucked it inside of my belt, under my right arm. Still moving swiftly, I opened up my suitcase and placed my pocket-book inside and zipped it back up. I got back up, and sat down just in time to see the vehicle pull up in front of me.

I was ready for war. I was only nineteen years old and was ready to kill a man if necessary, in order to protect my womanhood. The windows were still up. The door on the driver's side flew open and a tall, hideous man got out. He was young - older than me, but still young. His hair was uncombed and disheveled with the tail of a comb sticking out of it. He walked quickly towards me, smiling with gold teeth as if he knew me. His pants hung too far below his butt and his red Jordan sneakers were unlaced.

"What up sexy?" he asked still smiling at me.

I stood up without responding to him. He stepped closer towards me as if he knew me. I was now beyond irritated. I stepped back and watched as three other men got out of the back of the car. They all looked the same, and reeked of weed. Before long, these hoodlums had me surrounded. I quickly glanced up and down the streets. There were no cars in sight, and no one around.

"Dayumm! Shawty, yo ass is tight!" said the first hoodlum.

"Yeah, baby got some good tits too," said another.

"Dayumm, shawty, what else you got that's good?" said yet another.

"Yeah, I bet you got some good pussy!" said the first as he stepped up to me and grabbed onto my breasts. That's when I knew they all had to be out of their fucking minds.

"You all need to just back off," I said politely. They laughed.

"Ma', I like yo accent, where you from?" questioned the first hoodlum who continued to squeeze my breasts.

"Must be the Bahamas or some shit," replied the other who was behind me grabbing my butt.

"I'm gonna ask you one last time to back the fuck up!" I was outraged and my adrenaline was pumping.

"Naw, you back da fuck up!" said the first hoodlum who continued to squeeze my breasts as if I was his bitch.

He began to push me towards the back of the bus stop, while the others surrounded me and stole touches. I thought back to when my step daddy busted into my bedroom one night while Mom was still at work. There I was in the same situation, where hoodlums, out of nowhere, had stepped to me and had already begun to violate me.

"You heard me, sexy? Drop those pants and back it up for big daddy!" said the first hoodlum, finally letting go of my breasts and beginning to rip my pants off. I was about to be raped by four hoodlums, at a bus stop on the side of the street, where there was no one to come to my rescue.

While they pulled my pants down, one of them said, "Shit, is it da weed, or does she have socks on her hands?" The others began to laugh, showing off their gold teeth. Their armpits stank. I was horrified at the thought of them entering my body, one by one, viciously pounding, bareback. Someone began to rip my shirt off.

"Shit," someone else murmured, "She sexy as a mofo-"

"Let's see watchu got hidin' under those ugly ass jeans," said the one who had grabbed my breasts, obviously the leader of the pack. He proceeded to pull my pants down. "I'm gonna show you who's king of-" His eyes bulged as he stared at me then at the knife that had invaded his chest. I pulled it out quickly and he fell to the ground.

"Oh shit!" the others shouted, "she stabbed him!"

I clenched the knife and watched them scatter at first, overwhelmed with shock and confusion.

"Bitch, you stabbed him!" one of them shouted, his eyes now blood red from anger, or it could have been the weed they'd all been smoking. I positioned myself for more war, legs apart, stance appropriate. I stole a glance and saw a white vehicle in the distance heading towards us. I looked at the man that was lying on the ground in front of me, blood gushing out of him.

"Bitch!" his friends were yelling,
"Someone call the cops on this bitch!"
"Can't do that bro!" another replied.

"Why not?"

"There's still stuff in the car man!"

I stole another glance and saw that the white vehicle was similar to that which I'd been looking forward to seeing.

"Let's fuck this bitch up!" one of the hoodlums said, as they all got ready to pounce on me. The Escalade suddenly sped across four lanes of traffic, and over the median strip. Someone fired a gunshot and the hoodlums sprang into the Cadillac and drove away. Vaughnn and the others jumped out of the car and rushed towards me. I stared hysterically at the bloody body on the ground. Vaughnn quickly lifted me into the car, while his brothers grabbed my suitcase. I heard Vaughnn tell them to dial 911.

"Use this phone!" he ordered. The call was made and everyone jumped into the car. Vaughnn sped down the street and around the corner into a secluded parking lot. We all watched from a distance as the ambulance arrived several minutes later, with a fleet of police cars.

"How you feelin', lil' mama?" one of the triplets asked as he positioned his legs for me to lay my head in his lap. I was in the backseat with him and his brother. The third brother was in the front passenger seat while Vaughnn was behind the wheel. I didn't reply to the question I was asked. I mean, what the hell had he expected me to say to him? My entire body had gone completely numb at the thought of the crime I had just committed. I had attempted to murder a man by stabbing him and leaving him there at the crime scene. So many different thoughts flooded my mind. I had no idea that I'd actually ended up using the knife, at least not so soon. As a matter of fact, I'd bought it only hours prior to actually using it. It's a good thing I had bought it, too. I figured it would've been wise to carry it around on me for protection, just in case I ever needed it. My work schedule had gotten a bit hectic and I was required to work late-night shifts some nights.

My precious Uncle Desmond had made it his duty to let me know, he would no longer pick me up from work, not even on those nights when I had to work late. Therefore, I was out on the streets late at night trying to get my ass home.

Approximately one week after he'd told me that, I was on my way to the bus stop to catch the last bus home late one night, when I noticed that I was being followed. The driver of an old yellow car drove slowly along the other side of the street, boldly watching my movements through his car window. The creep was skillful too. I watched him as he watched me without looking at the road ahead of him while he drove. He saw me looking at him, but he didn't seem to care. Shit, you'd think I held some kind of special fucking powers that attracted all the crazy ass people that roamed planet Earth. It's as if I was a walking magnet for freaks!

Anyway, I continued towards my destination, the bus stop. I wasn't about to let that sucker get me so freaked out that I'd miss my bus. In fact, that might have been what he'd wanted. That possibly could have been the reason he'd made himself visible to me. I got to the bus stop and observed that only a handful of people were present. No-one seemed to have even noticed what was up. I also noticed that the creep had parked his car along the street-side, which was directly facing the bus stop where I stood.

My bus arrived shortly thereafter. I paid my bus fare and requested the driver to drop me off at the nearest police station. I also asked him to wait until I was safely inside of the building before driving away. The kind fellow did exactly that.

That night, I was escorted home by a very pleasant police officer. I made it a priority to purchase a knife for protection, and that's exactly what I had done. My knife was the "thing" I needed to purchase that evening when I went shopping at the mall.

He was caressing my face - an act I assumed was intended to soothe me. It didn't. Nevertheless, I appreciated it. My head was still resting on his lap and I thought about the softness of his touch. He possibly hadn't lifted even a straw a day in his life. He was using one hand to caress my cheek, and the other to hold my head in place.

I read the name that was tattooed on his arm. Stewart. His name was Stewart. I believed his brothers also had matching tattoos of their names. An Idea I considered to be very clever since it would help to distinguish among the identical trio.

Silence overwhelmed me. Someone once said that silence is golden, but there was nothing golden about this particular silence. Besides, the battle inside my head was deafening.

I pulled up closer to Stewart in order to make myself more comfortable. I felt my booty rub against the cold leather seat. It was then that I'd realized I was naked. Vaughnn and the triplets had had me strip down and out of my bloody clothes. I had sat inside the car and watched them as they set every piece of garment, including my socks, afire.

The irony was that I was sitting almost completely naked in only my panty and bra, nestled among four good looking brothas, after barely escaping the horrid violation of four others. The car was moving. That much I knew, however, I couldn't remember when exactly Vaughnn had left the parking lot from which we watched the ambulance carry my victim away.

CHAPTER FOUR
LEXI

After Vaughnn merged onto I-75, heading south towards Pines Blvd, I lost track of our route. I couldn't tell where we were headed since I had my eyes closed, and head resting on Stewart's lap. Stewart caressed my cheeks and stroke my hair. Though his action had required very little effort, I considered it a big deal. Never before had a man ever touched me, the way in which Stewart touched me, without sex being his ultimate motivation. Matter of fact, I'd never trusted anyone enough to allow them to touch me like that, right off the bat, especially if he was a complete stranger. Never in my life had I met a group of men as friendly as these four brothas and as affectionate as Stewart. Under different circumstances, I would have surely mistaken Stewart's warmth for something else. Vaughnn let the car windows down slightly and gusts of cool air suddenly entered the car and rapidly penetrated our pores, alleviating our tension somewhat. Besides the whizzing of the night wind against the window tips, and the loud roaring of the car which accelerated at an illegal speed of over eighty miles per hour on the highway, the silence within the car lingered.

The fresh air that had now infiltrated the vehicle, filtering out unwanted tension, was short-lived. Instead, the silence that reigned, thickened, clogging the air once more with its nothingness causing everyone's uneasiness to linger and proliferate. Vaughnn had apparently taken a sharp exit off the highway and had merged onto the off ramp that led to the main street.

I could easily tell by the car's decrease in momentum. Stewart continued to caress my hair while his brother, Stephin, sat quietly next to us.

A few minutes later the car came to a stop in front of a large house, nestled beautifully in front of a babbling brook. Vaughnn quickly opened up the door on his side of the vehicle and slid out. Stewart's brother, Steffaun, who sat in the front of the car followed suit. The door on my side swung open less than a few seconds later, as Vaughnn attempted to take me back from Stewart.

"Wait a minute, man!" Stewart protested.

"What?" Vaughnn paused for a moment, seemingly puzzled by Stewart's objection.

"Remember she's naked, man," Stewart reasoned, "one of ya'll should bring her a blanket so she can wrap herself up."

"Good lookin' out," Vaughnn said as Stewart took a step back and beckoned for one of his brothers, Stephin or Steffaun, to fetch a blanket. Steffaun fetched the blanket, while the quiet brother, Stephin paced back and forth outside, uneasily, wearing a hole into the ground.

Upon our arrival at where I believed was Vaughnn's superb six bedroom abode, one of the triplets, either Stephin or Steffaun ran and disappeared into the amazing house that now stood before us. The house overlooked a beautiful lake. I remained seated in the car, still naked and slightly trembling. Stewart was still sitting next to me while Vaughnn stood guarding the door. As quickly as he had vanished into the building, he had reappeared with a fleece robe, which he handed to Vaughnn. I read the inscription on his arm: Steffaun. My hypothesis was correct. They all had matching tattoos, which meant the quiet brotha who was now pacing the yard, wearing a hole into the ground had to have been Stephin, who must have also had his name tattooed on his arm, just like his two siblings. We were all silent.

Vaughnn accepted the robe then proceeded to clothe me with the snug piece of garment. His attempts failed as he was in an awkward position, so Stewart, who had been more than attentive to me throughout the entire journey, quickly jumped in and finished the job, by actually helping me into the robe.

Vaughnn had then lifted me out of the car and carried me into his house. I'd only just begun to absorb the splendor of this luxurious dwelling when my concentration was broken by the two women who were sitting in the corner of the living room by the bar. They were both very stunning. It's surprising how I hadn't noticed them the moment we'd walked in. They were both voluptuous and possessed Latin features. One of them had her hair up in a ponytail, and wore tight blue jeans, with a blue blouse that showed off her flat abdomen and full breasts. The other had her hair out which flowed over her shoulders and onto the chair on which she sat. She was rocking a short, tight, skimpy, red dress, which left nothing to the imagination. She reminded me of a video ho, or a stripper. She stared at me with dark eyes and watched as Vaughnn gently released me from his muscular arms. Her attention then moved to Vaughnn and she remained fixated on him. The other woman was a little more pleasant.

"Hola, hombres atractivos! I meest you so mosh," she expressed in a heavy, overly dramatic accent. The triplets rushed over to the women and hugged them.

"Hi, Lydia." They took turns hugging the woman wearing the jeans. She showered them all with loud kisses, as she spoke fluently to them in Spanish. I was almost certain that the triplets did not understand her words, but they didn't seem to mind. When they finished greeting her, they stepped over to the stripper bitch to repeat their affectionate greetings. She didn't seem to care because she was still stuck on Vaughnn. As a matter of fact, from the looks on her face, she had seemed livid.

"What's up, Vaughnn?" she finally broke her silence.

"So, it's like that?" Steffaun responded, while his brother, Stephin, smiled as he shrugged.

"So it's like what?" the video ho said, breaking her gaze and turning her head to face the triplets.

"So, we all walked through the door and tried to show you some love, and you ignored us for Vaughnn?" Stephin quizzed jokingly. It was the first time I'd heard him speak since the little incident we'd had at the bus stop. He'd been so quiet all night. He was the quiet one of the bunch.

"Why, are you jealous that Vaughnn is more of a man than both of you put together?" she challenged with a smirk on her face, her English much more refined than that of her colleague.

"Naw, man," Steffaun butted in, "we ain't jealous of the love you got for that loser. Right Stephin?" he nudged his brother into playing along.

"Right," Stephin responded playfully without looking over at Vaughnn.
They both bent down simultaneously, ignoring Vaughnn as they hugged and showered kisses on the rude, stripper-looking woman in the red dress. After their greeting, she redirected her focus to Vaughnn. I then observed that Stewart, who had been so attentive and affectionate towards me all night, no longer paid me any

attention. As a matter of fact, though he hadn't bothered to hug or kiss the rude woman who scowled at Vaughnn and me,   I watched as he gazed at her, while she remained fixated on Vaughnn. What on earth was going on? Why was Stewart so into her? And why was she glaring at Vaughnn? Just when I began to think that this mess was not what I really needed at this point, Vaughnn spoke up.

"Stewart," he grimaced as he broke his buddy out of a trance, "I need you to help out with Lexi."   His tone was more of an order than a request.

"Sure thing," Stewart replied obediently and without hesitation.   His demeanor quickly changed from spaced-out-love-struck-zombie-like, to human-like. Was I the only one noticing what was going on? Stewart looked over at me and smiled. It was a gentle smile that suggested he was about to resume the lovable role he'd been playing all night, where I was concerned, before he had gotten distracted by the rude woman in the red dress. I didn't smile back at him. I couldn't; however, his gesture calmed me. He walked briskly across the room to where Vaughnn and I were still standing. Vaughnn led him a few feet away and whispered to him. Stewart then walked over to me and took my hand.

"It's all good, lil' mama," he said soothingly as I followed behind him, "We all gotchyo back." I felt the rude woman's eyes pierce through my back as Stewart lead me up a couple flights of stairs. "You're in good hands now," he continued, "And you should be glad that Vaughnn likes you," he concluded.

"I hope he likes her enough to buy her a robe of her own," one of the women remarked. Her English was refined so I knew it had to be the ho. This bitch was beginning to piss me off! She was starting to get on my last nerve and was only two seconds away from getting bitch slapped. I ripped my hand away from Stewart's soft palm, and quickly flew down the stairs. Stewart also flew down the stairs in pursuit of me.

"You're a heartless woman," I heard Vaughnn say to her.

Before he could utter another word, I said calmly, "Would you please repeat what you just said?"

"Bitch, please go on upstairs and don't try to start shit you can't finish," she warned. Hadn't I been through enough for one night? Wasn't stabbing one person enough for one night? It had to have been close to 3 am - I felt spent. Before I could respond, Stewart embraced me.

"Shhh!" he hushed, "You have been through enough for one night. Let me take you upstairs."

"No," I insisted, "I think she's right," I glanced over at her and watched her lips curve into a wicked smile. I wanted to wipe that smirk off of her face.

"Lexi," Vaughnn stepped towards me, "let me handle this," He raised an eyebrow as he spoke. I had no choice but to obey him. I mean, it was 3 am in the morning and I was rescued by a man who'd not only kept his word about coming back for me, but also got rid of the evidence of my malicious murder attempt. On top of that, his friends were showing me the kind of hospitality I'd never dreamt existed.

"You know, you're right," I spoke carefully and cleverly, "I should let you take care of this."

"What were you gonna do, huh?" she asked dryly while her friend beckoned for her to cut out the nonsense.

I calmly asked Stewart to release me. "It's ok, she's right," I said sincerely hoping he'd believe me. He let me go and I walked over to Vaughnn.

"You know, Vaughnn," I watched as he studied me attentively, "your friend here is right," I smiled for the first time in days, not because I was happy, but because I felt a little bit victorious. I'd purposefully used the word 'friend' by accident.

"Bitch, who you calling his friend?!" she yelled from across the room. My mission was accomplished. I had successfully wiped the smirk off that so-called stunning face, without laying a finger on her.

I turned around to face Vaughnn and continued, "Vaughnn, you know what I mean. She has a right to be hostile towards me," I searched his face for an expression. I saw nothing.

"No," he responded, "and I apologize to you on behalf of all of us."

"Well," I pushed knowing what I'd planned to do, "just know that I understand that she has her right. Anyway, what are your intentions with me for tonight?"

"Trust," he assured, "my intentions are all good."

That response was enough for me.

Furthermore, he'd said it loud enough for everyone in the room to hear.

"Well," I reasoned, as I walked across the room
towards the rude woman in the red dress, "I won't be needin' this anymore," I undid the robe and pulled it off of my body. Once again I stood naked before a room full of strangers which seemed to have been one of my callings for the night. I knew I wasn't bad-looking; in fact, many had complimented me on my banging body, especially at times when I'd go for swims in the alluring beaches of Jamaica. For once, I thought my good looks had come in handy. I folded the robe neatly and placed it in an empty chair. I saw the blood drain from her face as she looked over my shoulders, clearly watching Vaughnn as he admired my beauty. I then turned around to watch as the men stared at me, mesmerized. Everyone was speechless.   As worn, worried and frustrated as I was, I found the strength to march up those stairs confidently, swinging my ass and bouncing my titties for dramatic effect. I knew my behavior was unexpected and inappropriate, but I'd enjoyed every moment of it. I'd left everyone behind dumbfounded.

CHAPTER FIVE
ANONYMOUS

You can call me anonymous. My name and background is nobody's business. Whenever people refer to me as sexy Boricua, I often get rather offended. I hate being referred to as such. It would be all good if I was Puerto Rican, but I'm not. I'm Jamaican. Born and bred. I wish people wouldn't be so ignorant, as to assume right off the bat, the nationality of others, just by mere appearance. I have a blend of Syrian, white and black in my blood. Though at times I may bear a resemblance to women of the Latin community, I am very far from being Latin. I embrace my Jamaican heritage and people, and it is for this reason I take such high offence to being associated with others of a different culture. Don't get it twisted; I have nothing against my Latin peeps. Matter of fact, my best friend Lydia is Cuban, and I love her to death. I met her here in the States shortly after I'd just met Vaughnn, and she'd been my road dog since then. While growing up, my father had insisted on my learning a second language. So now, I speak fluent Spanish.

That sums up my Latin characteristics, which have come in very handy. You see, Lydia speaks very poor English, and oftentimes has to relate to me in Spanish. I grew up in Kingston, around some of Jamaica's most elite. My father is a politician and my mother is a doctor. I grew up lacking for nothing. Being away from my family though, was a choice I'd made in my early twenties, out of rebellion. Now that I've touched thirty years, I'm not so sure I'd made the right decision. But enough said about me.

Like I said before, there's not much for me to tell about my background, work history, or accomplishments, for all of that shit is irrelevant. Your main concern should be Vaughnn and that stupid bitch he'd brought into our home on that fateful night when this whole drama started, or I should say, escalated.

Everything had started long before that night, but just escalated to a whole new level on that particular night. Now that I've cleared that up, let me explain to you what really went down.

I'd met Vaughnn approximately five or six years ago, when unfavorable circumstances brought us together.

Vaughnn was and still is involved in all kinds of illegal activities. I still, to this day, am not sure what those illegal activities entail. As much as I've investigated, I haven't been able to obtain any solid information about his activities. All I know is that he owns a number of mortgage businesses.

He's a criminal though, I was sure of it. Several times we've travelled abroad on vacation, and I've witnessed him studying people and their movements. Then he'd use his sophisticated methods of swindling them out of thousands of dollars. After which, we'd disappear together. That much I knew. I'd even witnessed him kill a man before. It hadn't bothered me much though because he'd given me a good explanation as to why he'd done it. Vaughnn had many people who worked for him. I still can't figure out how come, since he doesn't even have a college degree. It's amazing how much money can be earned from shifting your paradigm and branching off into doing things out of the ordinary; things you're not expected to do--no matter what those things are.

Vaughnn had become so successful that he had men and women at his every beck and call. His power has always excited me. So you can't be surprised to know that I will do anything to keep my man, and I mean anything.

I've fallen too deeply in love with him, and I'm not about to let him go without a fight, regardless of the risks involved. My love for him was the main reason I've become overprotective of my security with him. Until now, he couldn't get enough of me; however, over the past few months I'd noticed that things had changed in our relationship. He seemed to have lost interest in me, and my sources had informed me that he was on the hunt for another woman. I do admit that I'm a bit jealous, I've always been. I also knew in my heart that he was still in love with me. I just can't understand the reason behind his sudden loss of interest in me, especially after all the good loving I'd given him. My Cuban friend, Lydia, had told me that Vaughnn had clearly gotten bored of my pussy. She said he'd grown tired of fucking me. "But look at me," I argued,

"I'm as sexy as they come. What more could any man want?"

"It doesn't matter who you are, or how good you look," she replied empathetically, "If you give a man everything he asks for, he'll become bored with you."

"What do you mean," I asked, afraid of admitting that she was right.

"I mean," she explained, "that you're so beautiful he'd probably made love to you many, many times already. Possibly every time he laid eyes on you. Am I correct?" she verified.

"Si," I replied frustrated.

"And it may be safe to assume that you'd dropped your panties at his every beck and call, correct?"

"Isn't that what a good woman should do for her man?" I asked defiantly, rapidly losing interest in the nonsense she elucidated.

"No," she patiently continued, "Equilibrio. Balance is the key."

"Balance? We'd done a lot of that too - if you know what I mean," I attempted to lighten the tone of our conversation, because she was beginning to piss me off. I couldn't stand to hear all of that Dr. Phil nonsense.

"Unfortunately, that's the reason you're now in the predicament that you're in. Cierras las piernas!" she said bluntly, which means close your legs.

"Perdoname! Excuse me?" I certainly didn't appreciate her forwardness.

"You need to practice the art of giving a man just enough to keep him satisfied, while withholding a little part of you so he keeps coming back for more."

"What the hell?" I tilted my head to the side, screwed up my face and glared at her. She had the audacity to smile and shake her head at me pitifully, which made me even more pissed off.

"Then next time," she began again, "since you don't value my opinion, whenever your man continues to non-fuck you, keep that information to yourself. Callate--silencio!" Of course she'd said all of this in Spanish, since she could hardly speak a word of English.

I'd obviously been condescending in the way I'd reacted to her advice, and I could tell she was offended. But I couldn't help it. That girl knew how to push my buttons. Anyway, she'd always been my road-dog, and I loved her with all my heart. She'd been the sister I never had, my best friend and confidante. Vaughnn and the triplets had grown very fond of her too, though they couldn't understand what she said most of the times. Like I said, we'll just cut to the chase; you don't need to know specific details about me and my best friend.

Anyway, Vaughnn had seemed very distant over the past few months, almost a little too distant for my liking. I'd grown accustomed to him going out and coming in so when all of that suddenly changed, I immediately knew something was wrong. Vaughnn would have gotten rid of me a long time ago, but he knew it wouldn't have been that easy. Yes he could probably attempt to have me killed but it would never work.

I have people in high places, so he knew better than to mess with me. The problem was the little bitch he'd brought into our home.

I'd made every move to protect myself against Vaughnn, but not against this bitch. Anyway, one night recently, I decided to setup Vaughnn. I met with a couple of my friends from a very urban neighborhood close to Sistrunk in Fort Lauderdale, and arranged for them to trail Vaughnn. I paid them a deposit to follow him, and promised to pay a larger sum if they'd hurt and chase away whichever woman they'd caught him with. I arranged to follow behind them in a car I'd rented a few days prior. I intended to watch from afar without being a part of any potential drama. When Vaughnn headed out that Friday evening, I knew he wouldn't be returning home for at least a few hours.

My friends trailed him, while I trailed them, which worked out fairly well, since it was hard to lose sight of a big purple Cadillac.

Things had seemed pretty quiet for the first hour or so, until he tried to holler at some chick walking out of a store. I watched them exchange phone numbers and went their separate ways. As soon as she was at a secluded spot, my four sidekicks pounced on her, gagged her and threw her into the trunk of the vehicle. They parked to smoke some weed while I trailed behind Vaughnn. I used a prepaid phone to call them as soon as Vaughnn made a second stop. He'd pulled over at a bus stop and began flirting with a second girl. She looked young - much younger than me. I was livid. This time he left abruptly. His conversation with her did not last long. I thought he'd even give her a ride home, but she didn't get into the car. Once Vaughnn was out of sight, my boys attacked her. What I couldn't believe was how she'd managed to get herself out of being surrounded by four black men.

I knew things had spiraled out of control when one of the young men was stabbed. On top of that, I saw Vaughnn's car return to that same bus stop and that's when I left and went back home. I showered, slid into my sexiest red dress, and waited for Vaughnn to return. I intended to seduce him and give him the best lovin' of his life, then deal with that 'other' situation in the morning. None of those other bitches could compare to me. I was ready to do anything to hold onto my man.

I couldn't believe my eyes when Stewart, Stephin, Steffaun and Vaughnn all walked through the door almost two hours later; the bus stop bitch cradled in the arms of my man!

CHAPTER SIX
LEXI

As warm water streamed heavily from the shower head and pounded my worn body, I considered how endless the night had seemed. I'd been caught up in a string of unusual occurrences. The night had been filled with one bullshit event after another. The shit had worn me down. I felt like the whole world was suddenly resting on my shoulders. After a few minutes, I decided it would be best to block everything from my mind and be grateful instead for the refuge I'd found in Vaughnn. The triplets were cool, but I highly doubted that I would've met them, or been rescued, if it weren't for Vaughnn.

All the thoughts and unanswered questions that had been twirling around in my head, I'd forced to the back of my mind to be addressed at a later date. They'd just have to remain there until I'd gotten enough rest, and built up the nerves to deal with them. My eyelids felt too heavy for my eyes and I had to struggle to keep them open.   Twenty minutes later I'd finished showering and had wrapped myself with one of the fresh towels that Stewart had provided me. He'd smiled when I asked who the owner of the towel was.   His smile told me he understood what I meant, and his non-verbal response was the indication that the towel, or anything else I was using, did not belong to the ho downstairs. I'd never forgive her for the way she'd greeted or treated me.   By the way, why the hell did she have a problem with me? I'd been love-struck by Vaughnn from the very moment he'd stepped out of the car to introduce himself to me, but I'd have to suppress my feelings for him in order to focus on my unfortunate situation. Vaughnn was clearly into me, too.

It was obvious, or he wouldn't have brought me to his home. Was this bitch cock-blocking? If so, then why? I made an intelligent guess that Vaughnn must have been involved with her. If that was the case, why had he placed himself in such an uncomfortable position? How could he have been so bold as to have showed up with me at his house, knowing well enough he had his woman waiting there for him? Who was this 'Lydia' bitch who couldn't speak a word of

English? Was he screwing her, too? And last, but certainly by no means least, what on earth did Vaughnn do for a living? My mind was in overdrive. I decided to add these questions to the list of other questions and thoughts that had been stashed away in the back of my head. They'd just have to stay pending and plague me later. I used a towel to dry my hair, wrapped my head with a second towel, entered the bedroom, slid under the covers of the bed and drifted off into blissful slumber.

It was late at night. Real late. I didn't check what time it was because I couldn't. Vaugnn had weakened me with his deep, sensuous kisses, moments before he lifted me into his muscular arms and carried me into the bedroom. I was paralyzed with ecstasy. He placed me down on the bed face-up, and stared longingly into my eyes.

"You're so damn gorgeous," he said lowering himself between my legs while pushing my mini-skirt upward, exposing my pantyless mound. He spread my legs apart until he was satisfied. My pussy walls convulsed as electricity moved through me. Vaughnn used his middle and index

fingers to part my fleshy folds, then eased his tongue into my succulence.

"God you're wet- and sweet," he hissed, as he licked and sucked and feasted on me. In my frenzied state, I screamed and gripped the sheets tightly, surrendering to the powerful orgasm that overwhelmed me.

Before I could recover, Vaughnn positioned me on my side, generously lubricated his sizable manhood, and slowly entered me from behind. No man had ever touched me there before. Though I was a virgin - back there, I was relaxed, and ready for the experience Vaughnn was about to offer me. Slowly, inch by inch, he penetrated until nearly all of his thickness filled me up. I gasped. Our bodies then began to move to a slow, sensual rhythm that only we could hear. Moments later, Vaughnn pumped up the volume of our love making as he glided in and out of me. I reached for his arm and placed his hand between my thighs. I held my breath as his fingers cleverly manipulated my eager pussy that was already dripping wet. Vaughnn moaned and I could feel his hot breath on my shoulder. I turned my head towards him and his lips reached for mine. Within seconds our tongues were dancing together, wildly. I was using one arm to

*balance myself on my side, the other to massage
my breast and caress my nipples. All of our body
parts busily worked magic, until I experienced the
most powerful orgasm ever.*

The knocking on my door awoke me to my hot, wet pussy. I stirred in bed trying my best to properly gather my thoughts. I was shocked-almost embarrassed at myself for dreaming about anal sex with Vaughnn. I glanced at the clock on the wall and saw that it read 2:45. I immediately concluded that the clock was malfunctioning. It would have to be 2:45 in the evening and I knew I couldn't have been sleeping for that many hours. Yes, I knew I could throw down a mean sleep, however considering the events of the night before --well, considering the events of my entire life, how could I have slept for possibly over ten hours? The person standing on the other side of the door knocked again, bringing me back to reality. I jumped out of bed and walked to the door. That's when I noticed the note on the floor with my name on it. I picked it up and read it.

Dear Lexi, you seemed so peaceful I didn't want to awake you.

I know you needed the rest. Besides, it's only a few minutes after nine o'clock and you went to bed late-- or I should say early this morning. I hope you found my guest room quite cozy. I'm the only one who has a key and I locked you in before I left.

Though I did not anticipate additional drama, I had to make sure that you got the rest that you rightfully deserved. I'll be out for the rest of the day, but I left you breakfast on the bedside table.

There's also money underneath the tray just in case you decide to leave, though I'm hoping you stay. I'd rather you use the money to call a cab and go shopping instead (smiley face). I like you. I also already think that you and I have a lot in common. Stay sexy.

Vaughnn,
P.S. – the triplets said hi.

I smiled at the note and ignored the coldness between my legs. My stomach growled as I eyed the French toast, omelet and fruits that were on the tray, which sat on the bedside table. There was that knocking again, only this time, it was much more aggressive. I decided that, whoever it was, that person was unwelcomed. I spun around, walked back to the bed and sat down before the tray of food. A few hundred dollar bills fell to the floor as I straightened the tray. I dived into the delicious meal I'd been served, and reminisced about the wonderful dream I had.

"Bitch! You better open this damn door!" someone shouted.

I was happy at my decision against opening the door in the first place. I continued to devour my meal while she continued to bang on the door.

CHAPTER SEVEN
ANONYMOUS

"You hit me?" I screamed at him angrily, "you really hit me?" my eyes stung as tears welled up in them, and my left cheek hurt ten times as much from Vaughnn's heavy, unexpected blow. I wiped tears from my eyes as I glowered at him. More tears began to flow, not from the pain of being struck by him, but from the outrage that I felt within me. My fury grew even more when he displayed no signs of remorse.

He just stood over me breathing heavily and clenching his fists. I waited a few seconds for him to respond and when he didn't I gently touched the sore spot on my face. "You fucking hit me because of that street walker you picked up from the bus stop?" I continued miserably, looking up at him from where I sat on the bed.

"Stop that shit!" he demanded keeping his voice down to prevent everyone else from hearing our fight.

"Vaughnn, how can you tell me to stop this, when you're the one causing all these problems we're having?"

"What problems are we having?" he demanded.

"This is the problem we're having!" I cried pointing to my sore cheek and feeling the lowest I'd ever felt in my entire life. No man had ever hit me, not even my father. "You've changed. You're beginning to take me for granted. On top of that, you have brought a woman into our home--a nobody at that. Just some bitch you picked up from a bus stop!"

"You keep saying that shit!" he scowled.

"Saying what?" I questioned.

"You keep saying that I picked her up from the bus stop," he paused to study me for a moment, then continued, "how the hell did you know I picked her up from the bus stop?"

I realized that my ass was busted. I had really fucked up this time. I held my head down instead of answering.

"Now you see the real reason why we're having this problem?" Vaughnn stated scornfully, "I never knew you were like this."

I didn't respond. He stepped away from me and I looked up at him.

"If you try anything stupid," he declared, "you will regret it, you can bet your life on that. Don't you mess with Lexi!"

He'd sounded so final, yet everything was far from that. That's the shit I couldn't understand with men. One day they tell you how much they want you around, and the next they're ready to give you up in a heartbeat for someone new. He had the nerve to try to slap me into subservience, without apologizing for committing such intolerable act. Not to mention the fact that he hasn't explained why he thought it would be okay to bring an unwelcomed guess into our home.

Vaughnn had broken my heart. The worst part was that he'd discovered I'd been stalking him. *I never knew you were like this.* Those words had stung me even more than his physical abuse. I felt ashamed of myself for the situation I was in. I was also terrified of what could possibly happen if Vaughnn was to ever find out I was the life force behind Lexi getting jumped. Yet, I wasn't about to let go of my man that easily. Not after all the shit that we'd been through together. Certainly not after everything we'd built together. Vaughnn was a criminal, but he was my criminal. He was for me to love. He'd pursued me. I had groomed him into the man of my dreams, and he was going to have to accept that whether he liked it or not. If that bitch he called, Lexi, thought she could just waltz her tacky ass off the street and into my home, she needed to think again. I'd plan to come at her so hard, she'd never know what hit her.

"Open up the door, bitch!" I belched those words out at the top of my lungs.
Though Vaughnn had warned me to stay away from her, I knew that I wouldn't have been able to. That shit wasn't even right.

"Open up this damn door, right now!" I tightened my grasp on the cup I held in my hand, which contained the acid I was about to throw on Lexi's face. At first I'd knocked softly, so she wouldn't figure out it was me. But her ass was much smarter than I thought because she just wouldn't budge. I wished I had a copy of the key to the guestroom; however, in the past, Vaughnn had insisted on being the only one in possession of that key. I'd always wondered why, but now I was beginning to realize the logic behind his reasoning. I continued to bang the door, but to no avail.

Defeated, I returned to my bedroom and cried some more. I cried because I didn't know what the hell was going on, and I felt as if I was losing control. If I had wings, I'd just fly away. Once I had mentioned that to Lydia and she'd told me that no one was stopping me. She'd assured me that though I didn't have wings, many substitutes existed; such as airplanes, cars, bicycles or even my two feet. I just couldn't stand talking to her sometimes; however, I knew she was my rock and I needed her. It was her bluntness that'd kept me grounded over the years. Lydia was always right. It's just that, now, no matter how right she was, I wasn't really interested in whatever she'd have to say to me. Luckily for me, she'd already left for her English classes that morning, and Vaughnn had already left with the triplets. So I had enough time to myself to figure things out.

My first thought was to hammer down the door to the guest room, however that would've just heighten the tension between Vaughnn and me. Then I considered the idea of calling a locksmith who'd probably be able to pry the door open in a jiffy. I decided to let my subconscious marinate on that thought for a bit, while I picked up one of my many phones to make a much needed phone call. To my surprise, he'd picked up the phone on the second ring.

"Talk to me," the voice on the other end instructed.

"Sup with you?" I queried lightening my tone as best as I could in order to conceal my anxiety.

"Who this is?" my hood friend asked me.

"You know who this is," I kidded.

"Yo, check this shawty. You took too long to call and shit's about to hit tha fan. What took you so long to call?" he asked as if my reason for not having called earlier was of any importance to him.

"Why do you ask?" I evaded his idiotic question. Lydia had once told me that if I was being asked a question I didn't wish to answer, I should reply with the question, *"Why do you ask?"* I was surprised to see how well this technique had worked for me. It was hilarious to watch as inquisitive people scratched their heads trying to come up with a legitimate reason for being nosy, and then would change the topic subtly when they'd eventually realized how nosy they really were.

"Umm- well-"

"What do you mean by 'shit is about to hit the fan'?" I aided him by cutting him off.

"My boy was taken to the hospital late last night. He was admitted in critical condition."

"What really went down last night?" I interrogated.

"As if you don't already know," he countered. This jackass was getting on my last nerve.

"No. I don't know," I lied.

"Man, watchu mean you don't know?" his tone was rather offensive.

"I had driven off behind my dude's car so I could trail him. Remember?" I stretched out the word 'remember' for emphasis.

"Oh, my bad," he said in a more polite tone.

"Now take a chill pill and tell me what exactly went down last night."

"Ma, I don't 'preciate tha way you tawk to me, yo," he whined.

"Don't take it personal, that's just the way I talk. Go ahead, tell me what's crackin'," I assured him. Though my blood boiled, I had no intentions of adding fuel to fire, or fire to fury. I had to at least try my best to remain collected.

"Tha cops phoned Mama Dukes, yo," he explained ambiguously.

"Who is Mama Dukes?" I asked.

"She's his Mama, man."

"If she's his Mama, then why do you call her Mama Dukes?"

"She e'ry body's Mama, man. Yo, you gotta let me tawk."

"Ok, sorry."

"Now this shit got tha po-pos awl ova our neighborhood, man. Got Mama Dukes on tha verge of a heart attack. They trynna do finger prints and shit."

"Fingerprinting for what? People get stabbed every day. Besides, it's not like he died or anything."

"Ma-so you lied to me."

"What do you mean?"

"Thoughtchu said you wasn't at tha scene last night, ma."

"What do you mean?"

"How'd you know my boy got stabbed?"

"You just said so."

"Naw, man. I never said shit about my boy getting stabbed."

I paused to ponder on my stupidity. He was right.

"So now you can't tawk? What--cat gotchyo tongue or somp'in?"

"Listen," I spoke once more, "There's something that I have to talk to you about."

"Yeah. You right. We got a lot we need to tawk about."

"I also need to talk to your friend once he's out of the hospital."

"What friend you tawkin' 'bout, ma?" he asked.

"You know--your boy. The one who got stabbed," I replied.

"Ma? Where you been fo' tha past few minutes? My boy is dead!"

"What?!" I grabbed my chest.
There was silence on the other end of the phone.

"I thought you said he was in critical condition at the hospital," I debated.

"Was," he clarified.
We were both silent for a moment.

"Ma, you still there?" he asked.
Who the fuck was he calling ma? Did I look like his mama to him?

"Yeah, I'm still here," I whispered.

"Where should I meet you to pick up the stuff?" he asked.

"What stuff?" I played dumb.

"The money."

"But ya'll failed, and your boy died," I protested.

"Because of you, bitch!"

"Ok, ok. I'm sorry. Let's meet up in about two hours."

"Where at?" he asked, his tone letting me know he had me where he wanted me.

"The usual spot," I said.

"Down there by you, or Sistrunk?"

"Sistrunk."

"A'ight."

"Bring your other two boys with you."

"I copy that, ma."

"So see you at five then?" I verified.

"Yeah, five."

I hung up. *So you want me to pay you for fucking up and calling me a bitch?*

I picked up my purse, slipped into my heels, grabbed the contents of the box I had stashed away in a secret compartment and headed out the door. I scratched the idea of having a locksmith over. Lexi would just have to be dealt with later. Besides, she had killed this man and I was the one stuck with her mess. But I'd be sure to find the perfect way to make her pay later. Right now, I had a few things to take care of-- three to be exact, since last night, she had already taken care of one.

CHAPTER EIGHT
LEXI

The days, weeks and months went by quickly. My love for Vaughnn blossomed, as did our relationship. I must admit he was my first true love and he represented, in my life, 'THE father figure'; 'THE real man I'd never had'; 'THE stepfather who'd never raped me'; 'THE mother that'd never betrayed me'; THE uncle that never threw me out; 'THE friend unlike no other'; 'THE best lover of all times'--I suppose you get my drift. My friendship with the triplets was also blooming and I'd found solace in the beautiful relationship we'd shared and had come to value. I didn't know that things would have turned out as great the way they did, even if but for a moment, or I knew no situation on this earth was permanent. As a matter of fact, where I came from in Jamaica, people were taught from a young age, how to be grateful for, and embrace the good moments while they lasted as they braced themselves for the bad.

That never really applied to me though, because I'd never really known true happiness. Not until I met Vaughnn. The triplets were an added bonus, especially Stewart. I'd found the need to cherish the life I'd shared with such wonderful men. There were times in Jamaica when I was happy, but that happiness could not compare to the happiness I was currently experiencing. Besides, my happiest times back then were with JT, whom, in those days, was my best friend. I'd often catch myself smiling whenever I reminisced about the good times I'd had with JT. That guy was truly my homey. He'd always been there to support me whenever I needed him. He was the only one I'd shared the rape situation with.

"Lexi, you want me to do anything?" he'd asked me after I'd poured my heart out to him, walking him through my horrid experience.

"Do anything like what?" I asked, knowing full well what he'd meant.

"You know," he shrugged.

"No, I'd rather wait," I sniffed as I wiped tears from my eyes.

"Wait for what?" he asked as he helped me dry my tears.

"I don't know," I said after thinking for a short moment, "maybe wait for him to leave my mother."

"I'll always be here if you ever need me for anything," he promised.

I rested my head on his shoulder, closed my eyes and concentrated on the spasms that rippled between my thighs and throughout my uterine walls. Those spasms were the result of my previous night's encounter with Sir Rape. I now believed that the time was drawing near for me to take a trip back to Jamaica. I'd been keeping in touch with JT, and I knew in my heart that I'd probably needed his help after all. Whichever way I'd intended to unleash my anger upon my bastard of a step-daddy, JT would have to be there to help me pull that shit off, like he'd promised to do.

"Hey, there," Stewart's greeting interrupted my thoughts.

"Hey, you," I turned my head to look at him as he approached from behind. "Aren't you a sight for sore eyes," I joked.

"Can you say that to me later, when Vaughnn's around?" he joked back.

"Why? He'd only stomp you to death," I laughed, happy that Stewart had now joined me by the poolside.

"What? You think that I'm scared of Vaughnn's big ass?" he grinned, "'cuz I'm not."

"Ok," I retorted, "but you already know that you're all bark and no bite."

"Who you talking to?" he turned to look behind him as if I could've possibly been referring to someone other than him.

"I'm talking to you, dummy!"
He grinned harder as he lay back on the pool chair next to me. He was tall, skinny and cut. Those gorgeous green eyes of his were what I admired most about him, along with his charming personality. I'd often wondered why a guy, as easy on the eyes as Stewart, stayed single.

"What are you doing out here all by your lonesome sexy self?" he kidded.
"Just chilling, plus I needed to get some air."

"Can't stand the heat in the kitchen?" he asked diplomatically.

"Don't wish to."

"I feel you," he said nonchalantly.

"Why the hell is she still here anyway?" I
asked him.

"I ask her that same shit every single day."

"What's the answer that she gives you?"

"She doesn't."

We were quiet for a moment. I looked over at
him as he put on his shades and brought an
elbow up to his forehead to protect his face from
the sun. I couldn't understand that. I mean, why
are fair 'complected' black men and women
always hiding from the sun? Are they trying to
prove a point? Plus, why do my light skin brothas
and sistas always say, *"I'm going to get my black
ass out of the sun?"* especially when hanging
with someone of a much darker hue. I didn't
appreciate that shit. As much as I liked Stewart,
part of me resented his ignorant ass. Not that I
was hating on a brotha for having light skin,
however, I deeply rejected his narrow-
mindedness. I just knew I had to be careful of
him.

"I am not the enemy here, Lexi," he said,
looking up at me.

"What? Why did you say that?"

"Just the way you were staring at me. If I
didn't know better, I'd think you hated me. Of

course you understand I'm not the reason she's still here," Stewart explained, assuming he could read my mind.

"Why is she still here anyway?" I said, referring to Nita and making him no wiser.

"I believe you asked me that already," he said bluntly.

"I know, but if I were her, I wouldn't have been able to handle it. I would have left." I thought of how Vaughnn's ex-girlfriend had still remained at the house with us. She'd even kept her best friend from moving out. All Nita did, was throw nasty glares at me and talk smack and try to start shit. I know I had no say in who stays or goes, but I'd rather see her leave.

"Lexi?" Stewart said softly, "Are you jealous of her?"

"Of course not," I said defensively, "I just hate the fact that she has to be here with us. Why does Vaughnn keep her around anyway?"

"They have a solid history together, Lexi; they share bonds that are hard to break."

"I understand that. Since that's the case, why does Vaughnn always stops me from leaving? I sure as hell cannot deal with this any longer. Vaughnn needs to just let me be."

"He can't. You have Vaughnn whipped."

"Shut up Stewart."

"So, Lexi, I know you told us at your birthday party the other day that you're twenty years old. Was that for real?" Stewart questioned.

"Yes, you keep asking me that. Do I look older to you?"

"Naw--never that, but you seem older."

"How much older?" my words dripped with curiosity.

"You seem thirty."

"What?"

"Yeah, shawty, you seem wise beyond your years. You have to be older than twenty. You can't fool me."

"Fine," I got up and wrapped a towel around my waist.

"Are you leaving?" he jumped up suddenly to stop me.

"Yeah, I'm leaving," I said to him.

"I didn't mean to offend-"

"I'm not offended. I'll be back with my ID card."

I went inside to fetch my ID and had almost forgotten why I'd gone inside in the first place. The moment I'd stepped inside, Vaughn's ex-lover greeted me from the bar.

"Bitch, do you know who I am?" she asked me.

I turned around to tell her *yes, you're Vaughnn's ex,* but decided against it because Vaughnn had begged me dearly to ignore her. I continued on my journey to the bedroom Vaughnn had now shared with me. She continued to throw her insults.

"So now you think you're the head bitch in charge of this house? What? You think you're too high and mighty to speak to me, bitch?"

I tried my best to ignore her but she got up from her favorite spot by the bar and followed behind me, still throwing her insults.

"Oh, so you're going into my bedroom? Yes! That's right, bitch! That's my bedroom. As a matter of fact, do you know how many times Vaughnn had fucked me in that very same bed that you now share with him? Bus stop, heifer!"

Her words stung. I felt like attacking her. I wanted to shut her up permanently. How could I have stooped this low? Why the hell was I putting up with this shit? I was beginning to think that there were too many ironies in my life.

Why had I left my uncle's home, to come here and put up with this shit? I slammed the bedroom door behind me. What the hell did she mean by 'bus stop heifer'? How the hell did she know that Vaughnn had picked me up at a bus stop? I desperately yearned for that chick to leave the house. They say the best insult ever, is to ignore someone while they spoke. That shit had proven to be true.   Vaughnn's ex woman seemed angrier each time she saw me and even more angry when I ignored her vicious comments.

"Vaughnn is the only reason I haven't touched you yet, bitch!" she screamed at me.

After that, there was silence. I retrieved my ID card from my purse, opened the door and re-traced my steps back towards the pool. Vaughn's ex-woman had disappeared.   That bitch was crazy.

"What took you so long?" Stewart's lips parted into a huge smile, an indication to let me know that he was happy that I'd returned; his smile broadening as he saw the card in my hand. "Glad to see you in one piece."

"Here," I handed him the card and sat back down in my seat, massaging my temples. I was suddenly stressed out.

"This is you?" I watched as he studied my card.

"Yeah, that's me."

"You look so innocent here," he commented.

"What are you trying to say Stewart, that I don't look innocent in person?"

"You're far from innocent, Lexi," he chuckled, still studying my ID card, "I guess I have no choice but to believe you now," I replied, wondering why he was so intrigued by one stupid ID card.

"You got that right," I agreed, "I am who I said I am. I'm twenty years and lovin' it."
He handed me back my card, "It's time you update your ID card."

"What do you mean?" I asked.

"You need to update it with your new address."

"Oh, I never thought of that."

"That's because you're still young," he joked, "By the way, now that you know how to drive, you should consider getting your driver's license--let Vaughnn hook you up with a car," he said coolly.

I sat where I was and just stared at him in shock.

"Don't look at me with those bulbous eyes," he teased.

"Ok, you're still staring at me," he continued.

When I finally found the will to speak, I asked, "You think Vaughnn would really buy me a new car?"

"Baby girl, trust me when I tell you this, you hit the jackpot when you decided to get with a brotha like Vaughnn."

"Dayummm," I thought out loud, "I never even thought of that."

"That's because you're still young. By the way, didn't you pass your Real Estate course?"

"I did. Got my license and everything," I smiled, still thinking about the car idea.

"So what's your title now?"

"I'm a Real Estate Sales Associate," I informed him proudly.

"Good for you. Tell me somethin', how do you plan on sellin' Real Estate when you don't even have a car?"

"Whatever, Stewart," I said thoughtfully, "Stewart, can you tell me something?" I lowered my voice.

"What's that?" he asked.

"Can you tell me what Vaughnn really does for a living?"

"Why are you asking me? What did he tell you?"

"He told me about his mortgage companies, but it seems like there's much more to it than just that."

"Why do you say that?"

"You know--just the way you guys operate. I dunno--I'm just curious."

"Well, baby girl, if Vaughnn told you he's an entrepreneur, then that's what he is. Stop trippin."

"You're right. I do need to stop trippin'," I said getting up. Stewart's demeanor had suddenly changed. The last thing I wanted was for him to tell Vaughnn that I was snooping around.

I got back up from my seat, this time leaving the towel on the chair. I headed back towards the house, showing off my sexy two piece bikini that Vaughnn had picked out for me.

"Work it out girl!" Stewart shouted from behind me, "work it, work it, work it..."

"Shut up Stewart!"

CHAPTER NINE
ANONYMOUS

I smiled at the man who sat across the table from me. He smiled back at me; his face was agleam with pleasure, obviously from having the privilege of being out with a woman like me. Don't get me wrong, there was nothing wrong with him; however, nothing stood out about him either. He was just an average, older looking man whose looks were unrepresentative of the type of men that I usually dated.   It didn't bother me much though, especially since Vaughnn and I were separated--for the time being. Yes, I said for the time being. He may have left me for Lexi, but my plans for getting him back were already underway.

I was still living in the house because, though he had bought it and put it in his name, he'd promised to add my name to the deed, and I believed that a promise is a promise. Furthermore, we'd been through too much already and I'd found it absolutely preposterous to even entertain the thought of turning my back on such valued memories, and a lifetime of happiness in a home that held my past, present and future all in the name of pleasing a street walker. How could I turn over my treasures to Lexi? As for Vaughnn, he was afraid to ask me to leave. He dared not ask me to leave. I knew too much. The thought that he could have hurt me like this, disrespected me like this, was unfathomable.

"Penny for your thoughts," my date said in his baritone voice and heavy accent.

"Oh, nothing--just thinking of the great dinner we've just had," I smiled.

"I must say that I do enjoy your company," he praised in his heavy accent.

"Thank you, same here," I just couldn't get over his accent. If he was fifteen years younger and ripped, I would have jumped his bones, right there in that restaurant, without thinking twice. At least I'd been able to establish in my mind, the fact that I loved his accent.

"You know," I said, "I enjoy hearing you speak."

"You do?" he blushed lightly.

"Yes I do. You also seem very nice--easy to get along with. Are you usually like this with all the women in your life?" I questioned.

"Every last one of them," he quickly assured.
I nodded, to show I was pleased with his answer.

"Can I get you guys dessert?" the waitress asked us as she cleared our table.

"No, that will be all," I responded.

"Ok, then I'll just leave this here," she placed our check on the table, "I'll be back with you shortly," she left with the used plates and cutleries.

"I'll get that," I objected as my date motioned to pick up the check.

"Wow," he said, "I really love that in a woman."

I smiled knowingly. I pulled out two, crisp one hundred dollar bills from my purse, and placed them on the table.

"This should be enough to cover everything including, the liquor and tip, wouldn't you agree?" I asked rhetorically.
He raised his eyebrows and continued to smile at me in awe.

"Let's go," I instructed.

"Where do you want us to go next?"

"I already booked a room for the weekend at the Ritz in Downtown Ft. Lauderdale. We'll spend part of our night tonight on my friend's boat, by the Las Olas Riverfront; tomorrow we'll visit the Museum of Art, and then we'll bask in the sun by the beach," I responded, "That's if you have the energy to cope with all the fun."

"Damn!"

"Yeah, and the bedroom activities are not even included."

"Are you serious?"

"As a heart attack."

"Shouldn't I go home for an overnight bag?"

"What for?"

"You know--change of clothes-"

"Don't mind that, we'll shop once we arrive," I interrupted.

He smiled at me. I knew he was pleased at what he heard. Right there and then, I knew I had him where I wanted him. I smiled at how easy it was for me to control men. I had beauty, brains and money, but of all three of these, the latter held more weight. It's not shocking to know that men could be just as gold digging and trifling as women. Society's double standard is a bitch. We got into my Lexus, and I sped through the gates of the restaurant and onto the main street, headed towards I-75.

"What type of music do you like?" I asked the man who was sitting next to me.

"I'll listen to whatever music you select," he responded once again in that sexy accent of his.

"How about Bob Marley?" I held up Bob's album, Legend, so he could have a look at it.

"Wow, you listen to Bob?" he asked in a daze.

"Of course I listen to Bob. Bob's what's up!" I declared excitingly.

I inserted the disc into the player and turned the volume up. I looked over at my date, and we both smiled at each other as our eyes made four. I could tell he was having a good time, and so was I. While Bob Marley made melody on my CD player, my thoughts went back to Vaughnn and his bitch. The situation with them had driven me into doing things I'd never done before--well at least not on my own. I was out on a secret rendezvous with a man who was old enough to be my father. This man was a married man, but he didn't know that I knew that he's married. I should just pull over and bust a cap in his head for being a bare faced liar. However, he was more valuable to me alive than dead. For the first time in months, I felt as if everything was about to finally fall into place. Once I was liquored up, I would forget about his age, focus on his sexy accent, and allow him to take away my burdens for the weekend. Hell, why not? It was part of the plan.

I'd met him one Sunday evening when I was out and about by myself. I was having car troubles and had to park my car across the street from where he lived. I'd been in and out of that particular neighborhood for the past few weeks, allowing myself to become acclimated with its surrounding and its residents. In some ways, what I was doing was similar to what Vaughnn and I did from time to time, when sniffing out prospective swindlees, soon to be victims of Vaughnn's cons, after which we'd quickly vanish into thin air, leaving them both clueless and hopeless.

That Sunday, I knew I'd have no trouble getting help because, for some reason, most people stayed home on that day. I also knew that his wife wouldn't be home. She was a nurse, and she usually headed out to work on Sunday afternoons.

I parked my car across the street from his house because I'd been driving around for a while on busted tires. I got out and observed that the two back tires were flat. Apparently someone had slashed them and I'd been rimming it the whole time. Though I knew that the tires were the problem, I flew the hood of the car open and began checking out the engine. I needed to get his attention. A few minutes later, two men were passing by and offered to help me.

"Damn!" one of them sung, eyeing my legs.

"Do you need some help, beautiful?" his friend asked, staring at my breasts.

"No, my boyfriend is on his way here. Please leave," I snapped rudely.

"Well fine!" the first lashed out, clearly insulted, "with your stank attitude!"

"Yeah, you ain't that cute anyway," his friend agreed.

They kept moving, looking back with every other step they took. Their words didn't bother me one bit. I knew I'd hurt their ego. I glared at them.

"You alright, Miss?" I heard someone ask from across the street. I broke my rude gaze and looked directly ahead, into the direction of the voice I'd heard. It was him!

"I don't think so," I shouted, "Do you know anything about tires?"
He walked across the street over to where I stood.

"How did such a beautiful young woman get stranded by the street-side?" he inquired.

"I have not one, but two flat tires," I informed him.

"Do you have a spare?" he asked.

"I guess so," I said, doubtfully.

He smiled at my helplessness. My situation had provided him with an opportunity of a lifetime.

"I just had my shower, but I'll just have to get my hands dirty again," he stated as he inspected my flats.

"Sorry for the inconvenience, but I'd be so grateful for your help."

"Anytime," he offered.

"Do you want me to do anything?"

"Yes, pop the trunk open, meanwhile, I'll go back to my car and get you my spare," he briskly walked back into his yard.

"Thank you!" I shouted after him as I checked my hair and make-up in the side-view mirror.

Moments later he'd returned with a mini tire and some tools. He knelt down behind my car then went to work. After he was done, I showered him with gratitude and promised to repay him if he'd give me the chance to.

"No, mon. Everything cook and curry."

"I'm sorry, but what did you say?" I asked confused.

"Everything is everything, we're good. No problem, mon," he clarified.

"Where are you from?" I asked him as if I didn't already know.

"I'm from Jamaica," he said proudly.

"Wow, I heard that Jamaica is a beautiful country."

"Then you heard correct."

"So where in Jamaica are you from?"

"Beautiful Manchester."

"Wow, can you take me there with you one day?" I watched as his demeanor changed. He stared at me bewildered, "I'd like to get to know you better."

"Repeat what you said," he sounded baffled.

"I'd like to get to know you better," I honored his request.

"Are you serious?"

"Of course I'm serious. You're a very nice man with a very nice accent. You're also not too bad looking." I watched as his lips parted into a humongous smile.

"Ok, I'd be honored."

"So, can I have your phone number?" I requested.

"Sure, with all pleasure, mon," he said just before giving me his number.

"So, will you tell me all about Manchester when I see you next?"

"Anything you like," he replied.

"Great, I can't wait!"

"I didn't get your name."

"'A' for Anonymous," I said knowing he didn't care what my name was. I could tell from his glances, he was lusting.

"Interesting," he said as he rubbed his short beard, "I am not sure if that's satisfactory."

I assumed he meant that the information I'd given him about myself was not satisfactory enough for him to go out on a date with me. I handed him five hundred dollars, and thanked him for his help. I went back into my rental car and drove off.

Not satisfactory enough, huh? Yet here you are with me in the passenger seat of my car,

*heading to a hotel to spend the weekend with
me, abandoning your stupid wife, only one week
after you'd admitted to not being satisfied with
my evasiveness. Like I said, men can truly be
trifling.*

"That was some morning we've had, huh?" I
asked as I yawned from boredom. He smiled up
at me believing I was just tired from the lovin'
he'd put on me. I was pissed. Bet he thought
the sex was good, too! I wanted to slap myself
for being in such a ridiculous position. I knew
that what I wanted from him, I could have easily
gotten without giving him my body, but I was
starved and I'd reasoned that having sex with
him would have eased my famine and provided
me with something to gloat about later. But I
was wrong.

"Did I wear you out?" he questioned.

"Question is, did I wear you out?" I dodged
gassing his ego. I lay back on his arm and gently
trailed my index finger along his groin and up to
his lips. I wanted him to keep his mouth shut so I
could get down to business.

"You're making me hard again," he beamed.

"Tell me more about you," I ignored his unwanted comment.

"I must have done a number on you," he pushed.

"Let's put that on the back burner for now, 'cuz I wanna know more about you."

"Like what?"

"Like where you grew up, how long you've been here, if you have any kids, you know--the works."

"You really like me, sistrin?"

"I like to know about the men I sleep with."

"Well," he stared at the ceiling as he contemplated briefly, "I guess you're a good girl and I can trust you"

"Of course you can trust me," I lied.

"I'm from Manchester, like I told you before,"

"Did you stay there all your life, before you came to live in the States?"

"Yes, mon. You'll find that the country areas of Jamaica are the nicest spots. Manchester is one of those country areas. I was born there, grew up there, and lived there until I migrated."

"Are you married?" I asked the bastard.

"Why do you ask?"

"Don't you think I would need to know? I mean, if things between us should get serious, I'd like to know where I stand."

"Would it change anything?" he asked.

"I'm not saying that it would, but I'd like to be informed nonetheless."

"Ok, fair enough," he said clearing his throat, "I'm married. But I think I made a mistake with that decision."

"Are you saying you do not love your wife?"

"Well, it's not that I don't love her. It's just that, we've grown apart."

"You've grown apart," I echoed after him. I knew what this two-timing, adulterer was trying to do. He and his wife hadn't grown apart. He was just making shit up, justifying his actions. There were no justifications for cheating, especially on your wife. A woman was enough for you to take a vow before God and man to be faithful to her, and her alone, for the rest of your life. All of a sudden, she wasn't enough? My best friend Lydia was right. If you give a man your all, he will grow tired of you eventually. You always have to hold back a part of you. This man had grown tired of his wife's pussy and was trying to justify it. Or maybe he was just being a typical man, trying to have his cake and eat it, too.

"Yes, we grew apart," he confirmed.

"Why did you grow apart? Don't you guys have a lot in common, isn't she also Jamaican?"

"Yes she is. But, even so, we no longer love each other, as much as we once did."

"Sometimes when a couple grows apart, it's because of the children."

"Oh, we don't have kids."

"You don't?" I asked, surprised.

"No, my wife is unable to bear children."

"So you've never had the experience of nurturing a child?" I asked.

"Well," he answered, then paused for a brief moment deep in his thoughts, "I had the experience of nurturing a child, but that was short lived."

"Why, did that child die?" I asked.

"No, she left us. She just up and left. Just like that."

"Really? How old was this child? Did you guys call the police?"

"No, mon. She was over eighteen, and she left on her own accord. Very stubborn child."

"Don't you care that she's out there, somewhere, probably suffering?"

"Well," he laughed nervously, suddenly now aware of the bad impression I now had of him, "My wife and I did our best to make her feel loved and cared for. Wherever she is now, she'll always know that she has a home with us and that she's always welcome to come back."

"This young lady of whom you speak, is she Jamaican also?"

"Yes, she's my niece.   We are all from Manchester."

"So where are her parents, are they dead?"

"No. Her father is a deadbeat. He abandoned her. And her Mom still lives in Manchester."

"Ok, so what part of Manchester is she from?" I asked.

"Why you askin' me so much questions about where we're from?" He asked suspiciously.

"Relax," I said reassuringly, "I'm just curious about you. You're an interesting guy," I waited for him to continue speaking, but he didn't.

"I just wanted to know if I would like it in Manchester," I added.

"Of course you would love it," he said gleefully, taking the bait.

My mission was almost complete.

"Where in Manchester are you from?" I repeated and listened attentively to all that my mate had to tell me. That morning after I finally left the bed, I scribbled down the most important details in my organizer so I wouldn't forget. Then I took a long bath in the Jacuzzi.

My weekend mission had now been accomplished. I had obtained all the information that I'd needed from the man I was sharing my hotel room with. And the man I was sharing my hotel room with, was Desmond Jones, Lexi's uncle.

CHAPTER TEN
JT

It was after four in the afternoon and the streets of Mandeville, the capital of Manchester Jamaica, were crowded. Outside of the taxi window I could see people boarding mini buses and taxis. High school students dressed in their uniforms were browsing the colorful Mandeville market, admiring hand-made crafts and stylish clothing that were decked out on colorful carts. Market sellers were calling out the names and prices of their produce and pineapple lovers kept the pineapple vendor's hands busy, while filling up his pockets with cash. It seemed like the pineapple business was booming. As we drove outside of the hustle and bustle of Mandeville Square, a man suddenly ran up to the moving taxi and tapped on my window, hollering

"Toothpaste and carbolic soap married; yours for only two hundred dollars!"

"Get away from this taxi and leave my passengers alone!" the cab driver yelled. The passengers in the vehicle laughed. After that, everything was quiet again, and we were on our way to a little town in Manchester, called Christiana, which is where I lived.

Later, the passenger in the front seat of the taxi must have been lost in her own thoughts, because I saw her jump when my cell phone rang. I found it amusing how my Jamaican people were always pondering something. When left alone, they'd become consumed with their own thoughts and were more often times than not, spaced out. Take my mother for instance; she was one woman who was never afraid to find something new to worry about. Even if everything was perfect, she would think about what could be done if things should ever change--for the worse.

"Hope for the best but expect the worst," was one of her favorite sayings. Of course, I didn't see the logic in that. How could one hope for the best and expect the worst at the same time? Where's the faith in that? But I dared not challenge my mother.

My cell phone rang again. "Talk to me," I answered informally, already knowing it was Bishop on the other line.

"Is so you answer your phone, mon?" he asked me.

"Bishop, did you call to school me on phone etiquette?"

"No. The way you choose to answer your phone is none of my business," he chanted in his rich Jamaican accent.

"What you call me for?" I rushed. I was already running out of phone credit and needed him to cut to the chase.

"The ball game, my youth, we need you to play later, star. Seen?"

"Same place?" I quizzed.

"Yeah mon, same place as usual."

"Ok, I'll come through. What time?"

"Whenever you ready, boss. Just hurry up and come, bredrin."

"A'right," I accepted his invitation and hung up. I could never turn down a good game of football or soccer, as they call it in America. I smiled at the thought of kicking Bishop's ass. I was even surprised that he'd been the one to call and ask me to come by, being the sore loser that he was. I always beat Bishop's butt in every football match.

I concluded that Bishop had to have been in an extremely good mood, which was about to change as soon as I'd kicked his behind. My spirits were up as I looked forward to the game. I also looked forward to watching the girls in their short, pleated skirts play netball, a cousin of basketball, on the other side of the field. They were all so dainty and once I was around, they'd all put a little oomph into their game to catch my attention. If I wanted, I could have had every last one of them in my bed, but I wouldn't be that type of guy. A few of them in my bed was enough. I chuckled at my ridiculous thoughts.

"You alright back there, young man?" the lady in the front seat asked, while the other passengers next to me began to laugh. They must have heard my chuckles and thought I'd gone mad.

"One stop, driver!" I called out for the driver to stop. The car came to a stop and I got out. I paid my fare and walked away, glad to have escaped the embarrassment.

"Come back here!" the taxi driver yelled out.

I stopped and looked back at him, confused.

"Come back here!" He repeated.

I walked back over to the car and stood by his window.

"I'm going to give you the number for the Belleview Hospital," he began. There was uproar of laughter from the few passengers who were present in the taxi. They laughed so loudly I wanted the ground to just open up and swallow me. I felt so embarrassed. Without responding, I turned to walk away, but the driver wouldn't give up. "You need to check yourself in tonight," he warned as if he was actually serious. The passengers continued to laugh.

"Me a'right, mon," I shrugged, "everything cook and curry." I walked away hoping that he'd drive off, but he didn't. They were actually watching me. That's one thing I couldn't stand about my Jamaican people; they made so much of a big deal out of foolishness.

Once they got started on someone's case, there was no stopping 'until the fat lady sang'. I quickened my stride and prayed for them to go away. But it seemed as if the further away I got from that car, the louder and louder they laughed. I crossed the street and turned into the lane that led to my house. I sighed with relief, thankful, that I'd finally lost them. I decreased my speed and walked at much more comfortable pace. After all, I'd been busy at the hardware store all day and I deserved to take it easy. My cell phone began to ring again and just as I started contemplating on whether or not to take the call, I heard a car horn behind me. Unfortunately enough, it was the taxi driver with his passengers, honking his horn and trailing behind me. I couldn't help but laugh. Jamaicans can be so idle at times.

"We want to make sure you make it home safe, mon!" the lady in the front seat yelled. I stopped and watched them wipe tears from their eyes. That was it. I couldn't take much more of it, so I decided to run. Without looking back, I dashed across the lane and into my neighbor's yard. I sprinted over the fence and onto a shortcut that would lead to my house. By now I was in the bushes and out of everyone's sight. I stopped to catch my breath as I etched in my mind, the memory of the face of that taxi driver. I sure as hell did not intend to take his taxi ever again. After a few moments, I collected my thoughts and went home.

At home I decided against showering, since I would only end up getting sweaty and stinky all over again from the game. Instead, I slipped into my black, green and gold jersey, after which I slipped into my bobby socks and pulled them all the way up to my knees. Then I covered my knees with my shin guards, grabbed my house keys, and headed through the door.

CHAPTER ELEVEN
JT

"Hi, JT," the Netball coach smiled and waved at me as she sing-songed my name.

"Wha'appen, Empress?" I smiled back. I was going to walk past her without saying another word, but couldn't find it in my heart to do so. Her smile was so sweet and inviting, so I stopped to flirt for a minute.

"Wha'appen?" I asked again.

"Just here looking pon you, the better one," she replied as she eyed me up and down.

"Why you think I'm the better one?" I teased.

"It is obvious," she sang, "You have captured the heart of more than half of my netball team," she pouted her lips and raised her eyebrows.

"What about your heart?" I asked coolly.

"What about it?"

"Have I captured it yet?" I took a few steps closer to her and stared at her mini skirt.

"Why you looking at my skirt?" she asked teasingly.

"Why do you think? I want what's under it," I replied.

"You know what?" she rolled her neck, "don't flatter yourself."

"Are you wearing a shamai underneath?" I continued to eye her smooth, sexy legs.

"Why you want to know?"

"You haven't answered any of my questions," I was getting aroused.

"Yo, boss man, stop di flirting and do what ya come here fi do, mon!"
I turned around and saw Bishop approaching.

"We'll finish this conversation later?" I asked her.

"Only if you want to," she teased.

"I want to," I winked at her and stepped towards Bishop, wondering why the hell he was so interested in playing ball with me, and on top of that was being so unusually friendly. Behind me I heard the netball coach blowing her whistle, signaling for her players to get ready.

"What's up, bredrin?" I greeted Bishop.

"Deh yah pon di gullyside," he replied with a smug look on his face. We popped fists, and he turned to walk with me back to the football field.

"What's up with that gal?" he asked screwing up his face and referring to the coach. I didn't answer because I didn't feel I owed Bishop an explanation. As a matter of fact, I was beginning to feel a little bugged out by his sudden change in demeanor. My father had taught me before he passed away, that when your enemy suddenly wants to be your friend, you should watch him closely. I'm not saying that Bishop was my enemy, but he wasn't my friend either. In fact, nobody liked Bishop and his friends. He was the black sheep of our community that everyone was afraid of. That was, everyone but me. I wasn't scared of Bishop or anyone else. I knew how to take a blow and I sure as hell knew how to throw one. I made a mental note to watch out for this kat.

The rest of the men greeted me as they saw us approaching and we all braced ourselves for a solid game of real Jamaican football. Our teams were divided into Bishop's team which was the Reggae Team, and my team which was The Old Hits Team. The Reggae Team got off to a good start when Bishop scored within the first few minutes as he latched onto a pass from his teammate and fired past the goal keeper into the goal. My team, The Old Hits, rebounded quickly though, and after a fully charged game, defeated our opponents, coming out with a score of 2-1. I dropped to the ground overwhelmed by exhaustion and pride. I watched as my fellow teammates shouted with joy and fell to the ground, reveling in our victory.

"We kicked ass!" my teammates screamed as they chased up and down the pitch. Some of them had even gone as far as to chase behind our opponents, yelling out obscenities, and dancing lewdly hoping to get the Reggae Team riled beyond composure and at the same time make a point. And the point was that, once again they had gotten their asses whipped by us, the Old Hits Team. We were untouchable. I do not mean to be arrogant; however, everyone knew that the game wouldn't have been the same without my input. Now rested, I finally stood to touch fists with some of my teammates who'd approached me.

"Glad you could come out to play, mon," someone expressed, his voice oozing with satisfaction.

"Anytime, mon," I replied as I touched his fist, "You already know I never abandon ship." We all laughed together.

"So, you think you're a bloodclaut winner?" someone behind us asked angrily. I knew, almost immediately, without turning around, that it was Bishop. His voice sounded hoarse, more than likely from being a sore loser.

This was usually the case whenever he'd lost a game. We whirled around uniformly to face him, then I mocked, "What you mean?" I allowed my lips to part into a smug smile, "I don't think that I'm a winner, I know that I'm a winner!" I touched fists again with my teammates as we all laughed at him.
"Winner, my bomboclaut?" he raised his voice and sent me a vicious glare, "You walk around this place like a god!" he snapped.

"You're nothing but a piece of shit!" he continued to bark, all his comments directed at me.

I stopped smiling and looked at him, "Calm down, bredrin, it's just a game."

"Just a game for who? Did you think it was just a game when you kicked me on my foot so I would lose? Or was it when you finally won and walk 'round this place like you own we?"

"Calm down Bishop," someone else advised, "JT is right, it's just a game, my youth."

"Shut up your mouth!" Bishop silenced, "See your way out of this conversation.

This is strictly between me and this batty bwoy, JT!"

"The only batty bwoy standing here, Bishop, is you!" I was livid. I watched as Bishop grabbed the ball from one of his friends and slammed it into my face. It all happened so fast, before I knew it, we were wrestling in red dirt, me on top of Bishop beating him to a pulp.

His followers ran down on me and started throwing punches but I kept my attention on Bishop. Before I knew what was going on, my teammates had jumped in to my defense and an honest game of football turned out to be the beginning of my worst nightmare ever. When it was all over, many of us suffered minor bruises, however Bishop was laid out on the ground beaten almost to a pulp, by me of course, while his friends scattered. At that moment I wished I had never gone to play the game. I still couldn't understand it.

I was perplexed about the whole situation. What the hell was Bishop's problem? I knew he was a sore loser, but there was something else going on that I was amiss.

"Watch your back faggot!" someone shouted at me in the distance, and I knew it had to be one of Bishop's friends.

"You alright, sweetheart?" the netball coach sing-songed warmly, as she caressed one of the bruises on my face.

"You keep this up, then I'll be the one asking you that," I flirted as I squinted from the pain in my left leg, "Ouch!" I squealed surprised at the pain I felt. I wasn't about to deny the fact that Bishop had definitely stolen a few kicks and punches.

"See?" my warm hearted, long-legged, sing-songing, netball coach asked with a smirk.

"See what?" I asked slightly irritated by her mockery.

"See what you get for being, umm- what do the Americans call it? Oh, yes- a smart ass!"

"You alright, bredrin?" Biggs asked as he walked by with a few of my friends.

"I think I will live," I replied sarcastically, "Biggs, wait for mi up the street."

"No problem, mon," Biggs replied and kept it moving.

"Well if you need help, boss, you know where to find us," my other friends chimed in.

"Respect, mon!" I forced a smile, grateful for their support. They walked away backbiting Bishop.

"Now back to you," my attention now on little miss netball coach, "Where were we?"

"We were talking about how you're gonna sit in a tub of ice," she teased.

"I'm sure you're lying, nevertheless, I would sit in a tub of ice any day, if you were sitting on top of me."

"JT!" she pretended to scowl.

"What? You want me to stop?" I waited for her to respond but she didn't, so I continued, "you can stop me whenever it's too much for you to handle."

"Someone just tried to whip your ass; yet here you are being frisky instead of taking things seriously," she stated pragmatically.

"Why you keep dodging my invitation?" I said eyeing her sexy legs again.

"Excuse me, but are you okay?" someone from behind me spoke. My colleague and I turned to see who it was this time. The accent sounded different from what I was used to hearing.

My jaws almost dropped open when I saw the woman who now stood before me. Images of the netball coach's legs fled my mind, and were now replaced by the elegance of one of the most beautiful women that I'd ever beheld. The

netball coach must have seen the look on my
face, too, because she stepped off and wished
me a good night. Good for her.

"Cat's got your tongue?" she asked me in
such a cool, refined, sexy tone.

"Sp-speak again," I urged.

She smiled at me knowingly and repeated,
"Cat's got your tongue?"

"No, wh-what you said before," I stuttered.

"Oh, I asked if you were okay."

"Why do you care?" I quizzed, wondering who
the hell she was, and from where on God's green
earth she had appeared.

"I saw what happened; and I must say, you're
the type of man whom any woman would kill to
have by her side," she praised me in that sexy
accent of hers.

"Who are you?" I asked rubbing my eyes to
make sure that Bishop's stolen punches hadn't
gone to my head. I wouldn't be surprised if I
turned out to be crazy. After all, the taxi-man
did advise me to check into the mad-house
ASAP. So many people couldn't have been lying.

"Why do you ask?" she questioned.

"Because--well I don't know," I said.

"Ooo, check out that nasty bruise, can I have a look at that?" she offered.

"Why do you care?" I asked for a second time.

"Because," she began, "I'm here visiting from America with my friends. We were on our way to Hatfield and winded up getting lost. That's when we saw you guys playing soccer, and stopped by to watch the game. You play very well by the way."

"So why are you still here?"

"I like your style," she flattered, "I'm still here because I'm attracted to you. I had my eyes on you the whole time you played. You are so sexy, so vibrant, so..."

I lost myself in her words. They were so fluid. She spoke so eloquently and those words flowed from her sexy lips like water from a Portland stream.

"Did you hear me?" she interrupted my thoughts.

"I'm sorry, what?"

"I said, do you plan on standing here all night, or do you plan on going home to take care of your sore behind?" she smirked.

"My behind not sore, mon."

"Well at least let me and my friends give you a ride home, please," she insisted.

"Where are your friends?"

"Over there by that Range Rover," she pointed.

"Ok," I finally gave in. I mean, opportunity only knocks once. Right?

"I'm JT," I introduced myself to the three identical men who stood cool, calm and collected by the SUV.

"Guys, this is JT. JT, these are my friends; they're identical triplets," she pointed to me then to the triplets as she spoke. They all looked refined and wealthy.

"Sup, mehnn?" One of them spoke, "You can call me Stewie."

"That's fine with me," I replied, still a bit puzzled as to what was going on. We shook hands, and then they motioned for me to get into the car. I knew it was risky so I asked if my buddy, Biggs, could tag along. I knew that Biggs was always strapped and didn't put up with bullshit. After they'd exchanged glances, Stewie said, "Of course, mehn, without a doubt."

"Biggs!" I called out to Bigg's big backside, "Biggs!"

He spun around in my direction and revealed the person who stood before him. It was the netball coach. "Come here, mon!" I beckoned for him to join me and the strangers. He waved goodbye to the netball coach and hurried over to the Range Rover. My heart sank a little as I watched her walk away--disappointed.

"Are we all ready?"

"Yeah, mon," I told Stewie, breaking my fixation on the netball coach.

"Ok then, let's ride," He got into the driver's seat of the car, while my beautiful temptress sat in the front passenger seat.

I jumped into the back of the car after the remaining two of the triplets, followed by Biggs, who sat next to the window.

CHAPTER TWELVE
STEWART

"Call me Stewie," I told the tall, good-looking Jamaican brother whom Nita had pointed out to be JT. Nita had told him that we were lost, but we actually weren't. Nita was short for Bonita, which was the name of the love of my life. I would do anything for the love of my life, and that right there was the problem. I was in love with a ruthless, conniving woman, who was the ex-girlfriend of a man who was both my boss and my best friend. Nita would always introduce herself as Anonymous to nearly everyone she met. I'd do anything she asked of me, and the only people in the world that were aware of this fact were my two identical brothers: Stephin and Steffaun.

Though she was now his ex-lover,   I'd loved her since the day Vaughnn had introduced us, and I'd first laid my eyes on her. She'd been evasive about who she was, she'd never really given me a straight answer to any of the questions I'd asked. Even to this day, there's still so much that I do not know about her. However, this particular trait of hers seemed to have worked well where Vaughnn was concerned. It seemed as if he'd even loved her more because of it.

"Her mystery is good for my line of work," he'd always tell us, "Don't worry, I already know everything I need to know about her."

I'd grown mad jealous over that shit. I mean, I was the one doing all the dirt on her behalf, whenever she decided to go behind Vaughnn's back; yet I still didn't know half of the things that she'd revealed to Vaughnn about herself.

"I let you sleep with me, Stewart!" she once snapped, "Can't you just be satisfied with that?"

After she'd said that I could feel my heart ripping out of my chest. Though her body was tight, and her beauty was the kind of beauty that just made a brother wanna make love to her non-stop. I wanted to know as much if not more about her than Vaughnn did; I wanted her heart; soul--everything. I'd become used to hearing her tell strangers that her name was Anonymous. I bet the name Bonita was just a nickname she'd made up. I bet the few things she'd told me about herself were all lies and I also bet that Vaughnn knew what her real name was.

"Biggs!" JT called out to his friend. I knew that

Biggs was talking to someone, but we couldn't see who it was until he spun around to face us.

"Come here, mon!" JT yelled out at him. I was amazed at how obedient he was to this rude command. He'd immediately waved goodbye to the sexy girl whom we'd watched coach the netball team. Biggs moved swiftly towards us. Of course the plan was for us to get JT by himself; however, this dude was a bit smarter than we'd calculated. As a matter of fact, I was beginning to doubt that Nita's plans for him would work. Not only was he a cocky bastard, he also knew how to handle himself in any situation. *Come here, mon!* JT hadn't even said please, yet his big, rough looking friend moved towards him obediently. Yeah, I was beginning to have some serious doubts about Nita's plans. JT was a popular guy and that alone would make it difficult to get him exactly where we needed him. Biggs had finally caught up to us.

"Come with me, mon," JT told him.

"A'right then," he replied.

Then I watched as JT moved his focus from Biggs to the netball coach whom by now, was quite some distance away, walking briskly in the opposite direction away from us. Nita glanced over at me. I shrugged.

"Are we all ready?" I asked purposefully, breaking JT's gaze.

"Yeah, mon," he responded snapping out of his trance.

We all got into the car: she and I, JT and his boy, Biggs, and my two brothers. Good thing we were rolling in a Range Rover.

"So, where do you live," Nita asked JT.

"I live down the road," JT replied speaking half English, half Patois.

I started the engine and headed off into the direction JT had pointed out to us. I could feel Nita's eyes on me, but I dared not exchange glances, or else JT and his boy would have definitely suspected that something was up.

I kept my eyes on the road and did what Nita had instructed me to do, and that was to drive. As I drove towards JT's home, my mind wandered to the car Nita had rented a few weeks back--maybe even a month. She'd told me of her plan to seduce Lexi's uncle and that plan had included me slashing the tires of a car she'd rented a few days prior.

As conniving as she was, I didn't expect that the plan would have actually worked; but it did. However, Lexi's father had spotted Nita across the street from his yard, walked outside of his gate and into her trap.

The so-called car trouble that Nita had experienced was due to her two back tires being slashed by me, at her request. She rimmed it all the way to Lexi's old neighborhood and parked outside of Lexi's uncle's gate. Men are a lot weaker than I thought and Lexi's uncle and I were prime examples of that. Not only had I slashed a few tires, but I'd also connived to obtain Lexi's previous address. I hope you've been paying attention, because I had gotten Lexi's uncle's address from the ID card she'd shown me the day we were out by the pool. I silently sang her address so it would stick to my memory. Things worked out even better than I'd hoped when she got up and left to make a phone call to Vaughnn. As soon as she was out of sight, I scribbled down the address in my little black book, in case I forgot, and hoped it was still valid. Nita and I had been scheming for the longest while, to get some sort of information about Lexi, from Vaughnn. But Vaughnn had kept Lexi under his wings, and every piece of information about her under lock and key. I had finally succeeded when I coerced her into showing me her ID. I must admit that I'm not the perfect man, but let he who is without sin cast the first stone.

"How much longer before we get to where you live?" I asked JT. I had to ask because JT had told me his house was just down the road, which I assumed couldn't have been that far. But I'd already driven a couple of miles and he hadn't stopped me yet.

"Go through that lane," JT directed, leaning over my shoulders as if the Range Rover wasn't spacious enough. He pointed towards a little track on the right.

I stopped the vehicle dead in front of the so-called lane and waited for JT to tell me he was joking. But he didn't.

"Nope, I don't think this vehicle is gonna make it," I protested as I scanned the narrow trail JT had just pointed out.

"Trust me," he encouraged, "I have seen bigga trucks than this get through," he sounded convincing.

"And the drivers don't ever get ticketed, or even locked up?" I asked shocked at what I was hearing.

"Get locked up for what?" JT asked looking at me as if I was crazy. Biggs laughed.

"Just drive if you drivin', boss mon!" JT said shrugging and looking at me as if I was a punk for complaining about the jeopardy of our safety.

Nita giggled for the first time since we'd met. I continued to eye the narrow track that JT had called a lane.

"Him 'fraid, mon!" Biggs mocked.

"There's someone behind us, bro'," Steffaun informed. As soon as he'd said that the driver behind us began honking his horn.

"Come out of mi way!" he shouted at us, "You likkle battybwoy driva, come out of my way!"

"Why don't you get out and let JT drive?" Nita asked smugly.

The driver behind us continued to honk impatiently at us, so without hesitation, I quickly jumped out of the driver's seat and let JT take over. As I proceeded to sit in JT's spot next to Biggs, Nita spoke.

"Why don't you just wait out here for us?"

"Nita, what do you mean?"

"Just wait out here," she demanded. I slammed the door shut and walked towards the banking. Less than two seconds later my brothers joined me.

"That's fucked up!" they shouted.

"Did she ask ya'll to get out?"

"Naw, man, she knows better than that," Steffaun reasoned, "I'll slap that bitch, yo!"

I looked over at my other brother, Stephin, who was always the quietest of the three of us. He just screwed up his face and paced the ground. My attention went to the Range Rover that was now being skillfully maneuvered by JT. Somehow he'd managed to get the SUV into the middle of the lane and was cruising as if it were Sunday morning. I watched as the driver of a Hummer followed closely behind him, and stared in amazement at the ridiculous scene.

"Why do you put up with this shit?" Stephin finally asked me, still pacing.

"She'll come around," I assured him.

"But she's gonna fuck him!" he yelled, "Are you just gonna stand by and watch her do that shit?" He was livid.

"And for what?" he continued, "for her to get back with Vaughnn, the man she really loves!"

"That's where you're wrong," I interjected, "She's doing all of this to get back at Lexi!"

"Oh, yeah? And what do you think is gonna happen once she eventually brings Lexi down?" he snarled.

"I don't like your tone right now, Stephin," I said out of shame.

"She's trying to get back with her ex, and she's using your love as a tool!"

"She could never be using me!" I defended, "Everything I do for her, I do willingly."

"Yeah, that's because you're pussy whipped!" my other brother Steffaun counteracted.

"Pussy whipped?" I laughed nervously, "I have been celibate for over a month now. I wasn't about to have sex with a woman if I couldn't have all of her, so I'm definitely not pussy whipped."

"Do you hear yourself?" Stephin chimed in, "Do you really hear yourself?"
I didn't respond.

"So you're willing to fuck Nita while she's with Vaughnn, but now that she's single you choose to become celibate?" Stephin reasoned.   In response to that I held my head down pitifully. I knew my brothers were right. As for Stephin, he hardly ever spoke, but when he did, it was always some kind of deep shit, that could even make the biggest of person feel really small. We all grew quiet and I glanced back hopefully at the lane.

"See that shit?" Stephin blurted out angrily to Steffaun as he nodded his head and stared at me.

"See what?" I asked them confused.

"After all we've just said, your dumb ass is still looking out for that Range Rover," he shook his head at me scornfully. What they were saying was right. I silently questioned the man that I was, the man that I'd claimed to be. I thought I'd had things figured out, but it'd now occurred to me that I wasn't in control of shit. For right now, Nita was. I wasn't even in control of my brothers like I thought I was. They rallied around me only because of their love for me.

"Come here, guys," I waited as my brothers moved closer.

"I love both of you very much," I put my arms around their shoulders.

"We love you, too," Steffaun replied.

"I know that I've dragged you guys through a lot of mess. But check this, I got your backs. I'm not sure where this shit is headed, but I need you to trust me. A'ight?"

My brothers didn't respond, but I was happy that we were together; even if it meant being dumped off by the wayside in a third world country. My brothers weren't worried at all though. We all wore bullet proof vests and were strapped. Though my brothers and I were emotionally connected, we knew we had to be stone-hearted in order to survive.

CHAPTER THIRTEEN
ANONYMOUS

"Nita, what kinda of fucked up shit was that?" Stewart's brothers rebelled when they'd heard me tell Stewart to remain outside of the vehicle. For the first time in years, they'd finally managed to piss me off. I knew that shit was intentional, too. I wasn't pissed at the fact that they were looking out for their brother. I was pissed at them for calling me by my name in front of strangers. They knew how I felt about that shit. I wanted to have nothing to do with the strangers that were present in the car once I'd returned home, so why should they know my name? I mean, that was the name by which Vaughnn and Lydia, the two people I cared most about, had referred to me. Calling me Nita, in my mind, was very intimate. Now, because of Stewart, and his incompetent brothers, JT and his roughneck friend now had a name to go by.

The more I thought about that shit, the more convinced I was that they'd done it to get back at me. They'd also jumped out of the car before I could respond and that had made me double angry. But I had to play it off and keep my cool.

"You alright, Nita?" JT asked me, in an accent similar to that of Lexi's father.

"Yes, I'm okay," I forced a smile and held my breath, praying that the vehicle he was driving wouldn't get stuck in such a narrow ass track, and that he wouldn't use my name again.

"What was that about?" JT had the nerve to ask, as if anything was any of his business. Who the hell did he think he was to question me? I'd offered his ass a ride home, and rather than keeping his mouth shut and be grateful that he got the chance to ride in a Range Rover, he was being inquisitive.

"What was what about?" I asked back, irritated. I didn't have time to think about an answer for JT's sorry ass. I had more important things to focus on. I'd hoped JT would pick up on that but he kept pushing.

"You know--what was the deal with having your friends wait by the roadside?" he probed.

"Don't mind them, they'll be alright," I attempted to nip his nosiness in the bud.

"Not really," he responded.

"What?" I asked confused.

"Not really," he repeated.

"Not really what?" I was already beyond annoyed.

"Not really to what you said. They never seemed a'right to me. Furthermore, how could you do that to your friends?"

"Exactly. They are my friends."

"So what, you think you can just treat your friends coldly and they'll be okay?"

"I know how to handle them."

"If you treat them that way, how would you treat me?"

"But that's the point, I did it for you."

"For me?"

"Yes. I wanted to be alone with you."

"But you no know mi. You no know if I would rape and rob--even kill you."

"I'm willing to take my chances."

"But a beautiful woman such as yourself should be smarter than that, mon."

"Okay, I'll keep that in mind next time," I agreed hoping that would be the end of it. It was.

We pulled up to a big house with lots of yard space that was surrounded by greenery. Hibiscus flowers were everywhere. The windows and entrances of the house were protected with what Jamaicans referred to as grills. They were painted white, with many different patterns that made the house look even more beautiful.

"This is where you live?"

"Yup, this is where he lives," Biggs answered proudly on JT's behalf. It was the only thing he'd said to me since he'd gotten into the car. I ignored his ass and released the breath I didn't realize I was holding. I was relieved that we'd reached our destination in one piece, and also taken aback by the natural beauty that surrounded us. We all stepped down from the vehicle and I walked up to the house and picked a flower. I placed it in my ponytail.

"How do I look?" I asked the men who were now watching me, clearly pleased at my reaction to JT's home.

"Yu look nice, mon!" JT complimented, "Biggs, excuse us for a few minutes," he requested.

"A'right then," Biggs disappeared behind the house.

"Is this real concrete?" I asked touching the wall.

"Yes. The houses here in Jamaica are made with real concrete," he informed.

"But you have zinc for your roof?"

"Yes, mon. When we have hurricane, many times the strong winds blow off the sheets of zinc leaving our houses roofless. But we go back to the hardware store and buy more. It's not as expensive as it could be."

"How many rooms are in this house?"

"Four bedrooms, two bathrooms, a kitchen, living room, dining room and a verandah."

"Damn. And you own all of this? Or are you renting?"

"No. I own all of this, mon. My father left it in his will for me before he died."

"Sorry about your father."

"That's a'right, everything cook and curry."

"Do you live here alone?"

"For the most part, yes."

"What does that mean?"

"Let's not go there."

"So- if I wanted to spend the night, would your wife mind?"

"Of course my wife would mind--if I had one."

"So that means I can spend the night?"

"As much as I want to tell you yes, I have to consider your friends. Right now they're by the streets   waiting   for   you."

"So you're not gonna invite me in?"

"Maybe another time. But I mon want you to go back for your friends. They're foreigners standing by the roadside. It can't be the safest place for them."

"So, there will be another time?"

"I don't know, but thanks for the ride home. Biggs can drive you back out-"

"Can I at least have your number?"

"Sweetness, if I give you my number what will I use?" he smiled.

I laughed at that.

"Hold on," he jiggled his keys and hopped to his door. He was obviously still sore from the game and the fight. A few moments later he was back with a piece of paper that had his phone number written on it.

"This number only has seven digits. What is your area code?" I asked in pretense. I already knew what the area code was.

"There is only one area code for the entire island, sistrin, and that is 876. We only use that area code when calling from outside of the country."

"Wow! So everyone has the same area code?" I asked. But of course, I already knew that. I was from Jamaica.

"Yup, read this," he showed me a $500 bill that he'd just retrieved from his wallet.

"Out of many, one people," I read aloud.

"Exactly," he responded, "Biggs, come here!"

I laughed again. JT was a lot more interesting than I'd expected. I even think I kind of liked him. Plus he was sexy as hell. I could see why he was so popular. Regardless, I'd come back to Jamaica to get a job done. I wasn't about to lose my focus. I also wasn't about to reveal my true identity to JT. He thought I was American, and that's how it should be. Lexi was snuggling up with my man. That would be changing real soon.

"So I'll call you tonight?" I confirmed as I watched Biggs approaching us from behind the house.

"A'right then," he agreed, "You can call me tonight sexy, lady. Biggs, drop this sexy mama off on the main road," he ordered.

I smiled at his subtle flirtation. Just then, one of my cell phones began to ring. It was the private phone I used to speak with those whom I loved.

"Hello," I answered.

"I don't think I like the life you've been living,
Bebe."

"Dad, how have you been?" I replied,
shocked.

"I'm disappointed in you, Bonita."

"What did I do, or didn't do this time, Dad?" I
asked, stepping away from Biggs and JT, for
privacy. I was a grown ass woman, yet my father
spoke as if I was still a child.

"How is it that you're in Jamaica, and neither
your mother nor I know that you're here?"

"Who told you I was here?"

"So it's true. You're really here?"

"Dad, I came to wrap up a business deal,
that's all. I planned on calling you but I-"

"What kind of business are you running, that
you can't discuss with your own family?"

"I told you, I'm a mortgage broker."

"A mortgage broker?" my dad laughed
mockingly, "Is that what you've become, Bebe?
A mortgage broker? How's that coming along,
especially in these times when the real estate
market in the US has crashed? Seems like
whatever affects America, ends up trickling
down on other countries, like our little Jamaica.

And you're here cutting business deals? Child, what's really going on with you?"

"I'm thirty two years old Dad, I'm not a child."

"You'll always be our child--and you're the only one we've got. You know, all of this is your mother's fault," he said.

"Dad!"

"It is. This is all her fault. She spoiled you. Now you're in America doing God knows what. You've embarrassed us."

"Dad!"

"I won't let your mother know that you're here, but I'm sure that she'll eventually find out, and it will break her heart. Just don't let any of these reporters spot you like one of my guys did."

"Dad, stop it!" I paused briefly to make sure my dad was listening. "Dad, I'm sorry if you can't understand me. But this is my life. You have to let go and let me live. I'll say hi to you before I leave, ok? I have a few friends I want you to meet."

"Oh boy, it's a shame that I have to plead with you before you can visit us. That's one horrid mistake your mother and I made--to have only one child. I wish I had another child, to carry on my legacy. When will you return to live with us?"

"Dad, please, I have to go now, ok? I'll drop by before I leave." I clicked off the phone and fought back tears.

"Sorry for the wait," I told Biggs and JT, who were both staring at me cautiously. I forced a smile and said, "I'm ready now."

I told JT goodbye. Biggs and I returned to the Range Rover then headed towards the main street, to pick up the triplets.

CHAPTER FOURTEEN
JT

I slipped and fell on my behind as I raced from the back yard into the house to answer the phone. It seemed as if all I did was answer that damn cell phone and as a result I stayed replenishing my phone credit, which was now beginning to cost me more than one eights of what I earned weekly.

"Ouch!" I wailed as I tried to get back up. It was my fault though. I had forgotten to clean up the spill I had made from the coconut water I was drinking earlier. I took my time and tried to get up as slowly and painlessly as possible. By the time I got to the phone it had stopped ringing. "Damn!" I shouted angrily. I was mad that I had broken my backside for no reason. The phone lit up again and started to ring. I smiled, when I saw the netball coach's number dance across my screen. My boy, Biggs, had given her my number the same night of the fight which had been over a week ago, and she'd been blowing up my phone ever since.

"Talk to me," I answered informally.

"Hi, JT," she sang my name sweetly.

"You know I could get used to hearing you call my name."

"Why you always have to go there with me?"

"Because you invite me."

"What you mean by I invite you? I just got on the phone and barely said hi."

"That's all it takes for you to invite me, Empress."

"How are your bruises?"

"They're much better, but why you trying to change the topic?"

"Ok, what was the topic?"

"Can I see you tomorrow night?"

"See?"

"See what?"

"You always have to go there with me."

"I want to go even further," I listened for her to respond but she only laughed.

"Can I see you tomorrow night?" I asked again.

"Fine. You can see me tonight if you want to."

"I   can't,   at   least-   not   tonight."

"Why not?"

"Because I already have plans."

"Oh, you mean plans with the yankee girl you've been running around town with," her tone was sinister.

"She's just a new friend that I've met. She's actually one of my fans."

"Oh, so that makes it ok for you put her before the people you know?"

"Well, I'm getting to know her," I mocked in an attempt to lighten the mood. I didn't like the direction in which our conversation headed one bit. "Besides," I continued "the person I really want to get to know better is not giving me the time of day," I chuckled.

"Fine then, JT; spend your time with me tonight instead of that woman."

"As tempting as that sounds, I can't do it."

"Why not?"

"Because, Empress, I already gave her my word."

"Yeah, right! Good excuse indeed. You're acting as if you know that woman. So what if you break your word? You don't know her, JT. I have a strong feeling she's up to something."

"Ok, Empress, that's enough."

"What do you mean that's enough. You need to be careful with this yankee girl."

I   chuckled   once   more.
"Why you laughing?"

"Why do Jamaicans call American women yankee girls?"

"I wish you would take this seriously."

"Empress, I'll always take you seriously.   I realize now that you have mad love for me. But you can't get so jealous. I'm a grown man. You just have to wait until-"

"Until it's my turn?" she interjected,   "Until you're ready for me?"

When I didn't respond she said, "Ok, Mr. JT. I understand," she was being sarcastic.

"You a'right?" I asked hating myself for disappointing her. But I was a man used to my space. She was coming on a little too strong for me. Yes, I know that Nita was also coming on to me strongly. But that was different.

"What do you expect?" my sing-songing friend snapped.

"I just want you to take it easy with me, a'right, Empress?"

"I'm not your damn Empress, don't call me that."

"Well, whether I call you that or not, you'll always be my Nubian Queen."

"Before I hang up, you need to know the word on the street."

"What, you mean Bishop?"

"Oh, so you heard?"

"I've heard bits and pieces."

"Well, word on the street is, him and his friends are planning to chop you up."

"Let him try!" I yelled, as if it were Bishop on the other end of the line, "Bishop is nothing but a coward!"

"Well just be careful," she warned, "Plus, the people you're hanging with, place you at a higher risk."

"Higher risk for what?"

"Higher risk of having your life snatched from you."

"My God, you don't have to be so dramatic."

"Just be careful, JT," she hung up before I could even confirm whether or not she'd be coming over in a day like I'd suggested.

That night, Nita came by my house driving a Mini Cooper convertible. She was alone this time. I was already waiting in the yard for her arrival.

"Wow! You look smashing," I complimented as I embraced her warmly, "You smell really good too--as usual."

"Thanks, but you say that every time you see me," Nita replied.

"That's because it's the truth," I released her from my embrace and stepped back a bit to admire her. She was wearing a short black mini skirt, with a black halter top that showed off her huge titties and flat stomach. Her curvy legs glowed as if they'd been airbrushed. She stood five inches taller in the five inched heels she was rocking. Everything about this woman screamed sex and money.

"Seeing you looking as sexy as you do now, makes me want you really bad," I admitted honestly.

"We need to talk," she responded.

"Huh?" I was confused.

"Let's go inside," she demanded.

Inside, I offered her a drink of Red Label Wine, which she refused. I'd been hanging out with her and the triplets all week, and they'd never had a drink at my house.

"By the way, where are the triplets?"

"They're at a poolside party by the hotel."

"Oh, you sure you don't want a drink?"

"I'm sure," she smiled up at me with red, glossy lips, and placed her Louis Vuitton bag on the sofa next to her.

We both sat down together in my sofa.

"So, what's so important?" I asked her.

"We can't go out tonight."

"What?"

"We can't go out tonight."

"But I got dressed and was looking forward to-"

"Shhh," she hushed rudely, "Listen."

I'd been trying hard to put up with her rude personality and knew I had a long way to go. Sometimes I just felt like having somebody smack the shit out of her, but of course, it was just a feeling. I could tell she only acted that way because she was obviously used to getting what she wanted.

"The triplets need me tonight," she continued as she reached for her bag, "So I can't hang out with you tonight. I have something that will keep your mind busy though," she said reaching into her bag and then pulling out a 9 mm handgun.

I jumped up from my seat and tumbled to the floor.

"Don't tell me you're scared of such a small weapon."

"What you gonna do with that," I felt my eyes bulge from their sockets.

"I'm giving it to you," she said easily, "Here, take it."

"Take it and do what with it?"

"Take it and protect yourself with it."

"No! I've been managing fine without a gun, all these years before you showed up. Why now, do I suddenly need protection?"

"Don't be silly," she flashed me off, "Just take this and keep it. I'm by no means saying that you need it, it's just a gift from me to you-- and don't worry, it cannot be traced," those words flowed from her lips as easily as everything else she'd said to me.

"Who are you?" I now looked up at her from my place on the floor. My eyes moved wildly from the gun to her, then from her to the gun.

"JT, you are unbelievable. I saw you whoop some guy's ass with your bare hands, yet now you pretend to be scared of a gun?"

"Who are you?" I repeated. She rested the gun on the sofa. Picked up her bag and headed towards the door.

"Where are you going?"

"I'm leaving," she said firmly, "I've obviously overstayed my welcome."

She opened the door and left. I didn't stop her. As soon as I heard her car drive off, I jumped up and got my cell phone and started dialing.

"Hey, Biggs!" I was happy to hear my friend on the other end of the line.

"Meet me at the bar in fifteen minutes! We need to talk." We spoke for a minute before I hung up the phone. I then placed the phone in my pocket, picked up the gun and tucked it in my waist underneath my shirt, locked up the house tight, tight and hurried through the door.

CHAPTER FIFTEEN
JT

Friday nights were Wine Up nights at Horatio's Bar, and the large, crowded room was jumping off with loud reggae music blasting through speakers, and scantily clad women shaking their rumps to the good vibration. The DJ was pumping his best mixes from old school hits by Shabba Ranks and Super Cat, to new jams by Sean Paul and Serani. Horatio's wasn't just your average bar, because Jamaicans most times did things a little differently from everyone else. Horatio's was an all-purpose bar, so to speak. It had a club scene and was considered the perfect jump-off spot where people gathered to dance, hook up, hang with friends, play dominoes, drink and get drunk.

I passed by a group of men playing dominoes, and headed towards the counter, scanning the room as I moved through the crowd. Biggs was nowhere in sight. I was lucky enough to find an empty stool, so I sat down, greeted the busy bartender with a friendly nod and quickly turned my head in the opposite direction, pretending not to have noticed her double take.

I immediately regretted that little move, because as soon as I turned around, my eyes made eight with three voluptuous young women who stood in a corner winking at me. Over the years I'd learnt that there was a time and place for everything. Though it was the right place for meaningless flirtation, it certainly wasn't the right time. I turned away from their gazes and felt cold steel rubbing against my skin. My cell phone vibrated, distracting me from the coldness of the gun inside my waist. Already knowing that it was Biggs on the other end, I flipped the phone open and held it to my ear, without checking the number that appeared on the screen.

"You inside the bar, mon?"
I didn't respond to him because one, I was overwhelmed with angst; two, I knew he wouldn't be able to hear me; and three, why the hell was Biggs still on the phone when he clearly heard the loud music booming in the background? The call was disconnected and a few seconds later, a text message came in that read: *I'll come inside in a minute to meet you.*

I flipped the phone shut, stood up again, and headed back outside to meet Biggs.

Moments later, I was spinning around like a gig, frustrated and pissed off that I couldn't find Biggs.

"You look worried," someone said in a very familiar sing-song tone. I paused in place and wondered what the hell she was doing at Horatio's by herself. Certainly if she was with someone she wouldn't find time to come out and bust my chops.

"Turn around and face me, JT, I haven't grown horns," she demanded.

I slowly turned to face her. If she was looking sexy, I wouldn't know, because my mind had been elsewhere.

"I assume your lady friend stood you up?" she mocked.

"Are you asking me, or are you telling me?" I snapped. The last thing I needed was for Tanisha to provoke me.

"Calm down, JT. Don't take out your frustrations on me," she said, stressing the 'me' while rolling her neck, "I told you not to trust that woman."

I felt my cell phone vibrating again and welcomed the opportunity of being rescued from this harassment.

"Hello!" I shouted into the phone, hoping that Biggs would be able to hear me. The call was dropped. What the hell was going on? I stared at the phone in bewilderment.

"Earth to JT, come in!" Tanisha jeered.

"What is your problem, mon?" I asked irritably, as I jolted out of the daze I was in.

"I told you that little yankee gal was bad news," she persisted.

"Why are you so concerned about me and Nita?"

"Oh, so her name is Nita, huh?" Tanisha scowled, "Well your little Nita, is playing you."

"What's your problem?" I repeated.

"My problem is that you won't listen to me. I know you're in trouble, and Nita has something to do with it."

"Where you been, mon?" I asked, ignoring the netball coach as Biggs trudged towards us.

"Why did you come outside when I told you I was on my way in?" Biggs asked.

"I came out to meet you," I explained, relieved that Biggs had come through for me.

"Wha'apen, little Miss?" Biggs asked Tanisha.

"I should be asking you that question," she replied, throwing us an accusing glare.

"Biggs, let's go over there and talk," I butted in, pointing towards the bus across the street from where we stood.

"A'right then," Biggs agreed, without saying another word to Tanisha. We both walked away. Served her right. I hated it when a woman was being so damn pushy, and I'm a lover of my own space.

"What's going on, boss? You sound and look like you've just seen a ghost!" Biggs evaluated as he partially rested his massive butt on the brink of the bus stop wall.

"You're not going to believe the shit that I'm about to spill," I replied, leaning against the wall next to him, while stroking the cold steel that was securely tucked away under my shirt.

"Well, maybe you should just start spilling," Biggs responded glancing at the nearby bushes to mentally certify our isolation.

"Touch this," I raised my right hand and leaned towards the left, bracing my entire right side for easy access to the gun.

"What's wrong with your side?" Biggs eyed me quizzically.

"Just touch this, mon!" I ordered impatiently. Biggs reluctantly tapped my armpit then charily traced the palm of his hand southward. "What kind of battybwoy thing this?" he muttered as he slowly ran his arm down my side. "What's this?" he queried as he paused abruptly, recovered from his shock, and then began kneading the hard metal. "Is this what I think it is?" He asked, knitting his thick brows while staring at me puzzled. "JT, what the hell is going on with you?"

"A whole lot of shit," I sighed heavily as I resumed my stance.

"Talk to me, bredrin," Biggs urged.

"A'right. To make a long story short, I got into this fight with Bishop last week, but clearly the fight is not over because Bishop and his friends are out for revenge. They might try to kill me!"

"No bomboclaut way! Bishop can never touch you again as long as I live!" Biggs snapped.

"Wait, let me finish. Not only is Bishop after my life, but I received a call from Lexi a few days ag-"

"You received a call from Lexi-who?" Biggs interrupted.

"Lexi," I answered, wishing I could kick myself in my own ass for the slip of tongue.   Lexi and I had been corresponding with each other since she'd left for the States, however her calls had increased and our conversations a little too tense. My decision to keep this from my best friend Biggs was completely innocent. As far as I could recall, Biggs and Lexi never got along. Lexi hated Biggs because, according to her, he had too much chunk; and Biggs hated Lexi because she hated him. I avoided the subject all together to keep the peace. "She called me a few days ago," I white lied, pretending as if that was the only time I'd heard from Lexi since she'd left Jamaica. I paused and eyed Biggs from the corners of my eyes.

"Continue," he encouraged.

"Well, do you remember Everhard?" I asked.

"Who's Everhard?"

"The man who raped Lexi."

"Oh," Biggs nodded while playing with his invisible beard, "You mean Lexi's mother's man!"

"Yes. Lexl's stepfather," I verified, secretly wishing I could de-countrify Biggs and his less than sophisticated expressions.

"What about him?"

"Well, years ago--more like the day after he raped her, I had made her a promise."

"What kind of promise?"

"I promised her that I'd help to avenge the vicious death of her innocence." I stared off into nothingness.

Biggs waited for a few moments, then, overwhelmed with curiosity, he blurted out, "So?"

"So?" he repeated a few seconds later while nudging me to continue.

"Huh?" I mumbled jerking out of my deep thoughts and grabbing the spot on my shoulder that now throbbed from the impact of Biggs' heavy elbow. He was oblivious of course, to his painful blow.

"He raped her almost five years ago; you made a promise to her while you guys were still kids and she called you a few days ago. So what?"

"So, she's coming back to Jamaica, Biggs."

"To live?"

"No! To visit," I explained wishing that Biggs would catch on.

"So what's the big deal--oh shit! You mean she's coming back for revenge?"

"Not only that, but she wants my help, like I'd promised."

"What?" Biggs shouted.

"Shhh! That's just the start of it. She'll be arriving in the country tomorrow night."

"What?" Biggs shouted again.

"Shhh!" I hushed, "I don't wish to attract unnecessary attention."

"A'right, but is she crazy?"

"Biggs, you know Lexi."

"But didn't her stepdaddy break it off with her mother a few months back?"

"That's exactly why Lexi chose this time to return."

"But why now? You think she want fi kill him?"

"I don't know. All I know is that she thinks now is the best time to get her revenge, especially since he's no longer with her mother."

"That's some serious shit!"

"I know. To make matters worse, Nita gave me this gun, not too long ago and walked out on me."

"You mean you got that gun from sweet, sweet, Nita?" Biggs questioned sarcastically, "You think she's up to something?"

"I don't know. The netball coach seems to think that, but I don't know," I stared off again into the distance, but quickly recovered for fear of another blow from Biggs.

"Her name is Tanisha," Biggs spat, clearly disgusted for some unknown reason.

"Huh?" I responded, confused.

"Why do you keep calling her the netball coach? She has a name. Her name is Tanisha."

"Ok, ok, fine! Tanisha."

"So what are you going to do about all of this mess?"

"Shit if I know."

"Do you think Nita has something to do with some of this?"

"Biggs, you ask me that already and I told you I don't know."

"But, but, all this shit started to happen, one after the other, since Nita's arrival."

"I just don't know what to make of all of this. Plus, the netball coa- I mean, Tanisha, keeps pushing up on me and telling me how Nita is bad news for me. I don't know if I should believe it's her intuition, or if she's just pum-pum blocking."

"You're a popular man, JT. I guess someone wants to put out your light. But that will never happen as long as I'm alive! I will be your personal bodyguard. I'll call up my bredrin and let him know to be on the alert."

"What about the gun?" I asked Biggs.

"What about it?"

"What should I do with it?"

"Keep the gun, mon."

"K-k-keep it?"

"Yes, JT. Keep it. Come on! Let's go inside the bar for some drinks. You deserve it." Biggs shuffled his body from the wall and stood straight as he studied me.

"I guess you're right," I offered him a quick, nervous smile and we moved away from the bus stop and headed towards Horatio's.

As we both neared the bar, the music thumped louder, the surroundings appeared to be more festive and the women's smiles broadened. We entered the bar, moved through the thick crowd, and headed for the counter.

"What can I get for you guys?" the smiling bartender asked, her question directed more at me than both Biggs and me.

"Ray & Nephew Rum and coke," Biggs butted in, "And just keep it coming."

We watched as she turned away, obviously disappointed at my non-responsiveness. When her back was turned to us, Biggs chuckled and nudged me again with his elbow.

I staggered home, somewhat drunken from all the rum and coke I'd consumed over the past hours. Halfway through the night, Tanisha had moseyed her way over to our spot at the counter and whisked Biggs away into the night. I wasn't worried about that. If she wanted to give Biggs some of her goodies, then that would be alright by me. Or maybe it was the liquor talking. Anyway, I'd exhausted all the liquor I was left with, and had assured Biggs, four hours later, that I would be alright by myself.

"You sure?" he'd asked.

"Yup," I'd replied finding it difficult to utilize my, now, heavy tongue.

"Tanisha wants to talk, so I'll be back in another hour. Wait for me," he'd demanded for the first time in our many years of friendship.

Oh shhhit! He'd told me to wait for him. I chuckled at my absentmindedness and continued my lone journey down the dark, winding street. How could I have forgotten about Biggs? It had to be the liquor, I concluded again. I stopped, looked behind me, and then looked ahead. I'd come a far way, but I knew I still had somewhat of a distance to go. I thought about calling for a taxi, but dismissed the thought and chuckled again as I did so. I mean, calling a taxi at 2 a.m. in the morning? This was Jamaica for crying out loud! All the taxi drivers were at rum bars! I chuckled to myself again as I wobbled home, repeating to myself *this is Jamaica, not America, this is Jamaica....* I continued this for another five minutes, then paused again to look behind me. Damn! I'd obviously slowed down because I hadn't gone much farther than I was the last time I'd stopped. I felt tattered. I bent slightly to the side and tipped over. Awww! I screamed as I fell to the ground and twisted my ankle. Then I chuckled with relief since the pain signified my feet were still there. I could hardly feel my legs which is why I'd bent over in the first place to pinch them.

"Fuck you, Biggs!" I shouted. Then I proceeded with my arduous task of getting back up. One thing was positive about where I lay sprawled out by the street side--I'd finally come within reach of a street light. *That wasn't so bad,* I thought, *at least the power wasn't out at this street light.* I chuckled again and decided that the best way to get up would be butt first. So, I rolled over on my belly and went down on all fours. I then used my hands and feet to force my butt all the way up, then I lifted my hands from the ground with one quick movement. I staggered for a few seconds, then I was up! I marveled at my awesomeness. I decided to keep moving. The streets were horrifyingly quiet. Everyone had their lights out, and no one was in sight.

I wasn't as drunk as I could have been though, as a matter of fact, I was usually one who could hold his liquor. *What'd happened tonight? Oh, I hadn't eaten all evening.* I walked for what seemed to have been an eternity then stopped to look behind me. The stop light where I'd been a few moments ago was now well out of sight and the next one was some distance away. Though I was in the dark again I was pleased at my progress. I listened to the creatures of the night. *The crickets, bats, owl- shit! Were owls creatures of the night? And if so, did they have owls in Jamaica?* I chuckled again then paused to listen carefully. *Yup! There had to be owls in Jamaica.* That's when I heard the sound of leaves breaking in the bushes. I couldn't see what was making the noise, *but I was sure it had to be a goat, or maybe a cow. Shit! Did they have cows in Jamaica?* I marched onward for another eternity. I stopped when I approached the area with the bamboo trees. The sound of breaking leaves and grass echoed around me. *It was obvious that this cow was trying to follow me home.* I used my left hand to feel my right side, since I really wasn't in the mood to use my right arm. *Yup! The gun was still in place. If this cow decided to charge, I knew I'd be having steak for breakfast, lunch and dinner!*

Maybe it was the liquor in my system, or maybe it was the nearby gullies on each side of the street, but the constant resonance of leaves and grass breaking under the pressure of relentless footsteps, made me conclude that I was possibly being followed by more than one cow. I felt the pressure in my head intensify. I kept moving, while massaging my temples yearning for my warm bed and wishing I hadn't wolfed down all that alcohol in the first place.

My mind wandered back to the cows that were stalking me, then to more pressing issues that began to plague my mind. *I mean, who was responsible for the idea of making Ackee and Codfish Jamaica's National Dish? Why not Oxtail and rice and peas? Or even Steak. Or even Rundown with Yam, Breadfruit and Cassava. And why don't they have a National Day? There should be a National Day--set aside for men. Yeah, they could name the day PumPum Day, or something like that. A special day for us Jamaican men to-*

"So we meet up again, battybwoy!" a gruff voice from the bushes ruptured the darkness and menaced the air. My heart thumped from my immediate adrenaline rush. I was ready to run -- I mean; *could cows actually talk?* I tried to run but my feet wouldn't let me, instead I stood completely frozen with new awareness.

"Yo, JT! Didn't I just ask you a question?"

My heart thumped faster and my brows furrowed. *Not only could cows talk, but this one actually knew my name.*

"Turn around, you drunk bastard!"

I spun obediently in the opposite direction and took a quick look around. I was almost certain there was no one there. My eyes had grown accustomed to the moonlit night and I knew almost for sure, that I was either hearing things, or whatever or whoever was out there, had to be invisible. Then a dark figure suddenly leapt out of the bushes and bounded towards me.

"You think it was over between us?" he said as he charged at me wielding what I immediately recognized to be a machete. My drunkenness, now somewhat dissolved by adrenaline, dissipated and I ran as fast as my feet could take me in the opposite direction, towards the gully on the other side. My sober attacker was caving in on me fast, so I did the next best thing and chucked off into the bushes. My attacker was right on my tail and just as I landed with heavy force on grass and shrubs, my attacker delivered a sharp blow to the back of my head, and another to my spine. My body coiled in agony, but I knew I had to tune out the pain and move swiftly in order to protect myself. I rolled onto my back and looked up to gather my bearings. That's when I locked gazes with Bishop who shot me his most fiery grimace.

"Welcome!" he shouted, waving the machete in a wand-like motion as he twisted his cracked lips into a wretched half smile and glared down at me disdainfully. "Welcome to your worst nightmare!" He looked up to the heavens and continued to shout, "Lord! Have mercy on this sinner who's pathetic life I'm about to end! Amen!"

Before he could finish his sentence, I'd braced myself and rolled my body away from him, as hard and fast as I possibly could. I ended up rolling over the edge of the bank and gained momentum as I sped down the gully. My body was being battered against weathered stones and shrubs, but fortunately enough, there were no trees in the way. I felt the gun slip inside of my pants and lodged next to my groin. Like a drowning man catching after a straw, I reached out and grabbed onto a plant. As I clutched my lifesaver for dear life, the sudden movement flung my body violently from side to side and one of my legs collided with a rock. I heard my ankle crack. My body continued to sway until I'd finally regained some sort of equilibrium. I cringed as pain seared through my entire being. My face was soaking wet--a probable result of a head bleed, or maybe several bleeds. My eyes welled up in tears. I was a drunken man in a lot of pain and that was no chicken shit.

"Where are you, JT? Come out and face me like a man!"

This fool was really serious. He wanted me dead. I shook my head in an attempt to ward out any questions that would provoke my thoughts as to why a simple football game could possibly end up leading to something tragic. At that moment, as drunk as I was, I knew that one of us had to die. It was either going to be me or Bishop, and since I wasn't ready to go down like that, it would have to be Bishop. Furthermore, it was never my ambition to die drunk.

"JT! It's just me and you alone in this gully tonight. You can't escape! You might as well come out of hiding and get this over with!" his voice boomed, signaling he was close by. I fastened my healthy foot within the extended roots of a nearby tree, and let go of my lifesaver to rest my aching arms.

My head pounded, my injured ankle throbbed, my sore body stung and my face got wetter. I looked around and noticed that there was nowhere to run, plus I was too drunk to run. I was too drunk to even think. I felt something hard and cold rubbing against my crotch area. It certainly was something other than my dick. It was a foreign object. *What the hell?* I pulled down my zipper to fetch the unidentified object, and smiled faintly when I discovered that it had been the gun all along.

"JT, I can smell you!"

I peeped up just in time to spot Bishop swinging the machete in my direction. He missed. He jumped over my head in one skillful acrobatic motion, as if he was a mad man. Within moments he was only a few feet away from me. He stood before me, pissed off and well balanced, as if he stood on a flat surface. I figured that my struggle for stability was clearly more intense than his due to my inebriated state.

"You're a dead man!" he grinned and lifted the machete, ready to take a swing at my already bruised body.

The sound of the firearm going off was deafening--thunderous even, or maybe it was the alcohol in my system.

"You shot me?" he asked.
I didn't respond.

"You shot me?" he repeated with his eyes bulging and his neck sticking forward.
I watched as his machete slip from his hand like heated metal through butter. He grabbed his chest as blood oozed through his fingers. He fell to the ground. My hands shivered as I replaced the gun and retrieved my cell phone.

I dialed. He picked up on the first ring.
"JT, where are you?"
"Biggs," I grunted, "Come quick."

CHAPTER SIXTEEN
LEXI

I closed my eyes tightly, opened my arms widely and inhaled deeply, immersing myself into the purity of the Caribbean air. I held my breath for as long as I could, in hopes of absorbing as much as I could, of Jamaica's refreshing milieu. The fragrance of the Resort's garden blended with the hypnotic scent of the rich ocean breeze. This was indeed the almost perfect getaway. I considered it to be almost perfect since my mission here was rather business than pleasure, even though I knew I would be experiencing pleasure immeasurable, from the task at hand. Furthermore, I'd travelled alone despite Vaughnn's numerous attempts to stop me.

"Baby, since I can't talk you out of doing this, at least let me come with you" he'd pleaded as he gripped both of my arms.

"I can't," I replied looking away from him, "I have to do this on my own."

I opened my eyes and exhaled in satisfaction. As I stood in awe of the lush beauty that engulfed me, I grew more and more pleased at my decision to not only travel alone, but to also spend my entire two-week visit outside of Manchester. The Wyndham Rose Hall Resort, located in Montego Bay, Jamaica, stood tall in all its grandeur, overlooking acres upon acres of some of nature's most handy work. The healthy, bright green golf course was spectacular as it stretched onto the beach, kissing the white sand that glistened in the afternoon sun. The rocks near the beach were like exotic mini-mountains, which seemed even more exotic due to the continuous weathering caused by the sea breeze. All of this beauty was surrounded by even more beauty--flourishing vegetation and forests of tall trees that appeared to touch the heavens.

In the distance, across from the hotel, high on the hillside was the pathway that led to a Georgian Mansion which was considered one of Jamaica's most famous attraction spots. It was called the Rose Hall Great House, which is known for its legends and haunting.

The only person that was aware of my visit back to my island home was JT. I'd intended to keep it that way. I also trusted JT to keep this information private and not spill any of it. This mission was supposed to be top secret. I smiled at my silly thought and repeated the words in my head, *top secret.* I retrieved my cell from the pocket of my cargo shorts and flipped it open. I sat down on the ground and contemplated the idea of calling JT. There were several missed calls from the triplets and Vaughnn, but none from JT. This was very unlike him. I mean, I'd made it a priority to inform him of my arrival. Had he forgotten? No, it's not possible that he could have forgotten. I'd been planning my visit for weeks and I'd made it known to him. I knew JT like the palm of my hands. Could he have changed so quickly? I immediately dismissed the idea that JT had backed out of our plan and I decided to call him, instead of waiting for him to call me. I had never known JT to be a punk, so there had to be something terribly wrong with him. I counted as the phone rang four times. Someone, other than JT answered before the fifth ring.

"Hello"

I jumped, startled by the husky voice on the other end of the line that obviously didn't belong to JT, "Uh, hi, where's JT?"

"Who's this?"

"Are you JT?"

"No."

"Then give the phone to JT and stop asking questions," I barked.

"Lexi?"

"Wh- how do you know my name?"

"It's Biggs."

"Biggs?"

"Yeah."

"What's up?"

"A whole lot of things."

"Like what?"

"Can't say over the phone."

"Then give the phone to JT."

"Just calm yourself, mon."

"I am calm. I just want to know why you choose to piss me off by not letting me speak with JT."

"I am not choosing to piss you off!" he raised his tone and spoke defiantly.

I sighed and rolled my eyes, disgusted at Biggs and was tempted to hang up. I couldn't believe JT was still friends with him. Biggs needed to get his shit together. Yes, he had connections and all, but he was still a chump in my book.

"Ok, what's going on Biggs?"

"That's much better. I was beginning to think that America did nothing for you."

"I beg your pardon?"

"Yeah, your attitude when I initially answered the phone was uncivilized." He paused, clearly waiting for me to blast him. I didn't. I could see JT was schooling him well on how to speak properly.

"Are you there?" he questioned, disappointed at his failure at getting me riled.

"Where's JT?" I asked, my voice now a whisper.

"He can't come to the phone."

"Why not?" I could feel my temper sizzling as I struggled to keep it under wraps.

"He's at the hospital."

"What?"

"Yeah, he got drunk last night and tripped and fell over into a gully."

"That shit doesn't even make sense. How can someone fall over into a gully? Was he pushed?"

"Why don't we meet somewhere and talk, Lexi?"

"What?"

"Let's meet somewhere and talk."

"What do you mean by that? Are you insane?" I was consumed with distaste. How did Biggs know to ask me to meet him some place? For all he knew, I was still in the States.

"Lexi, I know you're here."

"So JT did blab his big mouth, huh?" I replied as my heart sank in an ocean of hurt. JT had been the one person on the planet that I could trust. He'd betrayed me by running his mouth off to Biggs, the sucker I'd hated for so many years. That was it! I would have to abort my mission right after visiting him at the hospital and saying goodbye for the last time. I was going to write JT off for life. I would return to the States and hire someone to assume my responsibility.

"Listen, Lexi, I know how much you love JT. I also know how much he loves you. You two were best of friends, but so were JT and I. Even though you couldn't accept me, I accepted you. You have to trust JT and the decision he made to tell me about your visit. He told me because he trusted me-"

"But I don't trust you!" I blurted out, tears streaming down my cheeks. I hated the hatred

I'd now felt for JT. I couldn't even blame my hurt on the buffoon that was on the other end of the line. I had no one to blame but myself. I was wrong for trusting JT in the first place. I should have kept my business to myself and trusted no one.

"Well, with all the shit that's happening now, you have no freaking choice but to trust me!" he attempted to yell, but failed due to his hoarseness. Biggs had never yelled at me before. He'd always been reserved and had always kept his distance.

"What do you mean, Biggs?" I quizzed, wiping tears from my eyes.

"Like I said, I can't say this over the phone. We have to meet up somewhere. Where are you staying?"

"Mo-Bay," I replied hesitantly.

"Mo-Bay? All the way in Mo-bay?" he asked emphasizing the word 'all', making me feel stupid.

"Yeah, at the Wyndham Rose Hall. You can meet me in the Square by KFC!" I snapped. I felt hopeful after all. Biggs did have a point. If JT's secrets were safe with Biggs then so were mine. There also had to have been a good reason for him to have gone behind my back. Plus, why was he in the hospital? My tears were drying fast as horror struck. What did Biggs have to say to me that couldn't be said over the phone? JT was clearly in danger.

"I'm gonna ask one of my boys to drop me off over there."

"Is JT gonna be ok?"

"The doctor seems to think so."

"This shit is serious, isn't it?"

"I'll be there in a few hours," he responded less than audibly and then he ended the call.

The meager bartending associate paused and frowned at my unusual request.

"Pour some Wray and Nephew rum into my Kola Champagne!" I repeated in annoyance.

I found her reason for frowning quite ironic. She wasn't frowning at the possibility of me being an under aged drinker. Her reason for frowning was due to the unpopular blend of drinks I had requested.

"Wonders shall never cease!" she replied forwardly, grabbing up my glass of soda, and trudging off with it, her steps stronger than her looks. Biggs chuckled, almost mirroring JT's contagious snigger. It's as if so much of my best friend had rubbed off on Biggs. The only thing that was left for him to do was to hit the gym. I was even surprised when he'd rejected my offer to have lunch at KFC. Biggs, turning down food! He'd opted for drinks at the bar instead. I guess what the waitress had said was accurate. Wonders shall never cease.

"When can I visit him?" I asked cutting to the chase.

"Maybe as soon as tomorrow," Biggs informed as he took a sip of the Baileys mudslide I'd gotten him.

"How is that?" I asked him, lifting my head slightly and motioning my chin towards his glass.

"Oh, this?" he smiled nervously as he raised his glass, "It's good, mon. As a matter of fact, I've had this drink before."

"I'm glad you like it," I replied, ignoring his lie. I knew he was lying because initially when I'd offered him the drink he'd pronounced it incorrectly.

"Would you like to try a mudslide?" I'd asked him.

"Yes, I'll have a mug side," he'd confirmed.

"Here is your order," the scantily clad cocktail waitress said as she slammed down my drink on the table.

I grasped the glass and slid it across the table closer to my lips. I took a sip. "Niiice!" I exclaimed with satisfaction, ignoring her. She stomped away and Biggs chuckled again. Again his chuckle reminded me of JT. As I stared over at Biggs, I wondered about his motives. I mean, he had to be in his early thirties, and JT was already in his mid-twenties. This meant that when JT was but a teenager, he was best friends with Biggs who was already a grown ass man. Why?

"So explain everything to me," I demanded when the waitress was out of sight.

"Gimme a minute," Biggs took one long sip, finishing off his mudslide, "Can I get another one of these?" He asked with eager eyes.

"Sure" I answered cheekily, "Right after you tell me everything."

CHAPTER SEVENTEEN
LEXI

It was all déjà vu--from the triplets and the mystery woman, to Bishop being killed out of self defense by JT. I'd asked Biggs for names, but he'd denied my request. "JT asked me to keep the names private," he'd objected.
"But I need names," I insisted to no avail.

I had kept my room open at the Wyndham, and booked another at an inn closer to Mandeville. It had been two days and three nights since JT's admission at the Mandeville hospital. He would have been discharged already, but the doctor wanted to keep him an extra night for observation. His ankle was broken and had required surgery. His skull had been fractured and had required several stitches. The rest of his body was bruised, but seemed to have been in great condition in comparison to his head and ankle.

"How are you feeling, beau?" I smiled empathetically as I gently kissed the white bandage that covered his head.

"Are you mad at me, Empress?" he asked winking his eyes at me comically.

"Never that," I giggled, casting my eyes at the cast that covered his ankle. "How's the leg?"

"I'll still be able to have sex," he chuckled.

"Same old JT," I took his palm into mine.

"I missed you," he admitted groggily.

"I missed you too," I leaned back on the small hospital bed and gazed at the curtains that enclosed us. Though I've never had anything against hospitals, I'd always had a thing against my being inside of one. Now here I was, lying in a hospital bed, supporting my injured friend while trying to play it cool as if everything was copasetic, when the truth of the matter is, I wanted to run away. I was becoming more and more nauseated by the minute. In my opinion, this could have been due to the strong, unpleasant smell of disinfectant colliding with the stench of death. I was tempted to make a dash for the exit, but willed myself not to.

"I want you to stay at my house throughout the remainder of your visit."

"I can't."

"Why not?"

"You know why I'm here, JT. It's better if I stay invisible."

"Well at least visit me often."

"Of course I will."

"JT, you have a visitor. Should I send her up?" A pleasant looking nurse asked as she smiled at JT. If I didn't know better, I'd say she was flirting with him.

"Yeah, send her up," he permitted.

"What are you doing?" I whispered, "What if it's someone that I know?"

"Relax, everything irie, mon," he closed his eyes and smiled.

"What kind of drugs are they giving you in this hospital?"

"Why you ask?"

"Because you're not thinking strai-"

"Hi JT," someone sang as she entered his room. I looked up and to my surprise it was Tanisha. I smiled up at her.   I never had any beef with that woman. As a matter of fact, she taught my class Phys Ed back in high school.

"What's good, T?" I greeted as she smiled back at me.

"Hi, Empress!" JT greeted her.

"Wait a minute! I thought that name was reserved for me," I scowled at JT playfully.

"That name is reserved for everybody with a coochie," Tanisha walked up to me and engaged me in a haughty hug, "It's nice to see you again, Lexi."

"It's good to see you, too," I patted her fondly on the shoulder before we released each other.

"Here," she said handing me a plastic bag, "I brought these apples for JT, but you can have them."

"Get out!" I said grabbing the bag of red, juicy, Jamaican apples. My mouth watered at the sight of the luscious fruits. Immediately, I thought about the market in the square, and smiled as I reminisced about the bright colored carts with huge umbrellas that protected the sweet oranges, naseberries and mangoes from the sun. "I missed all of this."

"That is why you're welcome to have JT's share."

"Hopefully, you'll give me something else to eat," JT said, smiling weakly.

"Shut up, freak!" I replied.

"He's half dead and still don't know how to keep his mouth shut," Tanisha laughed.

"Well, I'm outta here. I'll leave you two to catch up. Thanks again, Tanisha!"

"No problem, mon," Tanisha replied.

"Come by my house tomorrow night? We have a lot to discuss," JT yelled out after me.

"We sure do," I agreed and exited the room, grateful for the opportunity to finally escape those frigid walls. I couldn't wait to get back into the fresh Christiana air. It felt good to be back, if only for a while. When Biggs had picked me up in Montego Bay a few days ago, we'd travelled on the coastline to Falmouth, and then all the way through Bristol, to get to the hospital. Though I was concerned for JT, I'd enjoyed the scenic view of the ocean and greenery. This visit to the hospital had taken all of that away from me, so I decided, once JT was doing much better, we'd have to take a trip from coast to coast, halfway around the island to Negril.

One week later I decided to give Vaughnn a call. My mind had been playing tricks on me, and I was about to go insane if I didn't get some answers soon. On several different occasions I could have sworn I'd spotted Nita and the triplets either getting into cars, or entering buildings or some other shit. Just this morning, while I was on my way to visit JT at the hospital, the driver of the taxi cab I had chartered, decided to make a brief detour, to collect a crocus bag filled with breadfruits. I purchased half a dozen from him for JT and me, and he gifted me with two extra ones. On our way back, as we passed by Hotel Villa Bella, I thought I spotted Nita getting into a Mini Cooper. My eyes must have been deceiving me.

"Hello, I missed you so much baby," Vaughnn answered the phone.

"I missed you too, but I didn't really call for that."

"And they said chivalry was dead," he commented sarcastically. I didn't respond.

"What's going on baby? Tell me what's bothering you," he urged.

"I need you to tell me something."

"What do you wanna know?"

"Where are Nita and the triplets?"

"They're here."

"What?"

"They're here."

"What do you mean by they're here?"

"They arrived back from Puerto Rico a few hours ago."

"Are you sure?"

"Of course I'm sure. I know what they look like. Yup, it's them alright," he snickered.

"That's not what I meant, Baldy. Are you sure they were in Puerto Rico?"

"That I'm not sure about, why?"

"Because I think they were here."

"You mean there, as in Jamaica?"

"Yeah, I mean here as in Manchester, Jamaica."

"What? Baby, are you smoking weed down there?"

"No, Baldy! They were here in Manchester! What the hell were they doing here in Manchester, Vaughnn?"

"Ok, first of all, I need you to apologize for calling me Baldy, and secondly, I need you to put away the blunt."

"I'm not smoking, Vaughnn, a lot of shit has been going down. I think that Nita was here!"

"Wait a minute, what kind of shit? Baby, are you hurt? Is your friend JT ok?"

"No I'm fine," I replied frustrated. I wasn't getting very far with Vaughnn. I was also angry at my slip of tongue. I wanted to keep Vaughnn out of the loop until I returned home to him.

"Baby, did that man put his hands on you again? Did you get to complete your mission?"

"Vaughnn, I'll tell you about that later. I just need to know for sure that Nita was in Puerto Rico."

"Trust me, Lexi, I believe she was. I'm sure your eyes were fooling you. You have a lot going on right now and Nita is a big part of it. The mind is a powerful thing, baby."

"I guess you're right," I agreed, immediately doubting the images I'd seen over the past seven days.

"Alright now, baby, I need you to apologize for calling me Baldy."

"But, you are bald."

"Yeah, but that's by choice."

"Yeah, right!" I joked as I toyed nervously with the bluetooth device on my ear.

"You'll pay for that," he teased.

"I love you V. Gotta go," I disconnected the call.

CHAPTER EIGHTEEN
LEXI

"They did what with the body?" I let go of the plate I was rinsing and whipped my head around so fast I heard it crick. I now stood directly facing JT who stood before me, leaning against the kitchen wall, propped up on his crutch. We'd just gobbled up a tasty meal of jerked pork and roasted breadfruit, which we'd washed down with tall glasses of passion fruit juice. Throughout dinner, I'd been listening keenly as JT vividly described the duel between himself and Bishop on the football field. I continued to lend my audience while doing the dishes as he outlined his almost brief encounter with death a little over two weeks ago. For the first time in my ten days of being reunited with JT, he'd finally decided to open up to me and give specific details surrounding his injuries. However, I hadn't been mentally prepared for what he was telling me.

"You heard me," he replied, staring off into space. A new habit I assumed he'd picked up recently, since I'd never known him to be someone who just stares off into space. Since our reunion, he'd been doing a lot of that, as if he was constantly being bombarded by his own thoughts.

"You let Biggs do what?" I grilled, out of shock rather than lack of hearing.

"Not Biggs, but his boy," he clarified.

"And what did his boy do?"

"He poured kerosene oil over the body," JT explained to me once more, "then lit it afire. He then used an axe to dig a hole in the ground and buried the remains in it."

I stood in one spot unable to blink, "So no one had thought to call the police? You are aware you were only defending yourself, right?"

"The cops in this town are corrupt, Lexi. They'd lock me up regardless, and try to find a way to blackmail me. Everyone around here thinks I have huge sums of money stashed away somewhere. Plus, Biggs thought the illegal gun I used for my supposed 'self defense', would have caused me unwanted grief."

"So why didn't you get rid of the gun, or even plant it on Bishop?"

"Like I told you before, I wasn't there when all of this was going down. A friend had already taken me to the hospital. It was not until afterwards that I'd received the low down on everything."

"You're not even making sense right now."

"What more do you want from me, Lexi? You asked me to open up to you, so I did. Now you're questioning my murder ethics?"

"That's not fair, JT. I just can't see why your friends couldn't have planted the gun on Bishop, and then call the cops, instead of burning the body. You could have easily told the cops you'd wrestled with Bishop and shot him with his own gun."

"So what happens when they trace the gun?"

"So what? It wasn't registered in your name, was it?"

"I was drunk, Lexi! There was no way I could have possibly wrestled with crazy ass Bishop and actually win. The police would have found a way to drag my name into the dirt with this."

"Did you at least ask Biggs why he and his friends had decided not to get the law involved?"

"I didn't."

"Are you crazy?" I found it hard to believe that JT could have been so dull. He'd placed his entire future into the hands of dumbass Biggs and his monkeys.

"I trust them; they know what they're doing."

"Are you trying to convince me, or yourself?" I watched as JT hopped towards the living room. "So now you're walking out on me?"

"Just let it be, mon! I mean- are you planning to get the cops involved in the mess you came to Jamaica to create?" He plopped himself down on the sofa and stared at the muted television. I was dumbfounded. JT had just put my ass in check. I silently returned to the sink and resumed my activities with the dirty dishes. I couldn't think or feel. I was floored. JT did have a point though. Who was I to be dishing out moral advice? I knew that's what he'd meant to say, but didn't. Furthermore, I'd left a man for dead after stabbing him that night at the bus stop. Was that not out of self defense? Instead of calling the cops, I'd chosen to run away, with a man who'd covered my tracks. My whole body itched as I fought the urge to puke. Once again I was pissed off at Biggs. He'd given me a version much similar to JT's, but with a completely different ending. He'd told me that the cops had been summoned. My heavy burdens were abundant. There'd be no additional room inside my heart for disliking Biggs more than I already did. I dried the last couple of dishes and placed them into the cupboard and proceeded to join my best friend in the living room.

"I have something to share with you," I said softly as I sat next to him, reaching for the remote control.

"Let me guess. Your body," he smirked as he held my free hand.

"No, pig," I smiled as I unmuted the TV, "I'll tell you all about it once my mission here is done."

"That's fine with me," he nodded, "Just don't forget to tell me."

"I won't forget," I affirmed.

"I'm sorry for dissing you earlier," he squeezed my palm.

"I'm used to your disrespect," I smiled.

"That sure can't be good," he said conjuring his deepest form of Jamaican accent for dramatic effect.

I laughed, "No it's not, but I put up with you all the same."

"Kiss mi neckback! That's how I know for sure we're best of friends."

"Tell me how you know for sure," I jeered.

"I haven't taken you to bed yet!"

"What?" I asked alarmed, "And you used the word yet?"

"You never know what tomorrow may bring."

"You're such a whore," I said in mocking disgust.

"I'm a whore and loving it," he retorted.

"So," I said as I fidgeted nervously with the remote.

"So what?" he asked.

"Are you ready for our big night tomorrow?"

"I'll be ready as soon as Biggs come through with what we need."

"Ughh!"

"You better start loving Biggs, Lexi. He's the mastermind behind this plan."

"I know. I just wish there was a way for us to exclude him."

"We can't. Don't you see I'm one legged right now? I need his help."

"I guess you're right," I smiled, covering up my anguish. I was only hours away from accomplishing my biggest goal. I'd be face to face once again with the man I'd hated for so many years. Everything was finally falling into place. JT and I jumped in unison as a knock on the door detracted us from our thoughts.

"I'll get it!" I got up and rushed to open the door for Biggs.

"Goodnight," he greeted without making eye contact with me, "What happen, bredrin?" he greeted JT without waiting for a response from me. I didn't really care at all. I was just grateful that he'd come through for me, regardless of our differences; though I knew whatever he did, he did for JT.

"What's happening, boss?" JT greeted back as he popped fists with Biggs.

Cloaked with boldness and drenched in uneasiness, I knocked daringly on the heavy mahogany door of an old, secluded concrete house. I briefly eyed the seemingly countless mango trees that occupied most of the front yard, which, by the way, might as well have been the back. Inhabited by someone else, for instance, a non-rapist, the yard would have seemed a lot less eerie, and the front of the yard being no different from the back of the yard wouldn't have mattered so much. I glanced behind me one last time making sure that--well there was nothing to make sure of, I was going freaking nuts. I jumped as I heard the heavy door screech raucously on its hinges. Next, I was face to face with Everhard, the son-of-a-bitch who'd once claimed to be my mother's man.

"Bomboclaut!" he uttered, "If it's not the great Lexi!" He spread his lips wide open exhibiting most of his thirty-two teeth. He flashed his long dreads and hopped on the spot as if he was dancing to commemorate my unannounced visit. "Come inside daughter!" he invited.

"Have you seen my mother?" I asked ignoring his invitation, "I'm visiting for a few days to take care of some business, but can't seem to find mother. Is she with you?"

"How did you find me?" he inquired, puzzled.

"Come on, Everhard, these are modern days and this is Jamaica. You're not that hard to find. My mother on the other hand- seems to have disappeared," I dodged his question.

"No, she's not with me. Your mums and I parted a long time ago."

"What?" I pretended not to have already known this piece of fact.

"Yes, rasta! I couldn't deal with your mums any longer. She was stressing me out with her jealous ways."

"Meaning?"

"Meaning, she keep pressuring I mon about false allegations."

"What allegations are those?"

"Come inside so that I mon can talk to you, Princess."

"I need the fresh air, I prefer to stand right here," I observed as he gawked at my breasts and then at my legs. He then smiled a very disturbing smile once our eyes made four again.

"I want to give you a drink of Tia Maria, you sure you don't want to come inside?"

This perverted bitch had already gotten on my last nerve. It was taking everything I had not to kill him on the spot. "Ok, let's go for a walk," I said.

"Where?" he asked as he scanned our surroundings.

"Anywhere, isn't there a park close by?" I stared him dead in the eyes knowing he'd fall for the trap.

"Well, there's a river not too far from here!" He smiled in satisfaction.

"That sounds great! Let's go down by the riverside," I smiled, more at my choice of words, than at Everhard.

"Let I mon get I shoes," he rushed inside buoyantly, then reappeared within seconds wearing a pair of flip flops. He carried a red, green and gold headwear in his hands. As he locked his door with the key, I also observed something that hadn't been there before.
He was now wearing a pair of leather gloves.

I turned away and smiled to myself. All these years Everhard had taken me and my mother for fools. As I quickened my pace, his voice broke through my deep thoughts, "This way!" he yelled out, placing the headwear on his head. I spun around and walked in the opposite direction towards him, pleased that he'd bought the bait, and even more pleased at my acting skills.

"So what allegations were you referring to?" I asked when I'd finally caught up with him.

"Oh, you mean with your mums?"

"Yeah."

"Well, there is not a day that pass when she don't ask if I and I, if I really did rape you."

"What did you say?" My efforts to remain calm were major.

"I told her no, of course."

I stopped dead in my tracks and listened to the small voice in my head that kept saying *'Don't do it, Lexi. Stick to the plan.*

"Why did you lie to her?"

"Rastafari never lie!" he contradicted as he stopped next to me.

"But you said you told her that you never raped me," I softened my temperament, faked a smile and recommenced my stroll.

"What we shared was never rape, Princess. Your body was ripe, so I mon gave you what your body needed!" He flashed his locks again. As we travelled farther and farther away from civilization, the more I felt myself being pulled into a dark pit. There was no turning back now. It was only do or die from here on out. I knew exactly what Everhard's next move would be, and there was no running away from him.

"What makes you think that's what my body needed?"

"Don't act like you never want it."

"Want what?"

"Some good loving."

"At fifteen and still a virgin, I doubt good loving was at the top of my to-do list."

"So what you trying to tell I mon?" he asked infuriated.

"I just wanted to know why you continued even when I told you to stop."

"What you prefer?" he paused for a moment and rotated his head, his face taking on that familiar evil look.

"Huh?" I played dumb.

"I said, what you prefer? You prefer to give up your thing to a stupid school boy who would break your heart, or you prefer to give it up to a real man who know what to do with it?"

Though his icy tone ran my blood cold, I peered back at him through the dark, "I was only fifteen years old, Everhard," I spoke harshly, "You forced sex upon a fifteen year old child who was your own step-daughter. What the do you mean by that's what I wanted?"

I hadn't planned for my failure at sticking to the plan. My nerves rattled and my temper boiled. Though the serene sound of flowing water alerted me that the stream was close by, I felt we were still too far away from the river and shit was already about to go down. Everhard stopped in front of me, blocking my path, but I tried my best to play it cool. "Let's just keep walking," I gently pushed him to the side of the track. He moved on impact but grasped my hand as I passed by him.

"How old are you now?" he asked, in a tone as disturbing as his smile.

"I beg your pardon?"

"You said you were only fifteen when I first put my hands on you. I want to know how old you are now, since I plan to put my hands on you a second time."

"Let's go by the river, Everhard."

"No, Princess, our journey ends right here. Pull down your skirt."

"Excuse me?"

"Pull down your skirt! How you expect to show up in front of I mon, with them nice titties and not expect to get what you ask for?"
"I didn't ask you for anything, Everhard!"

"Princess, you're actually right. I'm ever hard for a nice girl like you. Now, pull down your skirt."

"Not in your dreams!" I screamed, attempting to move past him again. He grabbed my arm and placed me back into my original spot.

"What the hell is your problem?" I shrieked.

"There won't be any problem if you just do what I say," he stated as he stepped closer to me while undoing his belt to remove his pants.

"Fuck you!" I yelled out squeezing onto my purse for dear life.

"No Princess, fuck you! And I intend to do just that." With one swift movement he opened his arms and pulled me into him, locking my body into his tight, unsolicited embrace. My purse fell from my hands as he forced me down to the ground; then used one of his muscular arms to bind both of mine, while he used his free arm to rip my clothes off. He was moving faster than I could think--much faster than I'd prepared myself for. "I'll show you how a real man lay down pipe," he croaked into my ears.

"Go any further with this shit, and you'll never live to lay another pipe!" I snarled.

"Babe, though you're in a good position, it's definitely not the right position for threats against I mon," he ran his coarse palm over my chest, then trailed his fingers over my nipples. I quivered as I held back vomit. He snatched my skirt from my body and continued to trace his fingers along the frame of my curves, all the way down to my midsection, then pausing.

"What's this?" he quizzed, his luminous eyes now rapidly losing their shimmer.

"It's me being in the right position!" I managed to paralyze him by using my knee as my only weapon. I sent an unyielding blow to his groin. When I felt his grip on me loosen substantially, and he began to cower in pain on top of me, I managed to pull my never-failing butcher knife from its hiding spot on my inner thigh, reached for his nuts, and glided the back of the cold steel over them. This was a different butcher knife. It was the first thing I'd bought upon my arrival here in Jamaica. I had a very clever hotel worker get it for me. I tipped him well. "Do you still think I'm in the wrong position?" I glared up at Everhard through the dark.

"Bloodclaut!" he shouted panic stricken.

"Don't utter another word," I ordered in a soft whisper, still holding the knife against his penis, "Don't even move unless I tell you to." I quickly revoked that second order since the swine was still laying on top of me reeling in agony. Still clutching his manhood with the knife In my palm, I used the force of my body to roll him off of me. While he squirmed and squealed like the swine that he was, I sat on top of him, completely naked and waited for Biggs and JT to catch up.

"Pu-pu-please," Everhard stuttered, "If you going to cut off me willy, just kill me and done!" he begged and panted with his eyes bulging. I ignored his sorry ass. I knew that the proper thing to do was to have cut off his dick right then and there, and let him live with that shit. That was my plan originally. My plan was to make him suffer. But no, JT just had to find a way to deactivate my plan in order to use Biggs' plan instead, which to me was nothing that could ever be compared to the trauma I had experienced at the hand of Everhard. I briefly let go of his penis to rub the tender spot on my skin where the strap had held the sharp knife in place. No sooner than I'd let go, Everhard had pushed me off of him and began to crawl away bellowing with each movement, still crippled by my blow. My nostrils flared as my temper grew.

"Stay right there!" I shouted after him, "Didn't I tell you not to move without my permission?" I jumped up to my feet and went after him. I knelt back down and reclaimed his johnson.

"Your ass belongs to me tonight," I said wiping sweat from my brows. Where the hell were these fools at? I knew I hadn't been able to stick to the plan, but with all of my shouting and screaming and carrying on, I thought they would have run to my rescue by now. Everhard was recovering much quicker than I needed him to, and even with a knife to his balls, I knew I was no match for him. I had my mind made up though, even if he decided to kill me, I was going to cut off his menace to society. "You know," I spoke hoarsely, "The Bible says that if your right hand offends you, you should cut it off."

"What you want from me?" he asked submissively.

"Your dick offended me, Everhard, and I want to cut it off."

"Geez! Would you be so heartless?"

"Shut up!" I slashed him across his arm.

"Somebody help me! Murder!" he cried.

"I said shut up!" I used his locks to wipe the blood from the knife, "What do you know about having a heart? What you did to me- was that having a heart? What you were about to do to me again, was that warm hearted? Bitch! What you did to me five years ago, has haunted me every day of my life. Because of you, I go to my bed at nights dreaming of revenge. You have consumed my thoughts day and night. Do you think you're that important, to be occupying my thoughts?" I grimaced at him,

"Do you?" I heard voices in the distance and the sound of leaves crushing under footsteps.

"I'm gonna need you to do something for me," I continued, ignoring the approaching men.

"Wh-what?" he stuttered, then groaned under his breath.

"I said not to speak unless I tell you to!" I roared.

"Lexi! Hold on, we're coming," the voices shouted sounding much closer than they had before.

"I need you to apologize to me," I said, once again ignoring the voices.

"I'm sorry, Leh-Lexi," Everhard continued to stutter.

"What are you sorry about?" I slashed him on his other arm. He bawled.

"Shut up!" I ordered, using his locks once again to clean up my knife, "Now speak!"

"I'm s-s-sorry for raping you," his tear drops glowed in the light of the moon.

"And my mother?"

"Yeah, I'm sorry about disrespecting your mother too," he stared into my eyes, his expression pleading for mercy. I knew his pain didn't come from the wounds I'd inflicted on his body so far, but from the torment of him not knowing what I was about to do next. Not even I knew what my next move would be. It's as if someone or something had taken over my mind. I felt so lost and out of control. "I've decided to cut your dick off after all!" I smiled down at him, "And I won't kill you. You're gonna have to do that yourself." He shook his head violently, begging me not to.

"I'm gonna cut off the whole thing," I continued, my mind and thoughts still a bit misplaced. "Don't move," I carefully positioned myself correctly, revealing his massive genitalia.

"Lexi!" Someone shouted from behind me, "What are you doing?"

"I'm teaching this ruffian a lesson!" I heard myself reply. I brought the sharp knife blade to the skin of my prey, and proceeded to slice.

"Biggs, grab her!" A voice shouted behind me. Without missing a beat, I was swept up from my spot on Everhard's legs, into the huge, pudgy arms of another man I didn't like. I kicked and screamed, "Let me punish that son-of-a-bitch!" the knife fell from my hand and I watched as Everhard jumped up on all fours, and rushed towards the knife. By now, I had completely lost myself. I saw the man with the crutch limp towards Everhard, swung his crutch at him, hitting him across his back. He squealed and tumbled back over. He fainted. Blood spewed from his body. I was released from the pudgy cage I'd been confined to, and set to stand on my feet.

The man with the crutch turned to me and said, "Lexi, you ok?"

I stared at him confused. He stepped closer to me and gave me a hug, "It's ok, Lexi, Biggs and I are here now," he softly whispered into my ears.

"Biggs, what took you so long?" I asked a few moments later, finally coming back to reality.

"You still want to do this? I mean, look at him; he's pathetic," JT said, "Let's just let bygones be bygones."

"No. I want to finish this," I replied, determined not to back down. Biggs and I hauled Everhard's now flaccid body towards the stream, while JT carried my ripped skirt. When we got to the stream, Biggs retrieved the items from his backpack, bounded our victim with a rope, and poured cold water over his head. I got dressed, and we waited for him to revive.

"Do you know why you're here?" I asked, as Everhard slowly came to. I watched as JT and Biggs stepped away and out of sight. They'd made it a priority to confiscate my weapons, for fear of what I might do with them. I didn't really care at that point just as long as they were careful not to lose my knife. It now had sentiments attached to it.

"Bomboclaut, wicked gal," he mumbled, fighting with the rope around his hands and feet "You crazy!"

"No, I'm not," I objected, "Anyway, this is a ten inch dildo," I explained, holding up the fake penis for Everhard to see. I placed it in my lap, and reached for a pair of latex gloves. "Unlike me, your first time won't be so rigid," I continued while putting on the gloves.

"What the hell you talking about?" his eyes were wild.

"This is KY Jelly," I continued my illustration, "I will use it to lubricate the dildo," I opened up the bottle and poured its contents onto the ten inch matter that occupied all the space in my closed palm. I glanced over at Everhard who was watching me in bewilderment.

"You know what?" I reached for the backpack and retrieved a towel, "I'm gonna need you to keep your mouth shut," I said as I gagged him with the towel.

"Now roll over onto your stomach so that I can access your butt," I waited for him to roll over, but he didn't. Once he'd realized my intentions, he began shaking his head belligerently, his pleading eyes reaching out to me. With all my might, I pushed him onto his belly and sat on his back, facing his ass. Though he kicked and squealed and yelled and begged for mercy, there wasn't much he could do, because I had him bounded and under control. I realized he'd managed to spit the gag from his mouth. "You, my dear," I whispered, forcing the lubricated object into unfamiliar territories, "are in no position to plead with me. Now, you're nothing but a battybwoy. Isn't payback a bitch?"

That night, after I was through with Everhard, he was whimpering by the riverside like a little fifteen year old child, who had just been violated by a grown ass man with a ten inch dick.

"Remember, you did not see me or my friends here tonight," I'd warned before leaving him there, wishing I had strangled him to death and thrown his corpse into the stream.

CHAPTER NINETEEN
JT

The months following Lexi's departure from JA, were months filled with turmoil and constant worry. I was haunted by Bishop's death; disturbed by Everhard's predicament and plagued by constant death threats surrounding Bishop's disappearance.

My attempts at burying the evil memories failed, mostly because speculations surrounding Bishop's vanishing saturated the news. Bishop's friends had made it known to reporters, cops, and everyone who would listen, that they were almost certain of the individual responsible for their loss. I was being hassled from every direction. To make matters worse, Everhard had made a spectacle of himself by announcing to the press how he was *'de-masculinated by Babylon'*. He'd gone on to express his grief about not knowing how inhumane society had become.

"Did you see the face of the person or persons that performed this brutal act?" a reporter asked Everhard. He paused, thought for a moment, then looked directly into the camera and shouted tauntingly as he pointed toward the camera screen, "You know who you are!"

My phone was ringing off the hook. So many people had gotten a hold of my phone number. I was getting phone calls from the police station, reporters, friends of mine and of course, friends of Bishop.

"Don't worry about it, mon, this will soon blow off," Biggs assured. I wished with all my might that he was right. But this mess was nowhere close to blowing off. I was fired from my job the minute rumors about my involvement with Bishop's disappearance began to circulate. I knew I would survive one way or another. I was God blessed.

One day while sitting under the shade provided by one of the many coconut trees in my backyard, my cell phone began to ring for the millionth time that day. The screen on the phone announced that the caller had blocked his number. I had made a habit of not answering unidentified callers; however this time I went against my better judgment.

"Hello," I answered gruffly. I was startled by the sound of my own voice. It sounded as coarse as my appearance. I hadn't shaved in months, my hair was unkempt and my hygiene was at its poorest. I listened for a response on the other end of the line, but there was none. I cleared my throat and spoke again, "Hello!"

"So you think you can just kill my friend and get away with it?" Someone uttered bitterly.
"Who is this?" I questioned, knowing very well it was the enemy.

"We know you killed him, JT. What did you do with his body?" He asked chillingly.

"If you know I killed him, you should know what I did with his body," I replied, confused and frustrated.

"So you admitting that you killed him?"

"Who are you?" I asked again.

"You are a fool!" He shouted, "If you think you can get away with this, think again! You are a dead man." He closed.

I flipped the phone shut and stared off into oblivion. I was already getting used to these kinds of threats. I was even growing into the habit of constantly looking over my shoulders.

The police were all over Biggs and his friends. I knew something or someone would eventually give. It seemed as if there would be no way out of this mess. Just as I began to wonder how my life had so quickly spiraled out of control, my cell phone rang again. Tired of fearing every phone call, I decided to confront the problem head on. Without viewing the caller ID, I reopened the phone.

"I'm here when you're ready," I answered, disgusted, "Stop annoying me with your fool-fool threats and come face me like a real man."

"Damn, why don't you pick on someone your own size." The fresh voice of Nita warmed my soul.

"Wait, Nita?"

"Yeah, it's me. You sound awful. You alright?"

"Yeah, I'm superb," I replied sarcastically.

"Aw, why so gloomy?"

"Why did you call me?" I lashed out in envy, ignoring the sudden, unwanted bulge at the crotch of my pants, resulting from Nita's sexy voice.

For the first time in my life I went against my father's teachings and envied someone. I envied Nita. I also envied crazy ass Lexi. Both women had found a way to turn my life upside down and tarnish my good reputation, before returning to paradise in the great US of A. Not that I could really blame Nita for much, since it was her gun that had saved my life. But it seemed as if things had begun to fall apart the minute she'd showed up in my life. As a matter of fact, I was beginning to wonder what purpose she'd served in my life. My father always taught me to be careful of the people I allowed into my life. He always told me that everyone who came into my life served a divine purpose and could either bring me down, or build me up. I couldn't seem to pin point what purpose Nita had served in my life.

As for Lexi, I was glad her mission was completed and she could finally move on with her life and leave me the hell alone. On top of her cruelty, I'd also learnt she was a murderer. Somehow I wasn't surprised to hear her say that. After all, this woman was no longer the friend I'd once known and loved. She'd become a coldhearted stranger to me. That's why I envied both her and Nita. They had a refuge. I didn't. I felt like running away.

"I called to tell you that I have good news," she replied chirpily.

"Bishop came back from the dead?" I asked, sarcasm oozing from my tone. One night on my hospital bed, I had informed her of my run-in with Bishop. I'd also explained how her gift had come in handy, and thanked her profusely for her generosity. I ignored the fact that she wasn't shocked by any of the news I'd shared with her and concentrated on returning her kisses. Though we'd spoken several times over the phone afterward, that night was the last time I'd seen Nita.

"I don't care about Bishop coming back from the dead. Do you?" she asked coldly.
"Why did you call me, Nita?"

"Such grumpiness," she jeered, "Anyway, since someone is in no mood for small talk, let me just cut straight to the chase. What do you think about taking a vacation?" she asked. I didn't respond.

"Well," she continued, "I'm pulling a few strings to get you a visa. What do you think?"

"A visa?" I quizzed, stunned at her announcement.

"Yeah, and once you're here, I plan on taking you to South Beach in Miami. What do you think?"

"Miami?" I repeated after her in shock.

"Yeah, South Beach, Miami. You should be good to go within the next few months. Your first visit here should be a one month vacation, just in case my plan doesn't work."

"What plan?"

"Don't worry about that right now. Someone should be calling you within a week or so to explain the process to you. They'll tell you what you need to do."

"If you're serious, then you just made me a happy man."

"That's good. You'll need to work on getting a few documents together, like original copies of your birth certificate. Wait for the call from my father's friend, and do everything he tells you to. Then, I want you to close your eyes, click your heels three times and say, I wish I was in Miami!" She laughed at her own joke.

"You serious?"

"Do I sound like a comedienne?"

"So what must I do now?"

"Concentrate on your little vacation. I'll call you back in a few days to comb through our plan," and with that, she was gone. That right there was the highlight of my last few months. I closed my eyes, smiled for the first time in months and wished I was in Miami.

A few months later, just like Nita had predicted, I received my American visa and was gearing up for my little trip. I was even shocked at the number of Jamaicans she knew, but she'd warned not to ask questions, and to keep my mouth shut. And I adhered to those instructions. Nita had advised me to liquidate all my assets before travelling. I couldn't see the sense in doing all of that for a mere six week vacation in America, but I followed her orders anyway. I figured that she might have had something up her sleeves since I'd gotten a ten year visa. Plus, I was just thankful for still being alive and finally seeing light at the end of the tunnel.

Though visits from Biggs had dwindled significantly, I was grateful that he'd still kept all my secrets. I realized that I was on my own now. I was no longer at peace in my own home, and I had lost nearly all of my friends. I needed to keep my mouth shut regarding this upcoming trip of mine, and that's exactly what I did. No way would I tempt fate, by screwing with people who hungered to see me fall. I received a large sum from the sale of my inheritance, seven million Jamaican dollars to be exact. My father,

I'm sure was smiling in his grave, because he knew I was doing what needed to be done to save my ass. I purchased travelers checks with a million of that settlement, gifted Biggs with an envelope and deposited the rest of the ridiculous sum into a high yield accumulative account. I even made a will, using Biggs as my sole beneficiary. He deserved it. Though he'd withdrawn his friendship, I'd understood the reasons behind his actions. I was appreciative of the love and support he'd shown me throughout the years. Three weeks after converting my stocks, bonds, house, land, and furniture into cash, I relocated to Montego Bay. I decided it couldn't hurt to check out the Wyndham Rose Hall Resort that Lexi was so fascinated about. It was also very close to the airport, and I also knew I'd be safe there.

"I can charge you at the local rate," the high-yellow attendant crooned sexily as she winked at me over her glasses.

Here we go again, I thought. "I'd appreciate it," I smiled at her, "I'd also appreciate you memorizing the number of my suite," I flirted.

"Did you say suite?" she asked in awe.

"You heard me right," I responded confidently. If I was gonna leave my country for an unknown land, I might as well spend my last few days in style. I'd also be doing a lot of good for myself, society, and those involved, by showing these hot Jamaican women how a real man get down. After all, Nita seemed to have had something up her sleeve. So it was possible I wouldn't be seeing Jamaica for a while.

"How many days and how many nights will you be spending, Mr.-"

"Miller," I aided, "My name is Jeronemo Tyloweshuous Miller," I watched as she failed at suppressing her urge to laugh at my name, "But you can just call me JT."

"M-may I see your ID please?" she requested through low, controlled bursts of laughter, as she wiped tears from her eyes.

"You won't be laughing that hard when I hold you," I said easily, as I handed her my ID card.

"Aren't you confident," she stated, accepting my card.

"It's ok, have your fun," I replied checking the caller ID of my vibrating phone. My heart skipped a beat when I saw Tanisha's name dance across the screen. Hesitantly, I sent her call to voicemail. I knew I couldn't offer Tanisha what she was looking for. Tanisha wasn't ready for my kind of lifestyle. I was a rebel and I wasn't about to put her through unnecessary heartache. I didn't wish to make her just another conquest. I had too much respect for her. Though she reminded me of myself, with her killer physique, and voice of a hummingbird; though the sound of her voice made my dick stand up every time we spoke; though she saw me for who I really was, instead of just an acquired pedestal piece to be shown off to her girlfriends, she wasn't ready for me. Or maybe, it was I who wasn't ready for her. I also didn't like the fact that things turned out the exact way she had predicted. How was that possible?

I placed my phone inside my luggage and looked back up at the sensual attendant. Our gaze locked.

CHAPTER TWENTY
LEXI

"Did you sleep well last night?" Nita asked smugly as I strutted past her.

"I sleep well every night, Nita," I said, rolling my eyes and shaking my head in disgust. Over the past several months, since my return from Jamaica, she had been walking around the house with a smug look. I swear it had taken everything out of me not to wipe the floor with her face.

"Glad to see how you've come a far way--I mean from the streets, straight to my bedroom." She paused for me to chip in, but I ignored her comment and kept on moving. "I see you've blown up," she continued, following behind me, "But you can never be like me, bitch!"

Nita had crossed the line again. I admit that she had every right to be bitter over losing her man to me. The fact that I'd also taken over her bedroom was nothing to smile about either. However, lashing out at me was just plain dumb. She needed to bitch at Vaughnn, or take her problems elsewhere. "Are you listening to me?" she yelled.

"Nita, let's get something straight here," I said, rattling my car keys, "If I seem to not give a shit, then maybe it's because I don't." I opened the door, stepped outside and slammed it shut behind me. A few seconds after I'd shut the door, it flew open.

"What did you just say to me?" Nita snarled, "Repeat what you just said to me!" she yelled.

Without responding to her, I glided towards my brand new, bright blue Nissan Z 360 that sparkled in the early morning sunlight. Vaughnn had surprised me with it upon my return from Jamaica.

"I bet that soon you will be giving more than a shit!" she shouted after me, obviously not caring if the neighbors were listening or not.

I started my car, rolled out on the main, and revved the engine. As I sailed down Taft Street, I reminisced on how quiet things had been over the past few months. Certainly Nita and her friend had been acting strangely, walking around the house smirking and shit, but they had been staying out of my way. Stewart and his two brothers had also been keeping their distance.

It's almost as if they were avoiding me. I wouldn't be surprised though, if Nita had something to do with it. She surely had a grip on those three. It also wouldn't come as a shock to me if I found out she was screwing Stewart. I wondered if Vaughnn hadn't noticed the tie between those two. They were way too close for comfort. Something wasn't adding up. Shit just wasn't right. And why was Nita and her Non-English speaking friend still all up in Vaughnn's house? Why was Vaughnn so scared to kick their asses out? I had pushed those questions to the back of my mind when I saw things had quieted down. But now, just as I was about to accept the fact that there was a truce between Nita and I, she had gone and started more shit with me again this morning. I pulled onto the highway and headed north towards downtown town Ft. Lauderdale.

Vaughnn would definitely have to do something about his ex-girlfriend. If he didn't make her leave; then I would. *I bet that soon you will be giving more than a shit!* What had Nita meant by that? I concluded that she had to be up to something and I needed to keep my eyes opened.

I brimmed with new excitement. I had rescheduled all my property showings with clients, in order to take this trip. It felt good to have the day off. I had no clue that being a real estate agent could be so much of a hassle. It's not easy driving clients around all day; bribing them with free lunches and dinners; explaining over and over to them, the process and importance of purchasing a property; convincing them that now was the best time to buy or sell their properties; going over numbers and submitting offers that many times got denied. And when offers were accepted, the clients would choose to back out, for whatever reason. It's such a headache. I must say though, that I do enjoy the challenges that come with my job.

Today would be my first day in months since I'd taken a break from my job. In less than a couple of hours I would be re-united with my best friend again. The fact that he was actually here in the US was surreal to me. So many questions crowded my mind about him being here. I mean, how did he get here? I had no idea JT had a visa. When had he arrived? How long would he spend? Most of all I was curious to know how he'd worked out the 'Bishop situation'. It had been a while since I'd last spoken to him. Part of the reason was that I knew he was angry at me for involving him in the little incident with Everhard. Things had been so weird between us ever since. I'd stopped calling him altogether, and he'd stopped calling me. I was shocked when I received a call from him two nights ago. He asked that I visit him at the Sea View Resort. JT and I had so much to catch up on, and I could scarcely contain myself. I desperately needed a friend--his friendship. I'd always longed to relate with someone outside of the confines of my home. JT would be that perfect friend for me.

Thirty five minutes later, I pulled onto the downtown exit, and turned right onto Broward Boulevard. I drove a few blocks before reaching my final destination, the Seaview Beach Resort. I pulled up into the parking lot with my jaws literally dropped. If I had known, I would have brought an overnight bag--better yet, a suit case packed with clothes. The view was spectacular and the scent of the ocean breeze was magnificent. This just had to be some seriously luxurious shit! I mean, I didn't want to leave. I exited my car without the knowledge of doing so. My mind had been consumed with the impressive views that engulfed me. I snapped back to reality as thoughts of JT streamed through my mind. How was he affording all of this? I reached for my cell phone that had been lying in the passenger seat of my car, and dialed JT's number. I grew angrier by the minute. It's just not possible that he could have been squandering off his inheritance on this lavish way of living. I'm sure his father just had to be turning in his grave from JT's recklessness.

"Hello," his smooth voice pulsated calmly through the phone.

"Someone sounds relaxed," I greeted.

"Are you here?"

"Yeah I'm here."

"Wow, you got here quick, mon!"

"Well, I live here. Remember?"

"You live in Fort Lauderdale?"

"I mean that I live here in Florida."

"So?"

"So, I'm learning my directions."

"Ok, cool. I don't know if I'll ever learn how to find anywhere. America is overwhelming!"

"How do you know that? You haven't even been anywhere yet."

"Well, I've been to a few places so far. Everything seems so complicated. I prefer my lanes and hills and gullies back home in JA."

"Country bumpkin!" I joined him in his contagious chuckle, which I kept brief, since I had other issues to address.

"How do you like it so far?"

"I'll know as soon as you get me."

"Uh-oh!"

"Uh-oh what, JT? You mean you're still in your hotel room?"

"No comments."

"Listen fool, you better tell me where you're at!" I allowed the smile that parted my lips, as I mentally noted the room number JT repeated on the other end of the line. He was such a goof ball, and I could hardly wait to finally see him.

"You get it?" JT verified, referring to the number he'd just provided.

"Yeah, I got it."

"Good. So what you think?"

"What do I think about what?" I asked him.

"What you think about this place, mon?"

"JT, this place is sick!"

"Sick, meaning good- right?"

"Sick, meaning fantastic! It's beautiful here!" I shouted, ignoring the smiling tourists.

I wasn't sure if they were smiling because of my comment, or because of the fact that I looked odd, being dark hued and all. You know, people can be real "ignant" and prejudice at times.

"I'm glad you like it," JT said musically, "Let me hang up and call the front desk. I'll tell them I'm expecting you."

"Sounds like you're used to this lifestyle already," I replied sarcastically.

"Don't start with me today, Lexi," he said chuckling. With that, the call was disconnected. I flipped my phone shut as I sashayed across the lobby, and over to the tellers. I thought briefly of something JT had just said to me. *I'm glad you like it.* Glad that I like it? Why? He's squandering his money on unnecessary vacations, and he's seeking my approval? I'd be sure to give him a piece of my mind once I'd caught up to him.

"I'm here to see Mr. Miller, please," I explained politely to the cashier.
She smiled at me cheekily while sizing me up.

"Go ahead, he's expecting you."
I didn't move. I couldn't believe that rude bitch had just done what she did.

"Is there something on me that looks funny?" I glared at her.

She suddenly wiped the smirk from her face, appearing to be more professional, "No maam, I'm sorry if you got the wrong impression. I just think that Mr. Miller is rather popular with the ladies."

"Sapphire!" An older attendant scowled at her. "I apologize maam, Sapphire is a new employee here," she said, as she turned to face me.

"Your apology is accepted," I replied. The rude woman, who'd just been referred to as Sapphire, held her head down.

"What's going on here?" A tall, chocolate skinned, older man asked as he approached the ladies from behind.

I walked away, satisfied that the rude bitch had been checked. Whatever happened afterward was no business of mine.

I rode the elevator to the second floor; its doors slid open and there stood JT, with arms wide open. I inhaled deeply before stepping out into his welcoming arms. As we embraced, I closed my eyes and let go of the breath that I held. It felt so good to see him again.

"I can't believe it's actually you!" I shouted with excitement.

"You better believe it's me," he replied as he released me from our hug. He held my hand and led me towards his room.

"I really missed you," I said sincerely.

"I missed you too. I'm so glad that you're here."

I paused for a moment to take him all in. He was rocking a pair of dark-blue denim, with a white, muscle hugging shirt. His freshly polished Cole Haan shoes, gleamed smartly from his feet. He'd lost a little weight, however his physique remained superb. I smiled as our eyes became glued to each other. He smiled back at me. We resumed our quiet stroll towards his room.

"I see you've lost a little weight," I stated, once he'd locked us up securely inside of the room. I was hoping that my subtle remark would have encouraged him to open up to me at once. But it didn't.

"So have you," he replied, carefully dodging a solid response to my statement.

"I've been more than a little stressed out these days," I was determined to get JT to start singing like a bird.

"I know what you're doing, Lexi."

"What do you mean?"

"You know exactly what I mean."

"I'm just saying that I've been a little stressed out."

"If there's something you want to ask me, just ask. Don't beat around the bush."

"I'm not beating around-" I stopped mid sentenced when JT gave me a knowing look.

"Ok fine. You're right. I do have a lot that I'm concerned about."

"And you should, because you're my friend." I threw my purse on one of the beds and did a double take.

"Are there two beds in this room, or am I now seeing doubles?" I asked JT puzzled.

"Isn't this room nice?" JT asked me grinning.

"Nice? More like a little too much. Why do you need two beds?"

"It's a double/double guest room."

"Well, obviously. But you're a single, single man. Why do you need two beds?"

Ignoring me, JT walked across the room and pulled the drapes to the side, revealing the stunning view of the ocean. I gasped as I walked towards the window. For a brief moment, I stood there dumbfounded as I stared off into the Atlantic Ocean.

"I just don't know," I murmured, shaking my head in disbelief.

"You just don't know what?" JT asked, his facial expression giving away his annoyance.

"Nothing," I said, retracting all intentions of meddling into his affairs. I decided that JT was his own man. Why should I give a shit about his issues if he didn't want me to give a shit?

"This is all so dreamlike. Do you like it?" I asked. After all, he'd been seeking out my approval since the moment I'd set my feet on these grounds. I needed to make sure he was having fun, and I also needed to switch the topic.

"So now you're switching the topic?"

"Damn! I just can't win with you, can I?" I turned away from the Gulf view and plopped myself down on a sofa. I'd almost lost sight of the fact, that JT had known me for more than half of my life. My throat felt parched and my stomach growled. I hadn't eaten all day.

"Hungry?"

"Yeah, a little. What do you have here for me to eat?"

"You sure you want me to answer that question?"

"I take that back. Can we go somewhere for brunch?"

"Sure. After that, we can go by the beach and talk. I'll tell you everything."

"Sounds like a plan," I agreed while grabbing my purse.

Moments later we'd grubbed on pancakes, omelets, fruits, muffins and orange juice; and were on her way to the beach side.

"I'm really glad you came here, Lexi," JT said for the umpteenth time since my arrival.

I'm glad that he was glad to see me. But that shit was beginning to get on my last nerve. He hadn't said one word about why he was here in America. While my patience grew thin, my curiosity grew portly by the minute. What the hell was he dragging this shit out for?

"I'm glad to see you too, JT," I found myself declaring. I had to force myself to play along with him, hoping that he wouldn't drag this out much longer. "This is all so beautiful," I marveled.

"Is it as beautiful as the Wyndham in Montego Bay?"

"I won't answer that," I giggled, poking him playfully in the side of his head.

"Ouch!"

"That did not hurt; stop lying!" I shouted above the humming of the gusts of wind.

JT smiled at me intently, then quickly looked around, "Let's sit right here."

"I should have brought towels. I'm gonna get sand in my butt."

"That may not be such a bad thing," he smirked.

"Why are you so nasty?"

"I don't know, but the women love it."

"Whatever," I took off my halter top and sat on it.

"Nice bra," he complimented, as he sat next to me.

"I could get used to this," I closed my eyes again, laid back on the sand, and let the gentle wind caress my chocolate skin.

"Lexi, I'm in big trouble."

I opened my eyes, and sat back up to face JT. Finally the little sucker had caved.

"What's going on?"

"I keep asking myself that. But I can never find an answer that makes sense."

"Well, at least there's no one around. You can trust me."

"There's a woman."

"Where?"

"Here--in the US. She lives here."

"Ok, go on."

"Somehow, I just feel like she has something to do with everything that's been happening."

"What do you mean?"

"I go over this in my head a million times.

Things just seem out of place, when I really think about it. First, I end up in an unusual, un-called for brawl with Bishop and his friends."

"Ok."

"Then this mysterious woman show up in my life, immediately after, telling me how much she likes me." JT paused and scratched his head in agitation. "Next thing I know," he continued, "This woman gives me a gun. That very same night after she gives me the gun, I use it to kill a man," he paused again. I kept my mouth shut, so as not to interrupt his flow.

"Shortly after she learns about the 'Bishop Issue', she quickly flees back home to the States."

I dropped my gaze to the sand on which I sat. What JT was saying, wasn't making a lot of sense, but I'm sure by the time he was through, we'd both be able decipher all of it together.

"There I was, all alone, being attacked left, right and center, by friends of bishop; reporters and the police."

"Bishop's friends attacked you?" I asked quizzically.

"Not physically, but they sent me death threats and stalked my black ass over the phone daily! Then one day, out of nowhere, the same self-centered bitch who had given me the gun, called me with an offer to come to the States, courtesy of her."

I removed my gaze from the sand, and planted it on the horizon. At least she'd offered him a way out. That wasn't so bad.

"At first, I thought it was a great idea. You know--to get away from it all. She even told me she had plans for me to stay here permanently. After she took care of the paper work, and I finally arrived here and heard what her plan is, I was three seconds away from telling her to kiss my ass."

"What's her plan?" I intervened.

"Her plan is for me to find someone I can trust, someone who is a permanent resident here in America. She wants me to get married."

"Why should you get married?"

"She wants me to get married for a green card, so I can stay here permanently."

"What? So that was her big plan? And why does she need you to stay here permanently anyway?"

"I asked her the same thing. She said it wouldn't make sense for me to go back to JA. Everyone would just end up reading about me in the papers. She argued that I was even lucky to have gotten away, and that she has work lined up for me to do."

"What kind of work?" I asked, puzzled.

"She wouldn't say. But she remained adamant about me finding someone to marry, right away, while the vacation lasted; hat I should use my current stay here as an excuse to have met the love of my life and gotten married."

"But why does she insist on you getting married?"

"I don't know. I guess that's the only way for me to get a permanent stay."

"Do you think she wants to marry you?"

"I thought about that. But I don't get that impression from her. It's as if she's desperate for me to marry someone else."

"Who?" I asked.

"I don't know. One moment it's as if she has someone in mind. But the next, she's pushing me to go out and find someone."

"This is crazy, who's this woman, JT?"

"I can't say."

"What do you mean you can't say? Then how the hell am I gonna be able to help you?"

"I don't know the answer to that, but one thing's for sure."

"What?"

"That I can't go back home. My enemies would kill me. I'm stuck here."

"But Biggs would always have your back," I said matter-of-factly.

"Where have you been Lexi? Biggs withdrew his friendship when the kitchen got a little too hot."

"Shut your mouth! Biggs stopped talking to you?" I shouted in grave disbelief.

"Yeah! And to think that I was dumb enough to put him on my will."

"You did no such thing!" I fumed, "Does he know that?" I asked when I realized JT was actually serious.

"He knows now. I sent him a letter the day after I got here, instructing him to see my lawyer in Jamaica, if anything should happen to me."

"That's some bullshit! I thought you were smarter than that! Furthermore, God forbid you should die today, how in the hell would Biggs stay all the way in Jamaica and find that out?"

"You would tell him."

"Don't hold your breath! I hate that punk. I always knew he couldn't be trusted. You two were like brothers. If he let you down, why would you put his ass on your will? Did you include me on it?" I watched as JT held his head down shamefully. I shook my head in pity. My heart sank in disappointment; however, I was able to conceal my hurt.   This was his second time disappointing me, and frankly, it didn't hurt as much as the first when he'd taken the liberty of sharing my secrets with a man, who was now his enemy.

"I'm sorry, Lexi. My head isn't right. I'll call my lawyer and have him void those documents."

"You better do it sooner than later," I advised, "By the way, how long has it been since you've drawn up that will?"

"I took care of it before I left Jamaica," he replied slickly, volunteering very little detail of how long he'd been here.

"Do you think Biggs is in receipt of your letter?"

"Yeah, I'm sure he got it," JT replied.

"Did you use priority shipping?" I queried.

"Naw, mon, that's a waste of time and money. I sent it via regular mail."

I quickly did the math in my head. If he'd sent that letter via regular mail, it would have taken several days to reach Biggs. JT said he'd sent it off the day after he'd arrived in Florida. This meant that, when he'd called me two nights ago, he'd already been here several days before. If he'd missed me the way he said he did, then why had it taken him so long to get in touch with me?

My heart sank when I considered the possibility that he might not have even intended to inform me of his visit. If that was the case; why the hell had he invited me here? It didn't take long for me to add it all up.

"So where do we go from here?" I asked, faking my sincerity while eyeing him scornfully.

"I have a proposal," JT suddenly turned his focus towards me and jumped, reacting to the nasty look that plastered my face. "Lexi!" he screamed, frightened.

"What?" I said, quickly readjusting the expression that was on my face, "I'm just confused, that's all," I lied.

"Oh. You sure?" he double checked.

I drew closer to him and forced a smile, "It's all gonna work out," I assured him, rubbing his cheek gently with the palm of my hand. I watched as he relaxed.

"Now, what's your proposal?" I inquired, already knowing what the answer would be.

"Well," he began, "If I paid you-" he paused and scratched his head again, "W-would you marry your best friend for him to get his green card?"

"Wow!" I acted surprised, "This is all just too much for me," I stood, and began pacing, a habit I'd picked up from Stewart's brother, Stephin.

CHAPTER TWENTY ONE
JT

"Room service!" A lady hollered out in the hallway while banging loudly on my room door. If my memory serves me right, which I'm sure that it does, I had been sure to place the *"Do not disturb"* sign on the door handle. I didn't even recall requesting any kind of room service.
"Room service!" she repeated, still banging on the door.

I paused from the sexually stimulating motion picture that had consumed one hundred percent of my undivided attention, for the past forty minutes.

Candy, a caramel complected woman, with sumptuous titties and a graceful derriere, had been working wonders with a banana and a bottle of honey. I glanced at the clock on the side table. It indicated that the time was a few minutes after 9 am. It was way too early in the morning for someone to catch me watching porn.

"Not today!" I hollered back at the stupid woman who'd refused to follow simple instructions.

"Room service!" she continued to shout, banging even louder. I'd have to personally file a complaint to the manager about the crappy service I was receiving. Shit, this was America for heaven's sake!

"Wait a minute, I soon come, mon!" I replied, frustrated at my predicament.

I looked down at my hardened johnson that bulged through my under-pant, and became even more frustrated. I grabbed the largest shirt I could find and put it on. Hopefully that would hide the happy protrusion.

"Somebody's in a good mood," I murmured, referring to my dick, before pulling my shirt down to cover it.

"Room service!"

"I'm coming!" I was furious.

I was surely going to give this woman a piece of my mind. I stomped across the room and swung the door opened. I started to move my lips but the words wouldn't form on my tongue. I was dumbstruck.

"Close your mouth," she demanded harmlessly, "And let me in," she pushed past me and headed for the sofa.

I stood frozen as I watched her take off her shoes, then her jeans, then her tank top, then stood half naked in front of the TV.

"I'm naked here; can you please lock the door?"

I obeyed her command and locked the door, still surprised by what was in front of me. I remained fixed by the door, about to choke on my own drool, mixed with the words I had taken back about the cleaners of this hotel. She looked at me as if she thought I was stupid, then she laughed.

"I got you real good, didn't I?" her body spasmed through bursts of laughter.

I heard the door to the room next to mine open, and a guest stated,

"Where are the cleaning people?"

"I could have sworn they went into that room," another guest replied.

"Should we knock on the door?" the first guest asked.

I couldn't believe what was happening. Did someone just offer to knock on my door? All I wanted to do was watch some porn; now I was involuntarily thrown in the middle of some kind of Alice in Wonderland charade.

"They think I'm the cleaning lady," she whispered, still giggling.

I found nothing funny.

"Aren't you afraid of losing your job?" I whispered back, still unable to move.

Bang, bang, bang! I assumed the guests had decided to knock on my door after all.

"Who is it?" I questioned, already aware of the situation.

"We're staying next door! We just needed to speak to the cleaning lady!"

"Sorry boss, but she's already taken!" I shouted, hoping they would catch my drift.

"Oh shit!" the guest replied, "You mean your personal room service?"

I didn't answer.

"I get it, mehn!" they laughed, shortly after, I heard their doors shut.

The woman who stood before me was Sapphire, the sexy attendant I'd met in the lobby, a few weeks ago when I'd first checked in.

"What are you doing here?" I asked, watching weakly as she approached me with tits, ass and punany all out in the open and up for grabs.

"I see that Mr. Johnson is happy to see me," she smiled brazenly.

"Why did you come?" I repeated firmly. I've seen on the news back home in Jamaica, how these American women operated. First a woman shows up in a man's bedroom; then willingly offers up her pumpum. Once the man deals with the offering the right and proper way, she reports it as rape, after she realizes she scooped up more than she could handle.

"Why did I come?" she echoed, still staring down at my bountiful bulge. I could tell she was fascinated. But I wasn't. She needed to leave my room. Besides, hadn't she seen a grown man's erection before? Our bodies were now only inches apart.

"What do you mean by why did I come?" she stretched out her palm and grabbed my crotch, "I haven't come yet."

Suddenly regaining life in my limbs, I removed her hand from my crotch.

"Tell me why you're here, or leave," I said.

"Are you serious?" she mocked, glancing behind her at the TV screen, then back at me. I grinned at the image she saw, to cover my embarrassment. Honey dripped from candy's breasts. I finally stepped around her and went to fetch the remote. I pressed the pause button again, and Candy was back to work.

"Seriously?" Sapphire hissed. Apparently upset at my reaction to her nakedness.

I kept my eyes on Candy while I sat down on the edge of the bed.

"Are you Jamaicans always this cocky?" Sapphire asked, sounding a bit hurt.

When I didn't respond to her, she politely reclaimed her clothing from the floor, and slowly got dressed.

Don't get me wrong, Candy- I mean, Sapphire is a beautiful woman. But she was a beautiful American woman. I just didn't wish to take it there with her. Especially not after what Nita had put me through. I liked Nita; I even gave Tanisha up for that woman. In the end, what did I get out of it? Absolutely nothing. She had left me hanging. Now here's another American woman in my midst. All I'd done was smile and flirted with her a couple of times, and she was ready to hump. If I should take this woman to bed, she would definitely call the cops on me later. I wasn't about to go to jail. While other men were being deported over weed, cocaine

and guns, I'd be getting deported because of
pussy! No bomboclaut way!

"I thought you were nicer than this," she
complained.

"I am nice," I muted the ooh-ings and aawings
of Candy, and turned to face my pumpum donor.

"I thought you liked me," she mumbled.

"Listen, I think you're a lovely woman. But I
just didn't expect all of this."

"Who did you expect? Her?" she motioned
her chin towards Candy.

"Are you jealous of Candy?" I chuckled.

"You know what?" she said grabbing her
purse, "Here's my card. Call me when you're in a
better mood!"

She went to the door, popped her head out;
glancing up and down the hall before leaving.

I'd suddenly lost my appetite for Candy, no
pun intended. I was also losing my erection. I
switched off the video and slumped to the floor.
Sapphire was right about one thing she'd said. I
was in a real crappy mood, and hadn't even
realized it. Why else would I have turned down
real, live sex, for a porno flick? The fact still
remained though, I wasn't about to mess with an

American woman whom I just knew I wouldn't be able to trust.

My head began to pound as memories of the day spent with Lexi flooded my mind. It had already been over a week since her visit, and I hadn't heard from her since then. She was supposed to call me back with an answer. She'd told me things would be a bit complicated since she already had a man.   My situation was dismal. I was screwed. I hated having to put her in such a tight spot, when initially I had no intentions of stooping to ask her for a favor. In fact, I'd had no intentions of ever speaking to her again. Not after what she'd done in Jamaica.

Lexi had been cold hearted. I did everything except begged her not to hurt a fallen man. But no, she was way too blind sided by revenge to listen to me. It's almost as if she was possessed. What had sickened me even more was the fact that, after her mission was completed, she'd shown no signs of remorse. Show me your company and I'll tell you who you are. That's an old adage my father taught me. I was nothing like Lexi. Therefore, I'd consciously made the decision to cut all ties with her. However, after arriving in this country and getting caught up in several fights with Nita, I realized my only option now was probably to do as she'd suggested. And that was to marry someone I could trust. Lexi was my only choice now. Unfortunately, the love and respect I'd once had for her died. Her visit last week was living proof of that. I'd almost felt as if I was talking with a stranger. I was finding it really difficult to open up to her.

To make matters even worst, something happened by the beach, that scared the living shit out of me. After I'd explained to her how I'd made Biggs my beneficiary, I'd turned around just in time to notice the nasty look that crazy ass bitch was giving me. During my many years of being friends with her, I hadn't noticed that side of her. Surely she was a little firecracker, but she was a different person back then. Now she was all fucked up. For a brief moment I'd reconsidered proposing to her ass for a green card, but, if I couldn't trust her, who else in the US was I going to trust; certainly not Nita. I needed to think of something really fast, or before I knew it, my vacation would be up, and my ass would be back in Jamaica. I also had a weird feeling that, though Nita had been generous enough to stand all costs incurred by me so far at this hotel, things would be changing pretty soon. I didn't even know why she was doing all of this for me. Furthermore, we weren't even getting along very well. My ringing cell phone interrupted my thoughts. I quickly crawled around the bed, and snatched the phone off the nightstand. My heart raced when I saw Lexi's number pop up on my screen.

"Hi Lexi," I greeted, hopefully.

"What's up, JT?"

"Not much. Just here trying to take a rough life easy."

"I feel you."

"How are you, Lexi? I thought you'd thrown me away for good."

"Naw, never that."

"You sound down, are you alright?"

"Well," she sighed, "I've been better."

"Listen, Lexi, if this has anything to do with what I-"

"I'll be fine," she said, cutting me off in her acquired American accent.

"Ok, but only because you said so," I said, feeling like a fish out of water.

"JT, I've been thinking," she said dully.

"Go on," I urged.

"I understand that we've grown apart, and that's just natural," she reasoned, "I also know that right now, in this day and age, we are two very different people headed in different directions."

"You're right," I agreed, stepping out on the patio, and mentally preparing myself for the bad news.

"Regardless of how different we are today, our history is what matters most. You've meant so much to me over the years. Even while going through hell after leaving Jamaica, sometimes all I'd have to do is just think of you, and that alone would put a smile on my face." Lexi sniffed a few times then her voice gave way. "Memories of my life in Jamaica are still etched in my mind," she cried, "and you're the best part of those memories." She paused and blew her nose.

My heart twisted into knots. Lexi had blown me away with those words.

Suddenly every negative thought I'd been having of her dissipated. I'd forgotten just how much Lexi and I had once meant to each other. Lexi had been damaged. There was no doubt about that. She was still that little fifteen year old girl, trapped inside the body of a grown woman. A tear drop escaped my eye.

"I got you," she finally said.

"Huh?" I was still unfamiliar with American phrases.

In Jamaica, things tend to have different meanings than in other countries, I'm sure.

"I've got your back," she explained.

"Meaning-"

"Meaning that I'll help you, just like how you'd helped me months ago."

"So you'll marry me?" I leaned against the wall, in case I fainted.

"I got you," she repeated.

"What about your boyfriend?"

"Who, Vaughnn? He's right here listening to us. We'll get married right away, and take lots of pictures. I'll get an immigration lawyer, and apply for my citizenship right away. Don't worry, we'll figure something out," She sniffed a few more times. "I have to go now."

I stared at the phone in amazement, and pinched myself to make sure that I was awake. I sighed with relief. Things seemed to be looking up on my end; however, I knew this situation had to be a severe turmoil for Lexi. What she'd agreed to do could never be easy. I guess she'd turned out to be a better friend than I'd imagined. Like I said, if I couldn't trust Lexi, whom could I trust?

CHAPTER TWENTY TWO
NITA

"Stewart, you better get yo' narrow behind over here real quick!" I ordered playfully, euphoria dripping from my tongue.

"What's going on?" He quizzed, unenthused.

"Come see our hard work pay off, baby!" I invited.

"What are you talking about? Nita, what are you up to this time?" he sighed.

"Come on over! You wanna know what's going on, don't you?"

"Not this time, Nita. I have other plans."

"Now, what could be more important than what you're about to discover?"

"My date, actually," he said dryly.

"My date, actually," I mimicked, irritated by his rejection, "You have a date?"

"That's what I said."

"Who?"

"Who what?"

"Don't patronize me, Stewart. Who's your date?"

"Who cares to know?"

"What's your problem?"

"Problem? Let's see. I schemed with a woman to help her get her man back; this woman happens to be the love of my life, and to make a bad situation worse, the man she so desperately desires, happens to be my best friend!"

"Where are you going with this?"

"Vaughnn and Lexi's relationship is ruined! All because of you and the things you've done!" he yelled, stressing the 'you've done'.

"Correction; you mean the things we've done," I disputed.

"Wonderful!" Stewart exclaimed sarcastically, "So you've seen it too, huh?"

"Seen what?"

"The damn point! I helped you, because I was a fool! Now you've finally gotten what you've fought so hard and so long to get -- somebody else's man! You continue to live in a house with a man who dumped you. Tell me something, do you think that Vaughnn loves you, huh? Even if he stoops low enough to take your sorry ass back, how would it make you feel to know that every time he's making love to you, he's thinking 'bout Lexi?"

"Motherfucker, that's enough!" I released the phone from my hands and flashed my fingers as if they had just been caught on fire.

"What happened?" my best friend Lydia asked me in Spanish.

"Nothing important," I replied to her back in Spanish, determined to stay focused. The last thing I needed was to allow Stewart to screw with my head. He knew what the deal was from the jump off. Now he was trippin'. To think he had the nerve to school me on morality, when he had been fucking me for so long; me, his best friend's woman. I'd never even given him any idea that I'd give up Vaughnn to be with him. Stewart was nothing but my bitch.

I dismissed all thoughts of him and zeroed in on the pandemonium that was taking place inside of our living room. Vaughnn and Lexi had been going at it for the past few weeks. It had something to do with a man proposing to Lexi; and Lexi of course, accepting this man's proposal. This man happened to be JT!

"He's just a friend!" Lexi sobbed.

"Stop saying that shit! Stop lying!" Vaughnn scowled.

"I'm not lying! Everything I told you is true!" she pleaded.

"Let me get this straight. You want me to accept your engagement with another man; a man whom you claim to be your best friend?"

"Yes! That's all he is to me. I love you, no one else."

"You love me, but you're marrying him?"

"It's not like that, I'm just doing it to help him get his green card. I told you that already." Lexi blew her nose.

"Marry me!" Vaughnn shouted, "I want you to marry me instead of him!"

"Marry?" Lydia repeated after Vaughnn, staring at me with her eyes wide open in shock. She'd been listening to the bickering and had picked up on what was going on.

"Marry?" she repeated, trying to understand clearly.

"Yeah, giurrl, that son-of-a-gun just asked Lexi to marry him," I admitted to Lydia, in Spanish.

I was devastated. In all of our years of being together, Vaughnn had never once brought up the idea of marriage to me. I also found the situation a bit unjust. Lexi was barely twenty two years old. Vaughnn was more than ten years her senior, and I'm the same age as he is. What the hell did he see in that young, naïve bitch? Why would he disrespect me and our home like this? I covered my face with my palms and let the tears flow.

Surely, Lexi would never accept Vaughnn's proposal. I was sure of it. She'd already given her best friend her word, that she would marry him. And in doing so, she had successfully forfeited her relationship with Vaughnn. But none of that could take away from what I can only describe as a dagger that had just been plunged into my chest, and used to rip out my heart. I sat down on the bed and buried my face into my palms. Lydia moved closer to me, and held me dearly. She understood my grief.

The enclosed space we'd been occupying was beginning to close in on me. I needed to get out and get the hell away from Vaughnn and everything else that had something to do with Vaughnn. Outside of these walls, the man that I loved was proposing to a woman who was already engaged to some other man.

"Of course I'll marry you!" Lexi cried.

"Well, good. Then it's settled," Vaughnn sighed with relief.

"Vaughnn," Lexi sniffed, "Can we do this after he gets his green card?"

"What?"

"Let's get married after JT gets his papers."

"Lexi, you mean you're gonna put this JT motherfucker before me? And you expect me to believe he's just your friend?" Vaughnn snarled.

"I don't know what else to do," Lexi sobbed in defeat.

"Let him find someone else's woman to screw; or he can go back home to Jamaica!"

"He can't, they'll kill him!"

Vaughnn laughed wickedly, "If he stays here, I'll kill him! You know what Lexi? I love you so much. I love you more than anyone I've ever been with in my entire life. But if you marry that punk, know that it's over between us."

Besides the gentle sobs of Lexi, after Vaughnn had spoken those last few words, there was silence in the house. Lexi wasn't the only one crying though. I was crying too. Vaughnn had just professed his love for her.

There was no way I could compete with that. I just wished I hadn't gone through all that freaking trouble of breaking them up. I'd set up the whole thing, and then watched my creativity play out before my very eyes, like a video game.

Lydia had been in complete awe when I'd explained to her, how I'd gotten Lexi's background information from her uncle. She'd also marveled at my meticulousness, in setting up the fight between Bishop and JT. That was actually the easy part.

The triplets and I had asked around and gotten enough details to know that JT and Lexi were close enough for my plan to work. The plan in itself was also quite simple. If I could get JT into enough trouble to cause him to want to run away, then life would be perfect. The difficult part however, was when I met Bishop. I just knew from the start that he was no good. He seemed to have a taste for instilling fear into others, and carried a vicious facial expression, that made my skin crawl. It hadn't taken long to realize just how much he'd hated JT. So we paid hIm to start the fight. To be honest, we'd actually paid him to do a little bit more than just the fight. The agreement was for him to start the fight, after which he would send JT death threats, making JT want to leave the country. That's where I would come in. I'd run to his rescue; get him a vacation to the States, where

I'd coerce him into marrying Lexi for a green card.

This plan of mine had gone a bit awry, yet worked in my favor all the same. Bishop's jealousy and hatred for JT drove him into madness. After being mercilessly ass whooped on the football field that evening, he was determined to get revenge. He'd threatened to chop up JT, the star of my show, to smithereens. On top of this detour from the plan I'd paid him to follow, he also threatened to snitch on me and the triplets. Of course I wanted to kill him, but Stewart suggested we pay him off instead. So I did. The only thing I could do now was provide JT with a means of protecting himself, and hope for the best. Fortunately, things turned out perfectly. Well, at least that part of the plan did.

The next part of the plan was for Vaughnn to see Lexi for the stupid bitch she really was, and take me back. So much for that shit!

"Come on Lydia, start packing," I ordered fluently in Spanish.

"Start packing for what?" Lydia asked puzzled.

"I'm taking my ass back home to Jamaica, and you're going back home to Cuba!"

"No, I'm not."

"Say what?"

"No voy a volver a Cuba - I'm not going back to Cuba!"

"Giurrl, you crazy. Are you gonna stay here and keep Vaughnn company?"

"This is your home and Vaughnn is your man! We're not leaving. No voy a volver a Cuba!"

"So you suggest we stay here like pests? Huh Lydia? You want me to become Vaughnn's rodent?"

"I don't care! Think about everything you're giving up. You've come this far and are gonna give up all this because of a stupid heifer? Perra estupida! I don't know about you, but I'd rather be a rich rodent! Ricos de roedores!"

I smiled away tears. Lydia was right. Vaughnn's love for Lexi was irrelevant to me. I was this close to getting my man back, and there was nothing anyone could do about that shit.

CHAPTER TWENTY THREE
STEWART

I pulled into the parking garage of the Sea View Hotel in downtown Ft. Lauderdale. JT had roomed at this exact location, about seven months ago, before he'd married Lexi.

So there you have it. Lexi had followed through with her promise to JT. Looking back at the fool I'd been, I couldn't help but feel a sense of guilt. I'd done unspeakable things in my adulthood; however, scheming with Nita to break up my best friend's relationship had really tripped me up. Now everyone was miserable. JT couldn't go back to his lovely home in his beautiful country; Lexi had been subjected to carrying a heavy burden, and suffering the costs of losing her one true love; Vaughnn was all fucked up; my brothers hardly spoke to me.

It seemed the only person that came out of all of this smiling was Nita. I was beginning to wonder what I'd seen in that bitch in the first place. There was one thing that puzzled me though. There was no doubt in my mind how much Lexi loved Vaughnn. I also didn't doubt the fact that her marriage to JT was solely business. Yet, within less than seven months into her marriage, she was over seven months pregnant. My only hypothesis was that JT must have taken advantage of her vulnerable state. After all, the guy was a womanizer. But even with all of that considered, all hopes of Lexi and Vaughnn getting back together after this were now wiped out. No way would Vaughnn accept her betrayal, even though it wasn't her fault.

The knot inside my stomach grew. I stepped out of my SUV, and headed for the lobby. I was dropping by to see my new girlfriend, Sapphire, who worked behind the front desk of this hotel. She was the one good thing that had come out of all of this. We'd met back then when I was spying on JT on behalf of Nita, who'd once again seduced me into carrying out her bidding. She wanted to make sure JT wasn't getting overly close to anyone but Lexi. She'd also been clever enough to trick JT into believing that no one could be trusted, especially American women. She'd made sure to scare the shit out of him. Nita was extremely calculating, and she knew how to work that talent to her very own benefit. It felt good to have freed myself of that blood sucking parasite. I still don't know what I was thinking, to have messed with Vaughnn's woman. I seriously hoped that that decision wouldn't come back to bite me in the ass. On a more positive note, my life had been much happier with Sapphire in it. When we'd first met, I was taking a chance at finding new love. I'd made my mind up to move on from being with Nita, so Sapphire's freaky moves were timely. I'd decided to call down to the front desk to ask for assistance one day, after realizing I'd forgotten to bring my toothpaste.

"Don't worry Sir," the sweet lady at the front desk assured, "My shift has almost ended, and it would be a pleasure to personally bring you what you need." Twenty minutes later, she showed up at my door with a package.

"Here," she said offering me the package, "Hopefully this will suffice."

"Thank you Miss-"

"Sapphire," she said cutting me off, "I'm too young to be referred to as Miss."

"Is that so?" I asked, eyeing her very short uniform dress.

"Yes, that is so.   Furthermore, most of the older women that I know, wear panties under their uniforms."

"So what's your point?" I asked, intrigued. If she hadn't gotten my attention before, she certainly had it now.

"My point, Sir," she explained, lowering her voice, "Is that I'm not old, and neither is my pussy. Why cover it up with panties?"

I gulped down air. My 'johnson' became hard at the bold words of the very attractive woman that stood in front of me.

"Aren't you supposed to be professional?" I asked her.

"If I placed your penis between these luscious lips of mine, would you rather that I slowly, gently licked its tips with my tongue or would you rather that I sucked it ravenously?"

I stood at my room door flabbergasted.

"Ok," she continued mockingly, "It seems that I've offended you.   Let me apologize for not being professional," She smirked as she looked down at my stiffness.

"You're right," I agreed with her, finally regaining the ability to speak, "I think you should leave."

"I'll leave," she agreed stepping closer to me, then whispering into my ears, "Every time you take a shower, I want you to think about this bare, naked, wet pussy that's underneath my uniform." She walked away leaving me mesmerized. The mind is a powerful thing. Sapphire's wet pussy was all I could think about, every day after that. I desperately needed to know what was under her uniform. I drove myself crazy thinking about that shit, especially when I was in the shower. I ended up asking her out, and to this day I've had no regrets.
I entered the lobby and headed towards the front desk. My cell phone vibrated in my pants pocket.

"Hello," I answered after I'd retrieved the phone.

"Look behind you," she said in a sweet, sultry tone.

"Sapphire, whatchyu up to this time?" I smiled eagerly. There was never a dull moment with Sapphire.

"I said, stop walking, and turn around," she commanded playfully.
I stopped and turned around, but she wasn't there.

"Very good, baby. Now walk back to the garage."

"What? But I came here to see-"

"Shhh! Don't speak, just do as I say."

I shook my head, and smiled nervously as I headed back to the garage. I had to trust my woman.

"Ok, I'm here," I said moments later.

"Get into your car."

"What?"

"Shhh! What did I say?" she whispered.

"Ok," I said obediently.

When I got to my SUV and opened the car door, Sapphire was sprawled off on the back seat naked, with a bottle of chocolate syrup nestled between her thighs.

"See how it pays to obey me?" she teased, stroking the fleshy folds of her womanhood.

"And see how rewarding life can be when you give copies of your keys to the right woman?"

I stared at the delectable sight in front of me. "You know it's on, right?" I said as my mouth watered. Right there in the back of the SUV, in the parking garage of the Sea View Hotel, Sapphire and I got down like sexing was about to go out of style.

CHAPTER TWENTY FOUR
LEXI

I could hardly wait to give birth. Not because I was excited to do so, but because I was more than ready for this thing to pop right out of me. I couldn't stand it anymore. Before I'd gotten pregnant, my double D's were more than enough for me to handle. All they'd do is get in my way. But now, this everlasting stomach of mine was giving my breasts a run for their money.

I thought living with my uncle would be the most uncomfortable thing I would ever have to experience, besides being raped by Everhard, but this pregnancy shit was no joke! I swear it had taken me five whole minutes just to get up from my chair, and then another five to get to the bathroom to pee for the one millionth time for the day. Then another five minutes to get up from the toilet. On top of that, I was hungry again. I'd only eaten five minutes ago, and although I'd often attempted to starve myself and the greedy ass baby that grew inside of my fat belly, the cravings were too much for me to handle. Right now I had an unusual craving for Avocado, topped with whipped cream and peanut butter. I mean, what kind of shit was that? And then there was my face. What was up with my face? My cheeks were larger than an oversized beaver's. I had to literally turn my head sideways to see my ears; my nose had tripled in size and my lips kept moving.

I flushed the toilet and washed my hands. My fingers had gotten pudgy, almost as pudgy as Biggs'. Speaking of Biggs-

"JT!" I hollered his name as loud as I could, so I wouldn't have to call a second time.

"Lexi, I'm right here. Why do you always shout?"

"Well, ever since I got pregnant, you've developed this tendency of not hearing me whenever I call you."

"That's all in your head. I don't do that on purpose."

"Yeah, whatever. Anyway, did you remember to take care of that thing with your lawyer?"

"What thing?" the fool asked.

"What do you mean by what thing? The thing with having Biggs as your beneficiary," I snapped, unable to fathom how JT could not have picked up on that right away.

"Oh shoot!"

"Oh shoot what? Don't tell me you haven't done that as yet!" I screamed at him angrily.

"Please Lexi, don't shout. I can hear you from right here," he pointed out.

"Well, if you would just do what you're supposed to, I wouldn't have to shout in the first place," I scowled, rubbing my belly.

"I'm sorry, mon, I forgot."

"You forgot? How could you forget a thing like that, JT?" I looked up at him, disappointed. Before I knew it, tears began streaming from my eyes.

"Oh Lexi, stop crying, mon. I just don't understand, just a minute ago you were screaming at me; now you're crying. I'm so confused."

"I can't believe you, JT," I hollered, blowing my nose into his shirt, "I made the ultimate sacrifice for you. I gave up my one true love for you. Why did I do that, JT?" I sniffed, and blew my nose again, "I did that because I am a true friend. What did Biggs ever do for you? Nothing!

Yet, you wanna leave him everything you own. What about me?"

"I'm so sorry," JT apologized with regret covering his face, "Come here," he gently pulled me into him and hugged me awkwardly, I assume so the snot on his shirt wouldn't touch his skin.

After a few seconds, I wiped my tears and shuffled away from his cuddle.

"What now, woman?" he asked wearily.

"Now listen to me and listen to me carefully," I said, pointing one pudgy finger at him, "You're gonna make that call to your lawyer today. Do you hear me?"

"For a woman in your condition, you sure are abusive!"

"Don't play with me, JT!" I said walking over to my cell phone, then picking it up to hand it to him. "Here, make that call right now."

He took the phone from my hands and disappeared into one of the bedrooms on the other side of the house we'd rented. I sat down in my loveseat, elbows first. Yup, this pregnancy sure was a pain in the ass. We'd rented our home from a kind old lady who was relocating to Port St. Lucie, to live with her children. God definitely works in mysterious ways, because we'd stumbled upon the spacious two bedroom house by accident. JT had managed to charm the pants off of the old woman who owned it. She'd instantly fallen in love with him, so we got the place to rent at a very affordable price.

JT had also managed to get an off-the-books job at a lumber store, not very far away. We had been managing, despite the fact that Vaughnn had cut me off completely. Good thing I'd been secretly stashing away most of the money he'd been showering me with, while we were together. A woman should always have a secret stash. No matter how great things are in a relationship, the situation could eventually change, and the money would come in handy on a rainy day. I'd learnt that little lesson by accident. When I was saving all of this money, I hadn't anticipated any of this shit happening. I was just saving, because I didn't need to spend it all. Now it's paid off. I just can't understand why Vaughnn had chosen to stay angry at me though; it's as if I'd now become his worst enemy. He was so quick to kick me out of his home, even though I'd been forthcoming with him all along. While bitch ass Nita could run around the house and create havoc, even when he didn't want her ass no more. Why was he so hateful towards me? I was glad he'd allowed me to keep the car though. Man, I love that Nissan Z. As for all that other stuff, I really didn't give a two cents. As long as JT had agreed to take care of me and the baby, I knew we'd be ok. I was broken hearted though. I really missed Vaughnn. I hated myself for still loving him. He wouldn't even allow me to explain the baby situation to him.

He'd called me a whore, and told me to take my whorish problems to my curried goat-eating husband. What a damn shame. He could easily inform me of the whore that I was, but he couldn't see that Nita was running around his house, screwing his best friend. If I was a different person, I would have brought that shit back up, especially when I know now that Nita might get him back. But, I'mma let it slide. As low as she'd stooped to remain at that house and make life uncomfortable for me, she had nothing to do with my break up with Vaughnn. It's all good. She can have him. If it was so easy for him to walk away from me, then maybe they'd both deserved each other anyway. There was a knock at the door.

"JT!" I shouted as loud as I could.

"Didn't I tell you to stop shouting?" he stated insolently, the second he'd appeared out of nowhere.

"There's someone at the door," I informed him as I rubbed my belly.

"I'll get it," he sighed.

I watched him step off towards the door. I smiled to myself as I thought of how much I was being pampered.

I wasn't sure he was pampering me because of my pregnant state. He might have been sucking up to me, because of the green card situation. But it didn't matter. He needed to keep sucking up to me. As a matter of fact, he needed to stay faithful to this marriage until he'd gotten his papers straight.

Shit, if I couldn't be with whom I loved, because of JT, then JT sure as hell wouldn't get the chance to run around town, shooting off his dick and having all the fun in the world. If that were the case, then I would have to call off our deal. Should JT screw things up, it would be to his detriment. He should know by now that I don't play, and I wouldn't want to have to call immigration on his ass.

"Whaddup, boss?" he greeted, as Stewart stepped inside. Stewart's visits often surprised me. For some reason I just couldn't trust him. I'd also found it odd that he'd still remained friends with me after everything that's happened. He was still Vaughnn's right hand man, and Nita's fuck buddy. For all I knew, he could be here to kill me. But I was smarter than all of those bitches.

"Hey, Stewart!" I greeted cheerily, faking my sweetest smile, "How are you doing?"

"I'm doing alright, Lexi, how's the bun in the oven?" he greeted back.

"I'm just about ready for this bun to pop out of the oven," I replied with my palms on my belly.

"You want something to drink?" JT offered Stewart.

"Watchu got?"

"Heineken."

"Ok, I'll take one chilled."

"No problem," JT replied before disappearing into the kitchen, and reappearing moments later with a cold beer.

"Thanks, mehn. By the way, how is married life treating you?" Stewart asked lightheartedly.

"Well, just know this- everything that people say about marriage is true," JT replied.

"And what is it that people say exactly?" I asked, glaring at JT.

"Yo, boss, I'm just gonna leave you two to catch up," JT said, dodging my question.

"Thanks again, mehn," Stewart chuckled as he watched JT leave the living room.

"So, what brings you here today?" I asked.

"I was in the neighborhood, catching up on a few things for Vaughnn. I figured I'd drop by."

"That's nice of you."

"I see that you guys are doing well for yourselves," Stewart said, glancing around the living room.

"Well, it hasn't been easy, but we're trying to get by."

"That's the spirit!" Stewart replied, taking a sip from his bottle, Do ya'll have a name yet?"

"A name for what?" I asked.

"A name for the bun in the oven," he smiled.

"Oh, that. Well I was leaning towards JT, Jr."

"Are you kidding me?"

"That is kinda funny, isn't it?"

"Are you having a boy or girl?"

"I had wished for a girl, and gotten a boy."

"Well, call him Stewart."

"Oh hellz to tha naw!" I goofed. "I'm not naming my baby after your punk ass."

"I gotchyo, punk," Stewart chuckled, taking another sip of Heineken. One thing about Stewart and I, we always knew how to talk smack to each other.

"So, will you let JT help you name the bab-" before Stewart could finish his sentence, the home phone rang. I turned sideways and picked up the phone that was on the table next to me.

"I got it, Lexi!" JT hollered from the master bedroom.

"Hello," I answered anyway, ignoring JT.

"Hi, good afternoon," a female voice spilled through the line.

"Who is this?" I asked.

"Lexi, I told you, I got this," JT chimed in smoothly, "So like my wife just asked, who is this and why are you calling here?"

"Well", continued the bold woman, "I wanted to speak with Sapphire. I heard she was in need of a bedroom stimulus package."

"There are no lesbians living in this house, so we can't help you," JT replied hurriedly.

"Sorry about that," the woman replied, pretending to be sincere, "I guess I'll have to look for a bailout elsewhere then." She hung up. I placed the phone on the receiver and smiled to myself.

"Everything a'ight?" Stewart asked.

"Yup, just watch and learn," I said softly, still smiling.

I chit-chatted with Stewart for a few more minutes, completely unaware of what he was actually saying. I'd just nod my head in agreement with him, every now and again, and offered an occasional, "I see". A few minutes later, just as I'd suspected, JT hurried by us wearing a fresh pair of blue denim, with a white polo shirt.

"And where are we rushing off to all of a sudden?" I asked him coolly.

"I have to meet up with one of the guys from work. I'm late."

When he got to the door, JT stopped suddenly and whipped his head around," Can I borrow the car?"

"Of course not," I smirked.

"Come on, Lexi, I'm gonna be late. Where are the keys?"

"Like we were saying Stewart," I now shifted my focus back to Stewart and pretended to be uninterested in JT's escapades.

"Lexi, why are you acting like this?" he
whined.

"It's all good, mehn, borrow my truck,"
Stewart offered, throwing JT his car keys.

"Thanks a million!" JT shouted, catching
Stewart's keys.

"Let me ask you something Stewart," I glared,
after JT had left the house, "How do you plan on
getting home?"

"I'll have someone pick me up. Don't stress
it."

"So you're encouraging JT's infidelity?"

"What? No! I mean- infidelity to who? You? I
thought this marriage was-"

"Never mind about that."

"But you guys aren't in this for love," Stewart
reasoned.

"So you think that it's ok for me to give up
Vaughnn for JT, and be miserable for the rest of
my life, just so JT could have things his way?"

"What are you talking about? It's not JT's fault
why Vaughnn is being stubborn about this
marriage."

"Then whose fault is it, huh? Do you realize

that Vaughnn and I would have still been together, if it weren't for JT?"

"I guess you have a point, but shit happens, Lexi. Vaughnn could have still worked with you-compromised. But he chose not to. You can't blame JT because of that."

"Yes I can, and I do blame him. If I could make a sacrifice for JT's future, then JT should be willing to make an even bigger sacrifice. We made an agreement to make this marriage seem as real as possible. I will not have JT make a fool of me, Stewart!"

"I see where you're coming from. But that's kind of a ridiculous deal, but I guess the man has no other choice."

"I don't give a shit about what you think, Stewart."

"Even if JT was desperate enough to agree to such an arrangement; what would make you think he'd gone back on his word?"

"See, now you're starting to ask the right questions."

"So? Go ahead and spill your guts," Stewart urged.

Since when had he gotten permission to come up into my home, and talk shit? He was nothing but a two edged sword and I had the perfect plan that would put him in check.

"Well, some woman just called here looking for Sapphire."

"Sapphire? Wow, I didn't realize that name was so common. So this caller obviously dialed the wrong number. Correct?"

"No, it wasn't the wrong number."

"So, you know the person she asked for?"

"No, I don't know nobody by the name of Sapphire, dammit."

"Then- if you don't know who this Sapphire person is, why would you think the caller had not dialed the wrong number?"

"Because, the caller wanted me to think she'd dialed the wrong number."

"So, you're saying the call was like some kinda cue for JT?"

"I see why Vaughnn keeps you around," I smiled.

"Lexi, I still think you should give him a chance. A man has needs."

"And a woman doesn't?"

"Then you should consider consummating your marriage."

"Stewart, let's not go there," I said, nipping that subject in the bud. Stewart had been trying for a while to find out if I was fucking JT. I knew his question was a subtle way to get me to either authenticate or nullify his suspicions.

"All I'm saying is that fair is fair. You've got to either find another man on the side, or take it to the next level with JT."

"I had a man, Stewart. Now, I have a husband. If I find out my husband is being unfaithful to me, I will unleash my wrath. Do you hear me? JT will not hear the end of it. I'm the wife, and already I'm being disrespected in my own home. No shit!"
Stewart wrapped himself in his own thoughts for a while.

"So, you think the caller made the name up?"

"No, the caller's name was Sapphire. She just asked for Sapphire-"

"So JT would know it's her," Stewart said, finishing my sentence.

"Well, that's a coincidence," he continued.
"What is?"
"My girlfriend has that same name."
"Coincidence indeed," I nodded in agreement. I was pleased to see that he was finally catching up to speed. The moment that chick had uttered

the name Sapphire; it didn't take long to put the puzzle together. She'd been on my mind since our first encounter almost eight months ago in that hotel lobby. Somehow, I had a feeling this bitch would rear her ugly head again. It had to have been the reason why she'd been so blunt with me, the day I went to visit JT in his hotel room. I also wouldn't be surprised if she was also gaming Stewart. I mean, the poor guy just knew how to pick his women.

"I see congratulations are in order," I smirked.

"For what?"

"You've just claimed a woman. Do I hear wedding bells in the air, or a prospective bun in the oven?" I teased, attempting to lighten the air. I had a feeling Stewart's new flame would be very short-lived.

"Naw, it ain't even like that," he shrugged, still seeming a bit baffled.

"If you say so," I replied thoughtfully. "Umm-Stewart, I have a favor to ask of you."

"What's that?"

"Come closer," I invited. Stewart pulled his chair closer to me, and I whispered my plan to him. The plan, if executed correctly, would reveal Sapphire's true character. If she thought she could play me, then she would have another guess coming. I'd get my facts together, make sure that it was her, and that she was indeed messin' around with JT.

I advised Stewart of the plan--a plan so brilliant, if executed properly, I'd kill two birds with one stone. If it worked, then I'd be able to confirm that this chick really is whom I think she is, and in doing so, Stewart may just realize he'd just gotten played.

My plan was ingenious and bound to work. The first thing I needed to do was to copy that mystery woman's phone number from my caller ID, just in case JT was being slick and hadn't saved the number in his cell phone. This woman had been bold enough to call me without blocking her number, which meant she was obviously bold enough to handle the potential consequences. My plan would only work if Stewart found out about her. So I hoped she really was who I thought she was. The next step was to use JT's cell phone as a means of getting in touch with her. I waited until he was in the shower the following morning, after Sapphire called, then I sneaked into his drawer and retrieved the phone he'd so cleverly hidden. Whenever a man tries to hide his cell from his own wife, it means he's up to no good. I sent the first text message that read:

"Hey, baby."

Within less than two minutes, the screen lit up, indicating that a new text message had been received. I glanced around the room quickly, and listened carefully. I knew that if the shower stopped running, I'd have to quickly exit the room.

"'Sup, Daddy Long Stroke? Are you away from that bitch?"

This woman was sleeping with my husband, yet I was the bitch? Nonetheless I replied.

"Lol! I've been thinking."

"About me, I hope."

"Of course; but I also think we should meet up today."

"For real? Where? I can't wait to give you some of my best..."

"Hmmm... let's meet up at Rose's around lunch time."

"What will we have for lunch ;-)"

"Each other."

" Lol! I love the sound of that. See you around one then?

P.S.- what do you want me to wear?"

"Skirt. Wear red."

"You mean like a short mini skirt with no panties?"

"Hell, why not?"

"I'll be there in that mini skirt, sweetheart."

"See you then."

Just as I'd sent that last text message, the shower in the bathroom stopped running. I flipped the phone shut, removed the sim card, and replaced it with my mine. The idea was last minute. I wasn't about to take any chances. I replaced JT's phone in his drawer, and hurried out of the bedroom.

CHAPTER TWENTY FIVE
SAPPHIRE

"Yeah, right there, Daddy Long Stroke!" I moaned and writhed in ecstasy, savoring each and every one of my lover's overwhelming thrusts.

"You're gonna make me come," my lover grunted in return, as the sweet pleasure of my sex held his voice captive. His body spasmed outrageously on top of me, as the flexed muscles of my divine passage, clawed tightly onto his manhood.

"Oh! You feel so good. I'm-coming-I'm-coming," he groaned, frenzy stricken.

"Come for me, baby, 'cuz I'm getting ready to come with you," I whispered, anticipating our ever-so-explosive climax. I curled my toes and squeezed my eyes shut.

"Yes!" I screamed as his enormous member sank deeper and deeper inside of me; pushing past my pussy walls stretching towards my stomach, and filling vacant crevices not easily accessible by the average nigga. This brotha was working me like a Mexican on a melon farm.

"I love it when we come together," he moaned again. I fought off a giggle.

"You so stupid, baby," I replied, gasping for air and struggling to keep up with his wicked tempo. I dug my nails into his spine and tightened my grip on his anaconda. With sweat gushing from our pores, hearts racing and bodies quivering uncontrollably, my man and I climaxed together.

"That was great sex!" he panted.

"I concur," I replied, struggling also for breath, "Thanks, JT."

"No need to thank me," JT replied, placing a kiss on my forehead, before rolling off of me.

"Why shouldn't I thank you for great sex?"

"Because I'm just doing what comes naturally," he said smugly.

"You're so cocky," I smiled, pulling the covers over my erect nipples.

"You bet I am," he retorted, grabbing his crotch.

"That's not what I meant, fool!" I grinned, flushed with satisfaction.

"Doesn't matter, it could go both ways," he replied, rising from the bed.

"Where are you going?" I queried.

"I have to go," he replied, collecting his clothing from the floor.

"So soon?" I whined, knowing full well, JT had to go home to his wife.

"Let's not spoil the fun, Sapphire."

"Fine! Then go home to your bitch of a wife!" I yelled after him.

Without stopping or even dignifying my comment, he headed straight to my bathroom and politely closed the door behind him. I stared angrily at the ceiling, hating myself for failing. I had been failing miserably at luring JT out of his wife's grip. Sex with him was mind-blowing; however, no matter what I did for him in bed, it never seemed enough to get him to leave his wife for me.

I thought about the fight we had just before we made love. JT had been upset because I'd called his house, and his wife picked up. I, in turn, got upset at him for putting his wife ahead of me.

I removed my gaze from the ceiling, and retrieved my cell phone from my side table. I took it off of silent.

There had been six missed calls from my boyfriend, Stewart. I reluctantly dialed Stewart's number. He picked up on the first ring.

"Hey, baby," he answered.

"Hey Stewart, what's up?"

"You a'right?"

"Yeah, I'm cool; you still on the grind?"

"You could say that. I called your phone a couple times."

"Yeah, I just seen your missed call. I was watching a movie and had my phone on silent."

"Oh. You had me worried for a minute."

"Sorry," I laughed nervously.

"So which movie did you see?"

"Huh?"

"The movie you just watched, what's the name of it?"

"Um, I'll tell you all about that when I see you; right now I need-"

"Money- how much?" Stewart asked, finishing my sentence for me.

Call me a gold-digging, two-timing, backstabbing, arrogant, self-centered bitch. I don't mind. But my real name is Sapphire, and in terms of beauty, my name speaks for itself.

Therefore, the fact that I'm involved with two men, who both live in Pembroke Pines, should come as no surprise to you. Not that I'm trying to justify my actions, but you should know that both of these men, in my opinion, constitute one man. Both of them are also unaware of each other and that's the way I intend to keep it. As long as they each provide me with what I need, there'll be more than enough of me to go around for each of them. If that's how the thing is set, then that's how it's got to be.

Let me introduce my men to you. Meet Stewart. In bed, I call him Stewie, because that's where I find him the cutest. Now, that right there is my biggest dilemma. Stewart is too damn cute. He's way too much of a pretty boy for me. Though he's been blessed with enough of the right goods, he's never been able to satisfy me. At least not in the way JT can.

Now JT is the kind of brotha I like to refer to as a 'Maintenance Man,' that's right! Not only is he good looking, but JT has made it his occupation to consistently work my assets, using his finest skills to repair any and all of Stewart's mess-ups, while effortlessly polishing off my turf, leaving me feeling blissful and brand-new. I should write a book and call it 'The Joys of JT's Sex'. I've got it so bad for JT, but I also appreciate the qualities of Stewart. He has a good heart and he's got money.

Finding an affluent man who has a good heart is like hitting the jackpot. I deserve the best. I'm a beautiful woman and beautiful women deserve beautiful things. I'm very confident about my looks, and it is for this reason that I've chosen to only have friends who are either just as attractive as I am, or even more beautiful. Though this may seem arrogant to most, I know you'll understand the logic behind my decision. I hate haters. That's as logical as it gets. Unattractive women will always hate attractive women. So, instead of getting caught up in cat fights and trying to play down my beauty in order to please a friend or two, I'd rather be myself and hang out with chicks who can handle the competition. That's what it's all about-- competition.

I don't care what people think about me, the fact is, I'm what you may call, a wise gold digger. I've been holding down two jobs, just so I'm able to live comfortably, with or without a man. I've grown to learn that men tend to fall out of place sometimes, and for those times, a woman needs to be able to stand on her own. I work part time as a hotel clerk at the Sea View Beach Resort, in

Fort Lauderdale. I've had that job since forever, and I find it hard to give it up. It's fun and exciting, and I get to meet lots of new people, especially men. I also work as a paralegal for a small law firm called Stedman's Law P.A., on Pembroke Road. In other words, I get paid thirteen dollars an hour to do almost the same job my boss does for ten times the money I get. I like my boss though; he's cool. As a matter of fact, I'm quite fond of him. He's a tall, middle-aged Adonis, who divorced his wife about a year ago, and has been single since then. Word on the street is that Stedman divorced his wife after he caught her in bed with a woman. That's some seriously twisted shit. How the hell can a woman cheat on a man like Stedman--especially with another woman? Though I understand Stedman is a workaholic, there's just no justification for what she did.

Anyway, I could never be mad at the broad for returning fine ass Stedman back into the sea of women who are dying to just gobble him up. It's such a pity though. No one ever seemed to catch his eyes; not even me. All he does is work. If I was a lawyer, and in my opinion, technically I am, I'd be rolling in all that paper I'd be making.

There's no sense in working so hard, earning so much, and not being able to put all that money to good use. Money was meant to be spent. It's not like you could even take all that shit to the grave with you when you die. As for me, I have to treat myself every single day and live each moment to the fullest. That means lots of sex of course, spa treatments, weekly shopping, vacations in exotic places and such delight. That's why I have Stewart. Every last one of my financial needs have been met, since he came into my life. My cup has been over-flowing. Full-stop. Period. Before I had him in my life though, my lavish way of living would have still been maintained, courtesy of whichever man I was dating at the time.

Please, life is way too short to not be keeping it real. Plus, this body of mine makes life so much easier and fun-filled for me. They say you've got to work what you've got. And I definitely have a lot, which is why I can't understand why the hell Stedman still hasn't noticed me. I've always had my eyes on him, even when he was married, and there's nothing in this world I haven't tried in order to get his attention. At first, I believed it had to do with him being married, but after he divorced that heifer, I still haven't been able to steal his focus. I've tried the more subtle approach by wearing short skirt suits, smiling and making eye contact with him.

When none of that worked, I offered to take him out. He straight out declined my offer. I still have a ray of hope, since he doesn't seem to be particularly interested in anyone for that matter. Sometimes I can't help but get secretly pissed off at him. I mean, who the hell does he think he is, pretending not to be attracted to a dime piece like myself? One day I think I'm gonna have to ask him. My anger never lasts though, because who could possibly stay mad at a man as charming, good looking and accomplished as Mr. Stedman? He and I would look so damn good together.

I could see it now—my brand new double-D breasts against his broad chest; my slender, curvy frame beneath his two hundred pound mass. I often imagined him using his large hands to caress my silky soft skin. I envisioned the two of us in bed, making love, with my feet resting comfortably against his shoulders as his everlasting dick dances inside of me, with merciless abandon. Lips interlocked, tongues wrestling with the intensity of our bodies' rhythm. If I could ever get the chance, one chance to fuck Mr. Stedman, I would dig deep into my hat of tricks and give him the best sex of his life. I'm quite sure that after that one night, or day, he wouldn't be able to focus on anything else but me.

CHAPTER TWENTY SIX
SAPPHIRE

Another weekend had arrived. The weekdays seemed to go by more and more quickly with each passing week. We had been swamped with work at the office and I had a lot of investigations to do.

I welcomed the weekend with open arms, because finally I'd be able get some time to relax and sort things out in my head. All day long, JT and Stewart had been blowing up my phone. I had noticed their numbers assaulting my phone, every other hour since daybreak, and had been avoiding them both. The truth was, I couldn't get Stedman off my mind and I needed more time to focus on him. On top of that, I had received a series of romantic text messages during the week from my Maintenance Man, JT, instructing me to meet him at The Jerk Palace for dinner. I was also instructed to wear my red mini skirt with no underwear.   In my usual attempt to seduce JT, I'd decided to go all out and wear a thin, sheer top that would show off my luscious breasts. He'd stood me up. I'd sat there waiting for over two hours like a damn fool, calling his ass every other minute, and hearing those very calls go straight to his voicemail. JT hadn't bothered to show up or even called to cancel. Now, three days later, he'd decided to blow my phone up. I'd be foolish to even do as much as consider accepting his calls. To make matters worse, of all my weeks spent working at Stedman's Law P.A, the past week had to have been the most awful. I had spent the entire week trying the last few tricks in my mental book of tricks, to get Stedman to notice me, but to no avail.

I believe this chasing Mr. Stedman fiasco was beginning to wear me out. This shit was beginning to hurt. I'd gone above and beyond in making myself available to him; however, he'd refused to budge.

I pulled up into the garage of my townhome, parked my car and went inside. My cell phone continued to ring non-stop. I threw it over my shoulders and heard it land with a thud somewhere on the carpet. I climbed the stairs heavily; I felt weighed down. I needed time to think. I needed to find a way to create a new book of tricks that would effectively get Stedman into my bed and inside of me. I wasn't about to take his rejection lightly. I undressed, stared at my reflection in the mirror for a long moment and wondered what the hell else, could Stedman have wished for.

I also wondered why JT would pass up an opportunity to see me in my red mini skirt. I ran the water for my bubble bath and lit some candles in order to set the mood right. I needed my mood to be right if I was going to be successful in coming up with a bullet proof plan in getting Stedman's attention. I soaked in the bath tub in silence, closed my eyes, and breathed in the aroma of the scented candles. I then exhaled and allowed myself to relax.

Nearly an hour later, I had bathed, moisturized and clothed my body. I decided to stay in for the night and have some me time. I tuned out all thoughts of Stedman by thinking of what I could do while I was home alone. After successfully overpowering my thoughts of Stedman, JT popped up into my thoughts, pissing me off. I forced images of him to the back of my mind, picked up the remote control, slid under the sheets; turned the TV on and ordered a movie. I ordered 'The Women,' starring Meg Ryan. I watched the movie and was entertained while my subconscious devised the plans I needed to make my next move. As the plot thickened, I began to get carried away with the movie. I mean, this chick was unashamedly sleeping with another woman's husband and was behaving as if she was God's gift to men! It's as if she expected everyone to be okay with it because she was so gorgeous.

"Sapphire!" She had entered my home unannounced and slipped into my bedroom unnoticed. "I've been trying to get a hold of you all day!"

"Liz!" my temper boiled at the sight of her, "how did you get in?" I muted the television and sat up in the bed.

"I've been trying to get a hold of you all day, Sapphire!" she repeated, as if I was deaf. Who or what the heck had given her permission to show up at my home, in my bedroom, unannounced? So I asked again, "How did you get in?"

"Don't be rude, Sapphire," she scowled, "I'm only here because we all thought something was wrong with you."

"What do you expect? You just popped up out of nowhere in my bedroom, ready to give me the fifth degree, scaring me half to death, and you expect me to welcome you?"

"Like I said, we were worried that something may have been wrong, that's why I showed up here tonight," she dragged those words for emphasis.

"If you were so concerned, why didn't you call first? Don't you think that would have been the more appropriate action to take?" I tried desperately not to lose my temper.

"We have been calling you all day. We've been calling you non-stop for the past couple of hours," her eyes remained fixed on me.

"We who?" I questioned, matching her gaze. I immediately remembered that I hadn't checked my phone. *Where was my phone?*

"Kelly and I," she responded. She broke our gaze and quickly glanced around my room, as if to make sure nothing was wrong.

"Where's Kelly?" my voice indicating that my conscience had now gotten the best of me. I had been so pre-occupied with my thoughts of Stedman that I'd forgotten to check in with my friends as we usually did with each other every

Friday night. If we were all available, we would usually hang out together and catch up on the past week's events.

"She's on her way over here," Liz's tone was dismissive, "since you're ok, I'll let myself out," she turned around and waltzed out of my bedroom. A few steps later, when she was already out of sight, I heard her say, "Next time, remember to lock all your doors."

I know that my behavior was unsophisticated, but I couldn't help it. Liz was just the kind of friend that I could do without. I just can't stand her jealous, fake ass. On top of that, she's a hater... and like I said, I hate haters. We only remain friends because of Kelly. Now Kelly is my girl. She's beautiful, accomplished and confident. She loves me, and I love her. I believe Kelly is the foundation of our friendship. She holds us three together. I heard the door to my living room slam shut as Liz made her exit. I got out of bed to check the doors and to look for my cell phone. Oh shit, I forgot she said Kelly was on her way over here. If that's the case then she should arrive any minute and my cell phone was nowhere to be found. So much for having a relaxed evening, spending time alone in order to calm my nerves! I know you may think that I'm mean, but I'm not. I have no problem with Kelly; its Liz's dirty ways that I cannot stand. She's fake. This subtle war between us had begun a while back, however the shit got worst every time she chose to play herself. For instance, a few days ago she called me at work.

I knew immediately that she was calling to ask for some kind of favor, since she was the type of friend who remembered I existed only when she wanted something.

"What's up, what can I do for you?" I'd asked her.

"Hi Sapphire, how you doin'?" she responded, in a fake ass, screechy tone.

"I'm good. What's up?" I urged, forcing her to cut the small talk and skip right to the chase.

"Just wanted to see how your day was going," she lied.

"That's so thoughtful of you, Liz. What would I do without a friend like you," I said sarcastically. She cleared her throat.

"So are you really busy?" she asked me.
"Yup," I said, "I'll catch up with you later?"

"Sure. We'll talk later." I didn't hang up right away, so she said, "Um, Sapphire?"

"I'm still here," I replied, irritated.

"Can I ask you something?"

"What's that?"

"Can you loan me six hundred dollars?"

"Where should I get six hundred dollars from to lend you?"

"I'm behind on my rent and I promised my landlord he'd get all of the money by the end of this week."

"Ok," I said hesitantly, "I guess I could lend you three hundred."

"Just three?" she asked presumptuously.

"You can come by my office and pick it up," I said, ignoring her comment.

"Will you have cash?"

"Liz, I'm gonna write you a check, come by my office to pick it up."

"So I'll have to go all the way to the bank to cash the check; you sure you don't have cash?"

So, ya'll know I hung up the damn phone on her trifling behind!

Finally I found the damn cell phone I'd been looking for! It was lying in a corner next to one of my side tables in the living room. It must have been laying there since I'd arrived home and threw it down out of frustration. I quickly scanned it to make sure there were no physical damages, though that was the least of my concerns.

The phone seemed okay. I flipped it open to make sure it still worked. There were a total of seventeen missed calls, more than half of which were from JT and Stewart; both of whom I'd been trying to avoid. Only if Stedman could give me the time of day like these other brothas did, then I'd probably be the happiest woman alive. As I kept going through the list of missed calls, I ran a mental check on the callers. JT, JT, Stewart, Stewart, Kelly, Liz... and that's when I noticed the missed call from an unknown number. I hoped it was Stedman, so without checking the remainder of the missed calls, I immediately dialed my voicemail. This person who had called me with the number blocked, had to have left a message. I skipped over all the messages that were from JT, Stewart, Liz, Kelly— oh shit, Kelly was supposed to arrive any minute, according to Liz. I listened closely to the voices behind those messages; however, not one of those voices belonged to Stedman. Then who could have called me blocking his number? I concluded that whoever it was, may have dialed the wrong number. I was disappointed. I walked to the kitchen and retrieved a bottle of wine from the refrigerator. Kelly was on her way, and I needed to be a good hostess. I always went above and beyond for Kelly. She's always been my favorite friend. Now Liz on the other hand was a complete mess. I couldn't stand that chick.

My doorbell sounded, interrupting my thoughts of ungrateful Liz. I knew right off the bat that Kelly was at my door. I opened my door expecting to see Kelly standing there, with a stern look on her face, ready to give me the third degree for ignoring her calls. But when I looked outside, there was no one there. Puzzled, I called out her name, but no one answered. I was sure I'd heard the doorbell. I turned on the patio light, and quickly scanned the guest parking from where I stood. I didn't see her blue Corvette. I stepped back inside the apartment and locked the door behind me. Just then, my home phone started ringing; which was strange since I hardly ever gave out that number. Nearly everyone I knew had my cell number, and not even Kelly had been privileged enough to get my home number. That was my 'just in case' phone. I ran to the kitchen where I kept it and answered. There was no response on the other line. "Hello,

hello!" I repeated. There was still no answer. Just as I hung up, my cell phone began to ring. This time it was Kelly. Thank goodness! I sighed with relief.

"'Sup, bitch?" I greeted my girl.

"Don't 'sup bitch me! Sapphire, I'm outside," she snapped. She always snapped, which made it all the more fun for me to piss her off.

"Then come on in bitch, I'll get the door," I listened for a response but she'd hung up. I opened the door and watched her sashay across the parking lot and up the steps to my door.

"Scuze me," she pushed me out of her way and walked right past me into the living room.

"Wait a minute, did your Mama not teach you etiquette?" I smirked and observed as she scanned my home, just as Liz had done earlier.

"Why have you been ignoring our calls?" she inquired as she continued to scrutinize my apartment.

"Our calls?" I asked even though I knew she meant herself and Liz.

"What's going on with you?" she continued her investigation as she climbed the stairs that led to my bedrooms and bath. I didn't answer because number one: she hadn't waited for an answer, and number two: I didn't know what to tell her. I watched as her shapely legs disappeared up the stairs. Three minutes later, she was back downstairs, giving me the third degree as I'd expected.

"There's no one here," she stated.

I sat down on my chaise and chuckled as she stood glaring down at me.

"I don't see the joke," she continued, "and why aren't you answering my questions?"

"Chill out and have a seat," I smiled up at her from the sofa on which I sat. I stared in admiration at the way in which her breasts bulged through her baby blue, buttoned down, satin blouse. Her waist was small, and her ass was never-ending, graciously hugged by the low rider, designer jeans she was rocking. The hems of the jeans were turned up, exposing her shapely calves. Her shoes had three inched heels, which made her sexy calves look even sexier. If that wasn't enough, her freshly pedicured feet and toes peeped out through the stylish openings of her BCBG footwear. She had her long, thick black hair swept up into a ponytail, which appeared to be fake, but actually wasn't. Her mocha skin was smooth and her Barbie doll face--extremely stunning. On top of all that beauty, she was successful. Though she was smoking hot, I knew that I was much hotter.

"Love those shoes," I remarked and stood up facing her. I knew I was no lesbian. I was strictly a dick loving chick. But every time I saw Kelly, I wondered what it would feel like to kiss those cherry lips, and touch those breasts that were the same size as mine, but were real. Everything about Kelly was real. She had natural beauty. It was hard for me to even begin to comprehend how she could stay single. We were eye to eye, I knew she had a feeling about my curiosity, but was never bothered by it. She was the only woman I ever felt curious about.

"Do not patronize me, Sapphire," her beauty shining through her sternness.

"My, my, my, where's my lawyer friend tonight?" I licked my lips and circled her in a marauding manner.

"Sapphire!" she was clearly perturbed.
Ignoring her, I went to the door to make sure that it was locked, and then I resumed my flirtation.

Do not get it twisted! I am by no means gay. I consider myself to be completely heterosexual; or maybe a bit hetero-flexible, but not gay. I hugged her. She didn't hug me back, but she didn't push me away either.   I kissed her neck, caressed her cheeks with both my palms.   I waited for her to push me away. She didn't.

I undid a couple of the buttons on her blouse; unveiling her sexy Vicky bra. I gently kissed the nape of her neck again, and pulled one of her breasts from beneath her bra. I sucked on it. She gasped. I used my finger tip to caress her nipple and then I kissed her cherry lips. After I had kissed her, I gazed softly into her eyes. She returned my gaze. I knew she too was strictly dickly; however I also knew that, with Kay, her open-mindedness as a lawyer, had trickled down into other parts of her life. It was hard to believe that a woman as strong, stern and level-headed as Kelly could be so damn cool. Just by looking at her, it was hard to tell that she may be a freak; however, any man would be lucky to have her grace his bedroom.

"Are you calm now?" I asked, re-buttoning her shirt, after my little teasing game. No reply. I continued to straighten her up, though there was really nothing to straighten.   She was already almost perfect. I smiled as I watched her sit down on the chaise, obviously weakened by the effect of my touch. I sat down on the sofa, suddenly feeling uncomfortable due to the coldness between my legs. I desperately needed a man to finish the job I had just started. It also wouldn't hurt to have Kelly around while that job was being executed. That's something I'd never tried before, but if I ever should, it would have to be with Kelly.

"Girl, talk to me. What's up? Would you like some red wine?"

"Sapphire," her voice now softened, "What's going on with you?"

"What do you mean, Kell?" I asked knowing she wasn't referring to the little moment we'd just shared.

"You had us worried," she implored.

"I'm sorry, ok?" I attempted to put her mind at ease, "it's just that I had a long ass day today, and I came home with a lot on my mind."

"So you choose to ignore your friends?"

"No. I couldn't find my cell phone, so I bathed and ordered a movie."

"But you have a house phone, you could have still checked in with us."

"I know, but I forgot. Just have a lot on my mind that's all."

"A lot like Stedman?" she hit the nail on the head.

"Guirlll, you know me too well," I smiled at my friend.

"No, I'm just naturally smart," her lips parted into a smile.

"You are so full of sh-- " I was interrupted by the phone in the kitchen. I was beginning to feel more than a bit concerned about this phone ordeal. I decided to let the phone ring.

"Giurrl, whoever that is, must be real privileged to have that number. His dick must be squirting hundred dollar bills, and his lips spitting mad game!" she laughed uncontrollably.

"You know what, Kell?" I had to address her raunchy comment before addressing the matter at hand, "What I'd like to know is whether you use that kind of language in the courthouse."

She laughed even harder, "Don't try to flip the script and make this about me."

I waited for her chuckles to subside then I stated, "On a serious note though, I think there's something going on."

"Oh!" she shouted, "So something is going on!"

"Naw, not like that," I explained.

"What do you mean, not like that?"

"You probably think I'm sleeping with Stedman."

"Aren't you?"

"No, he's still not giving me the time a day."

"But, why should you care?"

"Why shouldn't I?"

"Let's see, you already have a boyfriend whom you're cheating on with that fine ass Jamaican brotha."

"You know Stewart alone can't satisfy me. I care about Stedman; and I need JT's fine ass. "

"But JT's married!"

"So? Marriage ain't nothin' but papers. I'll get him to leave his wife."

"Sapphire, you see the strong hold that woman has on JT."

"I intend to loosen that hold."

"How? My dear, he will never leave his wife for   you."

"Thanks a lot for the assurance."

"I'm sorry for bursting your bubble."

"It's all good, burst away. Tell me when you're through."

"I don't seem to be getting through to you."

"You're not."

"Ok, fine. Then if you're not sleeping with Stedman, what's the real deal?"

"See, now we're on the same page."

"Oh, just shut up and tell me what's going on."

"Can't do both at the same time, Hun."

"Will you just tell me what's going on?"

"Ok, ok, I'll tell you. Tuesday afternoon, I received a text message from JT."

"Ok, go on."

"He asked me to meet him over by Rose's Cafe for dinner."

"Ok."

"He'd also requested that I wear my red mini skirt- well, I made the suggestion and he agreed- but that's not the point."

"Then what's the point."

"The point is that, JT never showed up."

"So?"

"What do you mean, "So"?"

"Something could have possibly came up, Sapphire. You have to keep in mind that the man is married."

"Okay, whenever I need your opinion, I will ask for it."

"Gosh! Do you have stones for eardrums?
Plus, you did ask for my opinion."

"Anyway, like I was saying! I sat by the bar for
damn near over two hours waiting for this
nigga."

"Two hours?"

"Yes, two freakin' hours, and he didn't even
call to cancel."

"Did you call him?"

"I did; I mean, there I was, in my little, red,
mini skirt and high heeled shoes, sitting by the
bar, waiting for two hours for this married man
to show."

"And he stood your behind up. What was his
excuse when you spoke to him?"

"I haven't spoken to him."

"But you said you called him."

"And got his voicemail!"

"Then you should have called him again."

"I did, many times. I kept getting his
voicemail."

"Hasn't he called you since then?"

"He's been calling all day, today. But I've
been avoiding his bitch ass."

"So, is it safe to assume he's the one who's
been blowing up your house phone?"

"That's what I was about to get at, Kelly. I haven't given my home number to anyone. Not even Stewart; not even you."

"So who's been calling you?"

"I haven't a clue. But this shit has been happening since the day after JT stood me up."

"Do you think it may be JT?"

"JT, taunting me like that? It's not possible. He wouldn't do a thing like that."

"Maybe he found out you had a boyfriend and simply got jealous."

"But he has a wife. Remember?"

"So? You have to admit that you've been avoiding his calls. Maybe he thinks you've ended the fling, and wants to drive you up the wall. You know how Jamaican men are crazy."

"Can you hear yourself? I mean, you call what JT and I shared, a fling; then you disgraced his nationality?"

"Sapphire, I think I'm ready for some of that red wine."

"Oh, so now you're changing the subject?"

"Red wine, please!"

I uncapped the bottle of wine, and in silence, poured some of its contents into a chilled wine glass.

"I saw someone speeding from the parking lot, shortly before I arrived here tonight," Kelly stated after a few sips.

"You what?" I asked.

"Yeah, I never said nothin' cuz I saw that you were ok.   Furthermore, it could have been anyone."

"Damn!" I shouted, growing more concerned by the minute. The blocked phone calls, and the ringing doorbell, couldn't have just happened by chance and out of the blue. Someone was after me. I hoped the shit wasn't what I think it was.

"What's going on?" Kelly's expression mirrored mine.

"Do we have plans for tonight?" I asked, feeling the sudden urge to leave my apartment. I needed fresh air and fun, so I could clear my head. Kelly raised an eyebrow, staring at me as if I was crazy, "Well, I wanna get dressed and go out somewhere. We'll discuss this further over drinks."

"Well," she finally replied, obviously still concerned, "Get dressed and let's go out."

"Ok, gimme twenty minutes," I got up from the sofa and headed up stairs. My vajeje was still wet.

"Where's my phone? I need to call Liz to let her know what's up," Kelly stated, reaching behind her for her Gucci purse. It was a very cute, sophisticated purse. I hadn't noticed it when she'd initially walked in.

"You just made my mood worse!" I barfed at the sound of Liz's name.

"Be nice!" Kelly shouted from behind, "Oh, here it is," she finally retrieved her phone from her purse and began to dial. She was about to have fake ass Liz meet up with us somewhere. I went upstairs and got dressed for my night out with Kelly.   However, nothing could have prepared me for what would transpire next.

CHAPTER TWENTY SEVEN
SAPPHIRE

I was bumpin' to the booty songs that boomed through the loud speakers. My best friend, Kelly, had arranged for fake ass Liz to meet us at Skaterz, the best skating rink in the entire universe.

Letchyo booty bounce.... All the skaters on the floor were shaking what their mama never gave them, to the beat of the scandalous songs.

"You ready for this?" I pretended to ask both of my companions, but in my mind, I was referring to Kelly. I couldn't have cared less if Liz was ready or not.

"I still think we should wait a few minutes more," Kelly responded to my relief.
"Wait for what? We already have our skates on!" I shouted excitedly over the blare of the music. "I have some new moves!" I was eager to showcase my skating skills.

Kelly moved closer to me, and leaned over to my ear, "Don't turn your head right away, that brotha over there is checking us out," she said, looking straight ahead of her, sultrily. It was clear that Kelly was on the prowl and I didn't blame her. After all, she'd been single for over a year.

"Who's he looking at?" I asked, obeying Kelly's instruction to be subtle.

"Girl, I don't know, could be either one of us," she replied, looking back at Liz as she giggled, "Don't you think homeboy is foine?" she asked Liz.

"He's a'ight," Liz replied with a faintish smile. I turned slightly to acknowledge Liz, for the sake of being polite.

That's when I'd noticed her freshly done nails, and banging BabyPhat outfit. I wondered how much of my three hundred dollars, she'd used to get all glammed up.

"You look nice, Liz," I complimented.

"Thanks, Sapphire," she replied, her facial expression that of shock.

What the hell was there to be shocked about? I knew how to offer compliments; it was her that had issues, not me! I figured enough time had passed, so I finally removed my focus from that heifer, and gazed upon the man that Kelly had

been eyeing. From where we stood, homeboy
definitely looked like a show-stopper.

"Hot damn! I see what you're saying, Kell," I
said, gazing lustfully at the coco colored angel
who'd stolen Kelly's attention.

"Do you think he's with someone?" Kelly
questioned, joining me in my lust, and no longer
caring about subtlety.

"Doesn't matter," I said smoothly, "Can't no
one woman handle all that man."

"Giurrl, you are a mess!" Kelly shouted,
playfully pulling my weave.

We stood there, watching our eye-candy
watching us. No sooner than we'd started
gawking at him, a heavy-set, high yellow sista
approached him and they both exchanged brief
kisses.

"Oh shit!" Kelly said, turning her head away in
disappointment.

"Well, there's the answer to your question,
Kelly. He has his woman," I shifted my focus to
Kelly.

"Damn! Why are the good ones always
taken?" She whined.

"Kelly, let me tell you a little secret. No man
is ever truly single. Therefore, you have to tap

into the power you possess, and use it to get whichever man you want, regardless of his so-called status."

"So you want me to be a ho?"

"No! I'm not saying that."

"You want me to be a home-wrecker?"

"No. Damn, Kelly! Is that what you think of me?"

Before Kelly could respond to my question, Liz cleared her throat.

"Ya'll wanna skate or what?" She asked dryly.

"Go ahead, we're right behind you," I dismissed her ass angrily as she glared at me.

"Sapphire!" Kelly yelled.

"What?" I snapped.

"We all came here together, so we will skate together," she reasoned.

"How are y'all beautiful ladies doing tonight?" A smooth baritone voice stopped us dead in our tracks.

We turned around simultaneously and were breath-taken by the coco angel.

"We're doing alright," I replied with a smile, on behalf of my friends. I was feeling real good, just about then.

"That's good to know," he smiled back at me. Then he switched gears towards Kelly,

"And you are?"

"I'm Kelly."

"You're gorgeous, Kelly, extremely gorgeous," he remarked.

"Well thank you."

"May I have the pleasure of skating with you?" he offered.

"Thanks, but no thanks," Kelly declined.

"Why not?" he insisted.

"I don't want no drama from your woman."

"What woman?" he inquired.

"Ok, that's enough," I interjected. "Since Kelly won't skate with you, I will." I was pissed at the fact that he'd initially passed me up for Kelly. I mean, she's a nice girl, but I'm way hotter.

"Sapphire, may I speak with you for a minute?" Kelly requested.

"Can it wait?" I asked and watched as Liz grabbed her purse and stormed away. Jealous heifer!

"No, it cannot wait," Kelly stated.

"Where is she going?" I asked referring to Liz.

"I hope I ain't causin' no trouble," the sexy stranger interrupted.

"I had something I wanted to talk to you about," Kelly said, ignoring the sexy coco brother. I was offended on behalf of him.

"C'mon, Kelly, it can wait until another time. Let's have some fun!" my smile dissipated as Kelly turned away from us. She found a seat, sat down and began ripping the skates from her feet. Before rushing off behind her, I told the dude to hang around till I was through handling my business.

"What's up with you?" I asked her.

"Not a damn thing!"

"Then why are you taking off your skates?"

"Because our night out together has come to an end."

"Don't tell me you're jealous," I smiled awkwardly.
Kelly looked me up and down scornfully before speaking, "I'm going to catch up with Liz."

I couldn't understand why she and Liz were trying to kill my joy. I walked back over the sexy brotha with whom I'd already made up my mind to spend the rest of the night. I noticed him gazing after Kelly as she exited the building. It's as if I wasn't even standing there next to him. What the fuck? I decided to stand in front of him and block his view of her.

"Are you ready to have some fun?" I asked.

"Oh, that," he said absently, "Yeah, let's do the thang. By the way, your friend Kelly, can you give me her phone number?"

CHAPTER TWENTY EIGHT
SAPPHIRE

I was buzzed and lightheaded. I felt as if I was drunk, though I hadn't had a drink since hours ago, when I'd met up with the girls. I'd scored for the night and gotten the opportunity to skate with the hottest guy on the planet. Not for one moment had I blamed Kelly and Liz for being mad at me. Shoot, if I were them, I'd be mad at me, too.

"So, it's getting kinda late. What do you wanna do next?" my stud asked me.

"Well," I drawled happily, "I say we go back to my place," I suggested, smiling at him.

"I have no objections to that," he replied, gazing at a number of skaters as they left the building.

"Let's go then," I instructed, knowing deep down this man was probably still wishing he was with Kelly and not me. I'd just have to find a way to help him forget about her, and I knew exactly what I needed to do.

We finally arrived at my town home, and my

imagination had already been running wild about what I was going to do to this guy in bed, and what I would have him do to me. It had been a while since JT had cuffed me, since he'd been keeping me busy on my head top these days. To be honest, I really didn't have a need for this dude whom I'd brought home with me, but he was fine as hell, and I was turned on as hell. And for some odd reason, I just knew that when I was through with him, Kelly would be nothing but a distant memory. I opened the door to my living room and turned on the lights. I stood where I was, petrified at the scene before me.

"Wait a minute, have you been robbed?" he shouted. I couldn't open my mouth to speak. My home had been ransacked; everything was upside down. My sofas had been ripped opened, tables turned over; drawers on the floor; my crystal wares had been smashed to pieces, broken glass scattered everywhere. Who could have done this to me?

"Should I call the cops?" he asked. I stared at him. Who was he? I had brought a brotha home and hadn't even gotten his name.

"What's your name?" I whispered softly, finally sobering up. All my naughty thoughts of

him had vanished with a
quickness.

"What?" he asked, looking at me like I was
crazy.

"What's your name?"

"Mojo," he replied.

"Your name is Mojo?" I asked, puzzled. Given
the circumstances, I found it hard to comment
on his name.

"Listen, Mojo, can you call the cops for me,
while I check the house?"

"Tell you what, you stay right here and call
the cops. I'll check around the house," he
said, offering me a scratched, banged up chair.

"Thank you," I said faintly, too weak to stop
this stranger from roaming about my home.
What was he going to do now anyway, rob me?
Or was he going to ransack my apartment? It
was a little bit too late for that.

My hands and fingers quivered uncontrollably
as I dialed 911.

"The coast is clear," Mojo announced as he
treaded back downstairs.

"The cops are on their way, thanks for all your
help."

"You mean you want me to leave?"

"Of course I want you to leave, the cops are

on their way."

"You sure you'll be alright?"

"Yeah, I'm sure."

"A-ight, just be careful, ok?"

"Thanks again," I said, getting up to lock the door as he left.

"I should probably stay until the cops get here," he proposed.

"You probably shouldn't."

"Do you see that?"

"See what?"

"The words carved into your door," Mojo pointed to the words that were carelessly etched into my door.

'CLEAN UP YOUR ACT, TRICK!'

I was insulted by those words, but even more embarrassed that Mojo got to see that shit. Especially after the stunt I'd pulled on him and Kelly earlier that night. Anyone could have done this, but I was strongly leaning towards Liz.

"I think you should go now," I opened the door and let Mojo out. For all I knew, it could have been him that was stalking my ass, but that was a bit far-fetched. I shifted the blinds and saw the cops pulling in, as Mojo was pulling out. That was quick. I guess living in a white neighborhood counted for more than just a few things. Though I was numb, I pushed myself to greet the cops and explain everything I knew, to the best of my ability. I also explained to them about Liz's jealousy and how it had finally gotten the best of her.

"We'll certainly be questioning Ms. Rose, but please keep in mind that, at this time, we can't tell for sure that this was her doing."

After dusting for fingerprints and asking a series of routine questions such as, who else might have done this; when had the harassing phone calls begun etc., one of the cops handed me his card and reintroduced himself to me.

"My name is Officer Bradshaw," he said, "if anything else comes up, or if you have any questions or concerns, call me at this number."

"Thank you," I said, accepting the card.

"In the meantime, Ma'am" the other officer stated, "Is there anyone you can spend a few days with? Right now we wouldn't advise you to stay here."

"I can't stay here?"

"No, Ma'am, it's not safe," Officer Bradshaw replied.

"Well, ok then. Just give me a few minutes while I make a phone call," I said, slipping into the kitchen for some privacy.

My first thought was to get Stewart on the phone, but his phone had been switched off. He sure had been acting weird these days, it's as if he'd done a one eighty and changed up on me. So my next move was to call JT. I started dialing his number, but stopped midway as I recalled the big brawl between us, the day I'd called his house. He'd made it a point to put me in my place, by letting me know that I shouldn't fuck with his marriage by stirring shit up.

After apologizing to him and promising never to repeat the act, we had some seriously steamy, make-up sex. The next day he'd texted me to meet him at Rose's Caribbean Cafe, but he never showed up, or even bothered to call and cancel. I called him several times that day, but my calls went straight to voicemail, which meant that his phone was off. I'd been avoiding him ever since. What kind of life was I living? To be fucking with a man who couldn't even come to my rescue, in case of an emergency? I needed to put my pussy on lockdown. Let's see, who else might I call? Of Course! I speed dialed Kelly, but she didn't pick up. I wiped away the tear that fell from the corner of my eye. Defeated, I slowly stepped back into the living room to report to the cops.

"Found someone?" Officer Bradshaw asked.

"Yeah, I did. I just need to go upstairs and pack a few things."

"Let me accompany you," he offered.
We all showed up at Kelly's loft at a quarter past three in the morning. I pressed the buzzer, hoping with all my might that Kelly would let go of the petty bullshit, and help me out. The indoor lights came on, and the front door swung open. Kelley stood before us in a short, black, lacy nightie. Her nipples poked out at us inquisitively.

"Sapphire, what's going on? Why are you here?"

"Good morning, Mrs.-"

"Miss Benin, Kelly Benin- I'm not married," she informed arrogantly, which was unlike her. But I knew she was upset with me.

"Yeah- ar-hem! Umm- there has been a bit of an incident-" Officer Bradshaw began, clearly bothered by the sight of Kelly.

"Incident? Oh God! Sapphire, are you alright?"

"Yeah, I'm physically alright. Listen, can I spend the night? I'll explain everything to you."

"Oh, alright, come in," she said, eyeing me

cautiously, "Would that be all officers?"

"Yeah, sure-" they chorused together before she cut them off.

"Ok, well goodnight," she dismissed them, closing the door as I stepped inside. "Perverts."

"Giurrl, what's going on?" she asked me.

"I arrived home last night, only to find my apartment ransacked."

"What?"

"To be honest, I don't know what the hell to do. I won't be able to salvage much from the looks of things."

"You're kidding me!"

"I'm being for real, Kell, I told the cops that-"

"You told the cops that what?"

"Well, they asked me if I knew who might have done it."

"You told them it was JT, right?"

"Of course not! What's your hang up with JT, anyway?"

"So what did you tell them?"

"Nothing."

"Sit down, let me take your bags and get you a drink. Why don't you spend a few days here? At least until we gain some momentum on this case."

"That's mad love you're showing me, Kell. I appreciate it."

"What do you want to drink?"

"I'll take a cup of tea if you have any."

"Not a problem. Go ahead and freshen up. You can join me on the sofa once you're through."

Ten minutes later I'd showered, and slipped into one of Kelly's robes.

"I'm so confused," I whined, sipping on chamomile tea.

"So am I girl, but we'll get to the bottom of this. Trust."

"I sure hope so," I placed the tea cup on the table and snuggled up on the sofa. I wished JT was here to comfort me. To hell with Stewart!

"Remember while we were at Skaterz, I told you there was something I needed to talk to you about?"

"Yeah, I remember," I responded drowsily.

"Well, since you're here now, let me just tell you-"

"Kelly?" I said cutting her off.

"What?"

"Can it wait until morning? I'm so exhausted," I yawned.

"Uh- alright."

"You sure, Kell?"

"I guess it can wait. Sapphire?"

"Yes, Kell," I replied, annoyed.

"I'm gonna need you to tell me a little more about that guy you've been dating."

"Oh, pu-lease! What do you have against JT?"

"I'm not talking about JT."

"Then who are you talking about?"

"I'm talking about Stewart."

I rose the next morning at a few minutes past seven. If I was quick and lucky enough, I'd catch up with JT at CB Smith Park. He normally jogged for forty minutes between seven and eight in the mornings, before heading out for work.

I got dressed and left Kelly a note, alerting her that I was off to see JT and that our little 'talk' would have to wait a while. I jumped into my Audi and revved up the engine. My car and my townhouse were my reasons for holding down two jobs in the first place. My second job at the hotel was just a back-up plan, for when my men fell out of line, like Stewart did. There was nothing cute about working two jobs. I was seriously considering resigning from being a hotel clerk, but that was no longer an option since I'd lost so much last night. My household insurance would probably cover the cost of some of the loss, but I wasn't counting on getting back much.   Everything had been fucked up: my antiques, chinaware, crystals, even my jewelry. Most of my clothes had been bleached, or stolen.   Whoever had done this was out to get me and they needed to pay.

I spotted JT's fine ass zoom across a narrow trail by the park across the street, and disappeared into the forest of trees. A ray of hope lightened my heart when I saw him. There wasn't much JT could do for me, but maybe he could help me get to the bottom of all of this. Maybe now he would be willing to leave his wife, and take care of me. I pulled into the park and got out of the car and leaned up against the hood. Moments later, JT and I were hugging.

"I missed you," JT said, gasping for breath,

"Why have you been ignoring me? And you look scared."

"That's because I am scared."

"But why?" He pulled out a white handkerchief, and used it to wipe sweat from his brows.

"Someone broke into my apartment last night."

"What? Are you alright? Did you call the

police?"

"I wasn't there when it happened. Yes, I called the police."

"Dammit, Sapphire! Why didn't you call me?"

"Why? So you could ignore me again? Or so you could tell me how important it is not to screw with your wife?"

"That's harsh."

"You call that harsh? You wanna know what I call harsh? Telling me to show up at a restaurant and then abandoning me. That's harsh!"

"Who did that?"

"You did that, JT! How could you?"

"I didn't do that."

"You know what-"

"There's obviously a lot going on that I need to know about. We can't talk now. It's not a good time to talk. Why don't you meet me here later, around 1 pm. I'll come out here on my lunch break."

"No. Why don't you meet me at Rose's Caribbean Café? Bail out on me again, and it's over between us."

"What do you mean by, again? I've never bailed out on you before."

"So   now   you're   playing   games."

"I'm not; my shift starts in an hour, why don't I meet you at Rose's like you suggested. We'll sit outside and talk more about this. Do you need money for anything: a hotel, clothes, anything-"

"Later. Hopefully this time, you'll show up," I watched as he walked away, confused.

I sat in my car for a good twenty five minutes before leaving to go back to Kelly's house. I was ashamed of my crazed behavior towards JT, but I knew I had every right to be mad at him. He had been so nonchalant about my situation. *"I have to be at work within the hour."* Considering everything I'd been going through, you'd think he'd push work to the side for the time being. As I cruised down Pines Boulevard, a silver Mercedes Benz sailed past me and thoughts of Stedman, my boss, flashed across my mind. Stedman had a car similar to that one. I quickly dismissed my thoughts of him, and forced myself to focus on JT. He was my number one priority right now. Shameless to say, my Maintenance man had now taken priority over my boyfriend, Stewart. What was he up to anyway? Stewart no longer returned my calls, or came by my home to check up on me. I decided to forget about him and move on with my life. It's men like him that cause women to become dishonest in relationships. Not too long ago, Stewart had been showering me with adoration. Now, all of a sudden he'd fallen off of the face of the earth.

Forget Stewart! I still wondered if JT would ever leave his wife for me. I felt like I was fighting a losing battle where that was concerned. If he wasn't about to sacrifice a few extra minutes of his time from work to speak with me about an emergency that involved life and death; if he had so willingly chosen his job over me, then would he ever even consider giving up his wife? The more I thought about it the more enraged I got. *"Now is not a good time to talk."* Yeah, whatever. Now I started thinking of all the things I should have said to him, but never did. I just hoped he showed up at that restaurant today, so I could give him a piece of my mind.

I pulled into Kelly's driveway and parked behind a silver Mercedes Benz that hadn't been there before. It was the same car that had passed me in traffic, only moments ago--I was sure. Kelly's blue Corvette was parked next to it. I didn't know she was expecting visitors. I got out of my car and slowly walked towards the house, inspecting the car as I walked by. Again, thoughts of Stedman crossed my mind. And again, I dismissed those thoughts. I knew that once I'd resolved these issues in my life, I would find a way to make Stedman love me. I didn't have a key to get in, so I turned the door handle, and the door opened.

"S-S-Sapphire!" someone stuttered.

My name, Sapphire, is defined as a beautiful, precious, transparent stone, valued as a gem. I grew up believing that that name was just the right name for me. That name, Sapphire, defined who I was. And it now defined the woman I'd blossomed into. Beautiful, precious, valued- which is why, I found it hard to understand how, at this point, at this very moment, all of a sudden, I hated to be called by that name. Could it be the circumstances surrounding why my name was being called? Or could it be because of who was calling my name? Or maybe it's because, I wasn't feeling as valued as my precious name described. My best friend was wrapped up tightly in a very passionate embrace with her visitor, who was clearly the owner of the Benz parked outside.

"Sapphire! What are you doing here?" he asked, awkwardly releasing Kelly from his hug.

"Sapphire, I didn't expect that you'd be back so soon," Kelly said.

"Sapphire, I-"

"If any of you call my name one more time, I swear-"

"I'm sorry; I'm just shocked that you're here."

"Why, huh? Why are you so shocked that I showed up at my best friend's house? You do remember she's my best friend, right?" I asked as I glared at him.

"Listen, Sapphire-"

"Don't listen Sapphire me!" I shifted my glare to Kelly, then back to her visitor.

"Stedman! What are you doing here?" I demanded to know.

"I beg your pardon?" he asked, as if responding to being called Stedman, rather than Mr. Stedman, was beyond him.

"Sapphire, we need to talk," Kelly interjected.

"Do we, Kelly? I mean, you're supposed to be my best friend, yet here you are!"

"Wait a minute," Stedman butted in, "I'm sorry that my being here may seem to be a bit unprofessional-"

"A bit?" I asked, cutting him off.

"Well, maybe a lot," he said, studying me briefly, "You obviously have a problem with this, but why?" he asked.

I turned to Kelly and said, "I thought you were my friend. How could you do this behind my back?"

"I did nothing behind your back, Sapphire."

"Then what would you call this?" I asked, motioning at Stedman.

"This," she said, mimicking my movements, "is what I wanted to talk to you about."

"Wait a minute," Stedman said, "No disrespect here. But why do you feel you owe Sapphire an explanation about us?"

"Listen, Bill, we'll talk about this over lunch today?" Kelly told Stedman.

Was I hearing correctly? Had she just called him Bill?

"Ok, I'll just get going," Stedman said with a confused expression, "Sapphire, I'm sorry you're upset. I guess I'll see you in the office on Monday?"

"Whatever!" I snapped. I watched as Stedman walked away in his Diesel denim and a crisp white shirt. He was sexier than a mother-

"I'm so sorry, Sapphire," Kelly said, interrupting my thoughts. Damn her!

"What is he doing here, Kelly?"

"That's what I wanted to talk to you about. Yesterday when Liz and I couldn't reach you, I went by your job, but you'd already left. That's when Stedman asked me out."

"Bullshit, Kelly! You've been fucking Stedman this whole time! Right under my nose and I didn't even know it."

"You've got to believe me, Sapphire. I never knew he liked me like that; he asked me out yesterday, and I've been meaning to talk to you about it, and-"

"So that should explain why you're already all over him!"

"No, he's all over me. Listen, I don't even see what you're so upset about. You already have a man!"

"And it's my fault why you're desperate enough to screw my boss?"

"Excuse me?"

"Kelly, you know I've always liked Stedman," I said.

"But Stedman doesn't like you!" Kelly said.

"Excuse me?"

"You're excused, dammit! Who the fuck do you think you are? Do you think the world revolves around you? Get this in that thick, vain skull of yours; Stedman wants nothing to do with the likes of you."

"What?" I asked, shocked.

"You heard me! You're a selfish bitch! How dare you try to come into my home and tell me what to do! If you weren't so consumed with yourself, then you would have given me a chance to tell you about my man. That's right, Sapphire, he's my man! I don't care anymore! Stedman doesn't belong to you. He don't belong to nobody. I owe you nothing."

I stared at Kelly, unable to believe what was unfolding before me, "A round of applause to you!" I spat bitterly while clapping my hands,

"Some friend you are."

"You know what, Sapphire? I know you had a crush on Stedman. I'm sorry you feel betrayed. Is that good enough an apology for you? I have to get going now. Feel free to stay here for as long as you need," Kelly grabbed her Gucci purse and stormed through the door.

I felt like a damn fool. I slumped to the floor, chuckling nervously to myself. Sapphire and Robert, aka Bill Stedman have hooked up with each other. Son of a bitch! My world had finally come crashing down on me. I needed to bounce on up outta here. I was going to get up, get my things and go back home to my townhouse. Forget about the cops' warnings! At least I still had my home. I planned on cleaning up my apartment, and then meet JT for lunch. At least then, I'd be able to get some things off of my chest.

CHAPTER TWENTY NINE
JT

Sapphire and I met up at Rose's, as planned, and requested for the waitress to seat us outside. Someone was out to get her and she was mad at me for not being able to stand by her the way she needed me to. She'd seemed real pissed, with extra piss added. I've never seen her look this miserable.

"My name is Sophia, and I'll be your waitress today. Can I get you anything to drink?" the waitress asked us.

"Yes, bring us a bottle of Alize," Sapphire quickly ordered.

"Sure," the waitress said politely before scurrying off. I was nervous at Sapphire's request for an entire bottle of Alize. But, given the mood she was in, I dared not object.

I reached for her hand and kissed it gently, "I'm so sorry sweetness."

"You should be," she growled, pulling her hand away from me.

"You're taking out your frustrations on me."

"Well, I'm sorry I'm making you feel sad," she mocked.

"Stop the bullshit and tell me what's going on," I glared at her, thankful for being outside where there were fewer ears.

"Tell me something, did you have fun?"

"Did I have fun doing what?"

"Did you have fun making me look like a damn fool, JT!"

"How did I make you look like a damn fool?"

"I'll tell you how you made me look like a damn fool! I showed up here, just like your text instructed me to, wearing that short skirt, with no panties!"

"Shhh! People can hear you," I said, glancing around.

"I don't give a shit. JT, I'm so mad at you! You and your stupid wife! Imagine, you're sleeping with me, and I can't even call you in case of an emergency. What the hell is that, huh?"

"You're right. I'm sorry about that. I think I know what happened the day you received the text. My wife and I have the same phones, I think she switched them up, and used my phone to text you."

"Why would your wife text me to show up here wearing no draws, JT?"

"To make it seem authentic, like the text was coming from me. You don't know my wife."

"My wife this, and my wife that! Does your wonderful wife have a name? Don't throw your marriage   in   my   face,   JT!"

"I'm not-"

"Excuse me." Sapphire sprang to her feet, grabbing her purse. "I have to go to the little girls' room."

I sat there at the table waiting for her to return, and wishing I could go back to the days when I was just an innocent kid, and my father was still alive. I couldn't understand what had gone wrong in my life, and why is it that everything   I   touched,   seemed   to   get contaminated with grief.

"Here you go, Sir," the waitress said politely, while placing the drink on the table. "It's open." Here are wine glasses, ice- are you ready to order?"

"No, gimme five more minutes."

"Sure."

Someone had used my phone to text Sapphire. That could only mean one thing. My wife had found out about us. What I couldn't figure out is how she'd pulled it off. Now that she knew about my infidelity and my going back on our ridiculous deal, there's no telling, what my crazy ass wife would do next. Would she call immigration on me? Or would she kill me? Was she the one stalking Sapphire? I grabbed the bottle of Alize and took a generous swig, straight from the bottle. I was truly fucked.

The sound of gunshots shattered my eardrums. I felt something hit me, and on impact a sharp pain seared through my ribs. People screamed and ducked looking over at me in horror. As the pain registered, I tumbled out of my chair and onto the ground. I then realized I'd been hit by a bullet. A second bullet hit me, ripping through flesh and tearing through the muscles in my back. Blood spewed from my body as I crumbled. The pain was unimaginable. I wanted to die and live at the same time. My whole life flashed before me. Had this been an accident? Were these bullets meant for someone else, or had someone wanted me dead? The bullets moved through me, scorching my insides.

I slowly drifted away into unconsciousness. In the distance I could hear a woman's voice. She was screaming frenetically, "Someone, help! Stay with me, JT! JT, stay with me!"
Then all went dim.

CHAPTER THIRTY
STEWART

I ignored the red light and sped through the intersection, jumping ahead of the oncoming traffic. There was no time left now, I needed to get onto the highway and hurry the fuck out of Pembroke Pines! I could feel the whole world closing in on me. All the air was being sucked out of me, and my only refuge now lied anywhere outside of Broward County.

How the hell had things gotten so screwed up? Lexi had been nothing but trouble since the day we'd met her. Vaughnn should have left her ass at the bus stop that night, but he didn't, and now her husband was screwing my woman. No way in hell was I going to just sit back and take that shit. I hated that motherfucker. I despised Lexi also. She'd been aware of them two all along, and instead of telling me what's up, she conspired with me to set up JT and Sapphire. My blood ran cold as I reflected on the sinister look that had coated her face, the day she'd hatched up her little plan to "bring JT down." She sure is one crazy bitch, and I was going to find a way to get her back for this shit.

I swung onto the highway, and headed south towards Miami. My blood boiled as I thought of how Sapphire had sashayed into Rose's Caribbean Café, her face glowing as if she was on cloud nine. I did a double-take when her ass swayed across the room, wearing a short, red, mini skirt. Her smile was broad, as if she'd just won the lottery. It hadn't taken but two hot seconds for me to realize what was actually going on. With all the money I'd been raining down on her, she had all right to look so damn excited. Lexi and I had shown up there to see who JT's woman, Sapphire was. Lexi had orchestrated the plan, by instructing Sapphire to wear a short, red mini skirt to Rose's. When my woman walked in, dressed in a red mini skirt, I jumped up to confront her, but Lexi restrained me.

"What's wrong?" she asked, pretending as if she didn't know what was up.

"Lexi, what's going on? What is she doing here?" I demanded to know, through gritted teeth.

"You mean the lady that just walked in? Do you know her?"

"Don't play dumb with me, Lexi? How long have you known about this shit?"

"Known about what? Do you know that woman?"

"What the hell is Sapphire doing here, Lexi?"
"So, you mean the woman sitting over there, in the red skirt- is Sapphire- your girlfriend?" Lexi asked.

"Stop playing dumb with me Lexi- how long have you known about this?"

"Stewart, I had no idea," she continued to play dumb.

"How the hell could this be? Sapphire- my woman- was the woman who called your house?"

"Well- her text message did confirm she would be wearing a red mini skirt and a sheer top."

"You mean JT has been fucking Sapphire this whole time?" I asked in shock and disbelief.

"Stewart, I- I don't think JT is aware that she's is your woman," Lexi said, eyeing Sapphire from across the room.

It was hard to figure out if Lexi was being totally honest, and what her intentions were.

"You better start talking, Lexi- when did you

realize Sapphire was playing both of us?"

"Chill out and sit down. How was I supposed to know you were seeing that broad? It's probably a coincidence that your girl rolled up in here like this today."

"Fuck coincidence! Is that why she's wearing a red mini skirt too? I'm leavin', yo, I don't need no more of this shit!" I threw down a fifty dollar bill on the table, and stormed out of the restaurant.

I'd walked right by Sapphire too. Not caring if she'd noticed me or not. She obviously hadn't noticed me, because if she had, she would have come after me and ended her little ho-ing with that punk. I know she was still involved with him, because I've been stalking her dumb butt.

There was even that night when my brothers and I spotted her at Skaterz, rubbing up on some big, rough ass dude. Home boy was bigger than Vaughnn, so you know his ass was real big, lookin like he'd been poppin' steroids his whole friggin' life. I was devastated to see how Sapphire had been playing me. So I ignored my brothers' good advice to not do anything stupid, left Skaterz and went back to Sapphire's place to thrash her apartment. I broke the window to get in, even though I had a key. I took back the clothes, jewelry and all the expensive shit I could find. The stuff that couldn't fit under my arms, I smashed to smithereens. I banged up all her expensive furniture pieces and ransacked her rooms. No one uses Stewart and get away with that shit--except for Nita.

I'd gotten played. I didn't give a rat's ass whether JT knew she was my woman or not. His ass was married. He must have known Sapphire had to be some other man's woman. Who the hell did he think he was, to have his fucking cake and eat it? Fuck that!

I revved up the engine of my Mecedes Benz, which was one of the three vehicles that I owned. I had been in turmoil for days now, but today, I just couldn't take it anymore. My cell phone began to ring, interrupting me from my ill memories.

"Hello," I greeted, pissed.

"What's going on, bro'? Where you at?"

"I'm on my way outta town."

"Why? What are you running away from?"

"Steffaun, I don't have time for this shit. I have to go and clear my head."

"Clear your head for what? What did you do, Stewart?" Steffaun asked accusingly, pissing me off even more.

"I didn't do nothin', mehn! Why did you call me?"

"You did do something. Why else would you be running away?"

"I'm not running away, alright? I'm just going through some things."

"Stephin is here with me. Do you wanna talk to him?"

"Naw, I'll talk to him later. I'm in a rush."

"Stewart?" my other brother, Stephin, chimed in.

"We need to talk," he said. Now Stephin was the quiet one of the three of us. So when he spoke, I listened.

"What's going on?"

"Are you driving?"

"Of course I'm driving, I'm on the highway."

"Pull over."

"Can't do that right now, bro."

"There's been an accident today. I need you to pull the fuck over and park the car. Now!"

"An accident? What the-?" I said, surprised by the terror in my own voice.

I put on my emergency lights, slowed down, and pulled over like Stephin had instructed me to.

"A'ight, I pulled over. What's going on?"

"JT has been shot."

"Is that why you're calling me? Tuh! Is he dead? Do you know who shot him?" I asked, trying my best to sound nonchalant.

"That's why we called you."

"Wait a minute, you think I shot that son of a bitch?"

"We never thought of that, but now that you've mentioned it-"

"Don't bullshit me, Stephin! If ya'll didn't think I did it, then why did you call me?"

"We need you to turn back and meet us at the house."

"For what?"

"We have things to discuss. This has put the spotlight on all of us, since we're linked to JT. The last thing we want is for nosy investigators to come sniffin' around. You know the deal."

"No shit!" I chuckled nervously. I hadn't thought about that. There's no telling what they would find if we were suddenly investigated. And my brothers would be in a shit load of trouble.

"Do you guys think that I had something to do with this?"

"Just come back so we can discuss this, bro'.

This phone thing is not the best thing; you know that."

"A'ight. I'm on my way."

Twenty five minutes later I was caught up in a heated conversation with my brothers. I wished I had kept my mouth shut about my situation with Sapphire. I'd told my brothers what Lexi had done, and how I'd found out about Sapphire's little games. Now they had reasons to believe that I had shot JT out of jealousy.

"I told you to stop fuckin' around with those bitches, Stewie! We told you to leave Nita, Lexi and Sapphire alone," Steffaun snarled accusingly, "Now look what they've caused you to do!"

"I haven't been fuckin' around with them, and they didn't cause me to do anything!" I argued. If my brothers wouldn't believe me, then who would?

"Did you know that a lady showed up at Vaughnn's house recently?" Stephin asked.

"So?"

"What do you mean by 'so'? She was sniffing around, Stewie."

"Sniffin' around? For what? Did you take care of her, or did Vaughnn do it?"

"Take care of her? The woman was from the FBI or some shit like that; had Vaughnn jumpin' around like a fucking frog. Now he's as paranoid as a mofo."

"And ya'll are just now telling me this?"

"It doesn't matter; the point is that you've drawn a lot more unnecessary attention to us than we can afford."

"I wonder why the hell the FBI would be sniffing us out."

"And you know, once the FBI actually shows up at your door, it usually means they already have some solid shit against your ass."

"Something just doesn't add up. Cleaning up our tracks is what we do best."

"I'm tellin' you, Stewie, we need to do something before this gets out of hand. Damn, only if you hadn't shot JT. You could get charged for attempted murder! We could all be investigated- then all of us would go to jail!"

"Calm down, Stephin," Steffaun interjected, "Stewie, I need you to explain to us why you shot JT in broad daylight. Do you think there were any witnesses?"

"What the fuck! I'm done, man."

"So if you didn't shoot him, who did?" Steffaun asked.

Steffaun tightened his eyes and shook his

head dismally, "Yeah Stewart, if you didn't do it, who did?"

"I didn't do it! But I think we should pack our belongings, and leave Florida. I think I know why the FBI has begun to examine Vaughnn."

"Why?"

"It's highly possible that this may have something to do with a top secret computer project that Vaughnn had executed."

"Top secret?" Steffaun asked sarcastically.

"Computer project?" Stephin followed suit, "What computer project is that. How come we know nothing about it?"

"I'm not sure- I- I don't know."

"How could you not know? You're Vaughnn's right hand man."

"I don't fuckin' have time for this shit, Stephin! I said I don't know. Pack your things, both of you and let us leave Florida. We need to leave out tonight."

"Leave and go where?" Stephin continued to interrogate.

"We'll flee to a country that has no extradition treaty or diplomatic relations with the US."

"You mean like Mexico?"

"Naw- not Mexico."

"Then where?"

"Yeah, Stewie- where? I mean, isn't it now very difficult to find such a place? It seems as if the US now has extradition treaties with nearly every god-damn country in the world," Steffaun chimed in.

"Nearly, but not all," I verified, "I have a plan. We'll have to travel light. Pack only the things you need for a couple of nights."

"What about Vaughnn? Are you gonna just leave your best friend behind?"

"Screw Vaughnn! He got greedy and tried to pull off a scheme that was way too big for him and way out of his league. His cover got blown - he knew what he was doing putting all of our lives in jeopardy. Do you wish to stay back, Stephin, and see if you can help him?" I asked and waited for an answer. There was none.

"I thought so. This murder attempt does not look good on any of us. This shit happened at the wrong time, too. What makes things worse is that Lexi and JT are both linked to us. All hell is about to break loose. We need to leave Florida!" I demanded.

"Are you being for real?" my brothers asked.

"Yes, I'm being for real. I vowed to protect

you, and that's what I'm going to do."

"So, you really think we'll get away with all of this?" Stephin asked.

"All of what?"

"You know- what if the authorities stop us and throw us in jail?" he asked fearfully.

"Let's not panic. We need to try first. With my plan, we might be able to slip through the hands of the law. Furthermore, all the attention might just be on Vaughnn and whomever he was working on that scheme with."

"But he's your best friend. You can't just leave him!"

"Vaughnn might have been my best friend, but you guys are my brothers. I have vowed to protect both of you. So hurry up, get your shit and let's bounce!"

CHAPTER THIRTY ONE
LEXI

"Who shot JT?" Vaughnn asked me accusingly.

"How the hell would I know?" I snapped

"On the contrary, Lexi, you would know better than anyone else, who shot your husband."

"I don't think I like your tone, Vaughnn."

"Why Lexi, did I hit a nerve?"

"You're breaking my heart! How could you think that of me?"

"No! The real question is how you could attempt to kill the father of your unborn child?"

"I didn't, and would never attempt to kill my baby's father!"

"Yet he's lying in the hospital in critical condition and the doctors believe he will die."

"That's not true!"

"Are you that crazy, Lexi? What do you mean that's not true?"

"The father of my child is not lying in a hospital bed."

"Then where is he lying, crazy ass Lexi?"

"You, of all people should not be calling me crazy," I sniffed as tears flowed from my eyes.

"Do you realize that, because of this shit, the cops are gonna come sniff us out?"
He growled. I'd never heard him like this before.

"And you have the nerve," he continued, "to sit there and talk shit! Lexi, I thought you were smarter than that. But no, you just had to let your jealousy get in everybody's way, and now the father of your son is going to die!"

"Stop saying that!"

"I'm gonna say it, Lexi! And you're going to listen! Whether you're baby's father dies or not, we will all be investigated for attempted murder. That means unnecessary attention on me, you, Stewart, and everyone else whom we're involved with!"

"I didn't try to kill my baby's daddy!" I wiped tears from my eyes.

"Yes you did! I know it for a fact because I know you like I know the palm of my hands. You attempted to have JT, the father of your own child murdered!"

"No I didn't!" I cried, "JT is not the father!"

"What?"

"JT is not father of my baby, Vaughnn," I held my chest and waited for him to call me a whore for having cheated on JT. But he didn't. There was silence on the other end of the line.

"What kind of fucking games are you playing with me, Lexi?"

"I'm not playing games with you."

"If JT is not the father, who is?"

I gripped the phone tighter and trembled uncontrollably, "You are my baby's father," I said, knowing deep down, how ecstatic Vaughnn would be about the news he'd just heard. But he wasn't.

"You little bitch. You would do or say anything to save your ass now, wouldn't you?" Vaughnn said viciously, "Listen to me carefully. You need to go to the police and confess that you tried to murder your husband."

I gasped as tears flowed from my eyes, "Vaughnn, you don't mean that I-"

"I do mean that!" he said cutting me off, "I loved you once, Lexi, but you left me for that son of a bitch, and I hate you now. I always knew your wonderful JT would be nothing but trouble.

Now, because of him, you'll have to sacrifice yourself, in order to save everybody's ass!"

"Vaughnn, you don't mean that," I whispered weakly, "I didn't try to kill JT. And you already know why he married me."

"Yeah? Is that the same reason why you paid to have him followed? Just to make sure his ass wasn't cheating on you?"

"Who told you that?" I asked overwhelmed with shock and disappointment.

"You better believe that Stewart called me and told me everything. I know that he caught JT cheating on you with his woman."

"See? So if Stewart caught JT with his woman, what does that tell you?" I asked, relieved that I just might be able to get through to Vaughnn after all. Make him see that Stewart must have been the one who shot JT. This was also finally beginning to make some sense to me. It was Stewart who'd done it! "Vaughnn, listen to me. If she was Stewart's woman, and he caught her with JT, and now JT is in the hospital; that could only mean one thing."

"Yeah, that your ass is gonna confess to attempted murder!" Vaughnn interrupted, just before hanging up on me.

CHAPTER THIRTY TWO
LEXI

I was out in our yard struggling to get the lawn chair in just the right spot, next to the once beautiful garden whose glory was now gradually fading. Neither JT nor I had a green thumb. I was in such a foul mood.

"Be careful with that heavy chair!" Mrs. Woodstock warned from the other side of the fence, "You've come too far now to jeopardize that healthy pregnancy."

"Ok, Mrs. Woods. I heard you," I said dryly.

Mrs. Woodstock was our old, nosy, next door neighbor. She and her husband were now retired and had nothing to do now but just chill.

They had money too; loads of it. I was in no mood to be polite, so I positioned the chair, so that when I sat down, I would be facing away, and my back would be turned to her. Frankly, the way I see it, I would soon be going to prison while she and her bourgeois ass husband would be living it up. As far as I was concerned, she could go to hell! I ain't heard one more word from Mrs. Woodstock. I guess it was safe to assume that she'd gotten my message loud and clear, and had walked away.

How could Vaughnn have been so cold? I knew he meant what he'd said to me about turning myself in to the police. Vaughnn wanted me to confess to attempted murder, a crime I never committed. I was so stressed out over this, not to mention the fact that my husband was in the hospital, fighting for his dear life. It's a good thing I'd taken out a health insurance policy. I was certain that once all this was through, hospital bills would overwhelm us, or should I say JT? I would soon be incarcerated, once I'd confessed.

I felt my baby kicking inside me. I gently rubbed my tummy and sobbed softly. Crying was the one thing I could do right now, to relieve some of my stress. Kee-keek! A black Navigator pulled up into my driveway, behind the Z. Immediately, I panicked. Perhaps Vaughnn was ready to kill me. Maybe I'd taken too long to carry out his bidding and he'd decided to make good on his threat. Would he really do it? Would

Vaughnn really kill a pregnant woman— his baby Momma, in cold blood? I'd already given my statement to the cops, letting them know that anybody could have killed my husband. I didn't give them anything to go on. At least, not yet. So, as far as who was coming to visit me in that vehicle, I was clueless.

The car door swung open and a tall, skinny Caucasian woman, wearing a black pant suit stepped out. Vaughnn must have sent her to kill me. I was too afraid to get up and run, so I remained where I was, and watched as she approached me.

"Good afternoon," she smiled pleasantly.

"Yes, how can I help you?" I asked, trying hard to conceal my fear.

"May we go inside briefly? What I have to say to you, needs to be said in private."

"Naw. I'm sure I'm not interested in anything you have to say to me."

"Well, you should be."

"Excuse me? Who are you? Did Vaughnn send you here?"

"My apologies, I'm Lisa Cartright, a federal agent. So you're quite familiar with Vaughnn Gibbs, I'm guessing?"

"What would the feds be doing at my house?"
I asked as a new form of panic took hold of me.
She glanced around until her eyes became
fixated on something, or rather someone, over
my shoulders and over the fence. I immediately
knew that Mrs. Woods hadn't left as I'd
assumed. She was still there nosing around.

"Listen, why don't we step inside? Here's my
badge. You're Mrs. Miller, correct?"

"Yes," I said, glancing at the badge as I got up
from my seat.

"How well do you know Vaughnn?"

"Who's Vaughnn?" I asked.

"I see you have a good sense of humor."

I decided to walk with Lisa towards the house.
I began reflecting on how my grandmother once
taught me about being guilty by association. It
was obvious that I was potentially in a shit load
of trouble, so cooperating with this nice FBI lady
was the least that I could do. I purposely turned
suddenly to look back at Mrs. Woods. She jerked
when she realized her nosy butt was busted. I
cut my eyes at her and turned back around.

"Nosy neighbor?" Lisa commented.

"Yeah, nosy neighbor," I sighed, rubbing my
belly.

Once inside, Lisa wasted no time in getting to the point.

"Mrs. Miller, like I asked you before— how well do you know Mr. Gibbs?"

"I don't."

"But while we were outside, you asked if he was the one that sent me to-"

"I know what I asked- but I was referring to a different Vaughnn."

"Sure you were," Lisa said thoughtfully, "Let me ask you this- what do you do for a living?"

"I'm a real estate sales agent," I replied proudly. If this woman thought I was a criminal, she'd better think again.

"For what company?"

"New Day Realtors and Brokers," I said.

"Right," Lisa said, "For which Vaughnn is part owner, correct?"

"I guess so," I said taken aback. I'd completely forgotten that Vaughnn was part owner of more than a few mortgage companies.

"I'll ask you this question one last time, Mrs. Miller, how well do you know him? And while you're at it, tell me how well you know Stewart Nicks."

I didn't respond. All of a sudden my legs felt weak. I took a seat on my favorite sofa and stared at the floor.

"Mrs. Miller I do not--"

"I'd like to cut a deal with you," I said, cutting her off.

"A deal?" she raised a brow.

"Yes, a deal—before I say anything."

"So you are admitting that you know something."

"No, I'm just requesting that, I get some sort of protection. You know—so that whatever I say to you won't incriminate me."

"Let's see here—you are requesting that the FBI grant you immunity from prosecution, before speaking."

"You could say that—yes."

"Even though you say you do not know Mr. Gibbs?"

"Well–"

"Would you be willing to testify in court, Mrs. Miller?" She asked, cutting me off.

"I don't know. What would I be testifying about?"

"I think you already know. But since you claim that you don't, let me break it down a bit for you. Mr. Gibbs is suspected of committing mortgage fraud. He's currently being investigated."

"Mortgage fraud?"

"At this time, we cannot disclose how we've acquired our information," Lisa paused briefly, then spoke again, "Right now we are working on gathering all evidences to crack down on these malicious schemes of Vaughnn Gibbs."

"Ma- malicious?" I stuttered.

"Mortgage fraud is a very serious crime, Mrs. Miller, especially with the economy being the way it is today. As if that's not enough, Mr. Gibbs is suspected of committing multiple murders," Lisa said, staring me dead in the eyes. I gulped.

"That's not all," she said, "The FBI has been working closely with our partners, including the US Secret Services. A few weeks ago, a major trading company's computer system was hijacked, and sensitive internal communications were accessed. Trade secrets were stolen."

"But– Vaughnn is not that smart," I said, shocked.

"Actually, we have reasons to believe that Vaughnn may be linked to this crime. Vaughnn will be charged with several counts of manslaughter; counterfeiting of US currency and identity crimes."

"You mean identity theft?" I verified.

"Yes, along with a slew of other identity crimes such as access device frauds, computer frauds and fraudulent commercial instruments."

"Oh, God! So—why are you here?"

"Vaughnn was picked up early this morning. Stewart Nicks and his brothers have already fled the country."

"The triplets are gone?"

"I suggest that, whatever you know- you spill, since you have ties to these men."

"What do you mean by ties? I have nothing that ties me to them!"

"For starters, your previous address."

I was speechless. I was always aware of some of Vaughnn's criminal exploits, but nothing of this magnitude.

"Mrs. Miller, who do you believe shot your husband?" Lisa asked.

"Why don't you tell me? You seem to know everything."

"I suggest that you cooperate with me. Given your present condition, conspiracy to committing any of these crimes is the last thing you wanna be charged with."

"I'm innocent!"

"Try proving that in court."

"What do you want from me?"

"Simple. I need your cooperation. Who is this woman your husband is speaking to here?" she asked, handing me a picture.

"Let me see this!" I grabbed the picture from Lisa and did a double take when I recognized Nita's face immediately. I had no idea JT knew about Nita.

"Why do you have pictures of my husband? Is he being investigated?"

"Not yet. But the woman is."
I sighed as I returned the picture to her.

"Are you ready to talk now?"

"Will Vaughnn get bail?"

"That may be a possibility."

"How soon can you hammer out a deal?" I asked.

"Why don't you come with me to the station? I'll need all your contacts-all the 'intel' that you can honestly provide. If it turns into something substantial, then we'll work out a deal."

For a brief moment I considered contacting a lawyer to represent me. For a brief moment-- only.

I was convinced, now more than ever, that Stewart had shot my husband. Normally he wasn't that sloppy with his work, but who knows, the man was desperate. And now he'd fled the country with his brothers?

There was something missing from this puzzle. These crimes of Vaughnn are very serious and meticulous crimes, and serious enough for the FBI to get involved. It was obvious they were still combing through, or working on acquiring evidences, or Lisa wouldn't have shown up here today. She was even willing to see about drumming up some sort of deal, to hear my side of the story. What was going on?

I picked up the phone and dialed Vaughnn's number. The phone rang once and then went straight to voicemail, so I hung up. A few minutes later, my home phone was ringing. The caller ID indicated that the phone number was unidentified.

"Hello," I answered.

"Hello," Nita said.

"I see you're still at Vaughnn's house," I said, realizing she'd obviously seen my missed call, and called back from one of her many phones.

"Yes bitch— I got my man back, why are you calling my house?" she asked rudely.

"Remember the old adage 'he who laughs last, laughs best'?"

"Really? Is that why I'm laughing so hard now, Lexi? Huh? Tell me something– aren't you supposed to be in jail? Vaughnn told me last night, while he was deep inside me, that he had something very nice in store for you."

"Is that so? And what did he tell you this morning when his black ass was being hauled off to jail?"

There was silence on the other end of the line, so I continued to speak. "I called to ask you three questions, Nita."

"Make it quick, I have important things to attend to."

"My first question is why you aren't you in jail with Vaughnn? Secondly, why have you been screwing Vaughnn's best friend, Stewart, and lastly, what is going on between you and my husband?"

There was no answer on the other end of the phone line, so I ranted on through gritted teeth,

"Listen to me bitch, I'm gonna make sure Vaughnn knows of your little 'sexcapades' with his best friend. How do you think he'll feel about that? All this time you've been calling me a bitch, when the whole time, you've been a whore. Tell me something, you filed for JT? How the fuck did you come to know him? I'm sure as hell gonna get to the bottom of this shit! What? You think I wouldn't find out? I'm his wife and best friend. It wasn't that difficult putting two and two together. I saw you in Jamaica, bitch! I know that you and Stewart set me up—"

"So whatchu gonna do?" Nita asked coldly, cutting me off, "What can you do? Just be glad you still have your life--you and that bastard baby you're trying to raffle off. You better watch your back! Vaughnn is gonna make bail soon, and when he does, he'll still need you to confess to shooting JT. If you tell Vaughnn about Stewart and me, you won't live to regret it. You better keep your mouth shut about everything you know! Do you hear me! Things didn't change just because they locked Vaughnn up. They have no proof, no witnesses, nothing!"

"Is that what you think?" I mocked, but I was suddenly introduced to the dial tone.

I needed to do something and fast. I couldn't trust people who had nothing to lose. I placed the phone back on its receiver. *Ok Nita and Vaughnn, Stewart, Steffaun and Stephin! Ya'll wanna play rough? It's on now!*

CHAPTER THIRTY THREE
SAPPHIRE

"Why on earth would I kill JT?" I asked the strange woman who had called my phone, claiming to be JT's ex, and claiming her name was anonymous.

"You wanted him to leave his wife for you, did you not?" she asked, "He kept turning you down, and you got obsessed with him."

"Who the hell are you, and where did you get your information?"

"I told you, I'm anonymous," she replied, then paused, waiting for me to get riled up. Though I was freaking out, I didn't. So she spoke again.

"I am friends with both men, JT and Stewart. JT told me you two had been arguing for a while. He said you're never pleased, that you're always asking for too much. Stewart caught you messing with JT, and now he knows you're nothing but a ho."

"Stewart knows about me and JT? This doesn't even make sense!" I yelled, "And how are you friends with both men?"

"Coincidence, my dear," she said, "This is a small world and your insatiable appetite for money has now become your downfall."

I couldn't believe it. I ended up fucking two men who somehow had ties to each other. Someone attempted to murder one of them and now he was fighting for his life in the hospital. This crazy bitch was on the phone telling me she was certain I had something to do with it.

"I would never do something like that," I protested.

"Do something like what? Sleep with a man for his money? Or be a ho?"

"No, heiffer! I would never try to kill anyone." She chuckled, "you obviously don't know me very well, so I'm gonna let your little name calling slide. I called you for one reason and one reason only."

"What's that?" I asked, as if I could take much more of all that had been happening.

"Someone has been stalking you for a while now, right?" she asked.

"Who the fuck are you?" I asked again, stunned.

"I believe you asked me that already. Anyway, it's Stewart who's been stalking you. Just thought you should know."

"Stewart?" I asked shocked, "But- why are you telling me this?"

"Because I believe in doing good. Now I need you to return the favor."

"Return the favor? What do you want from me?"

"See? Now you're starting to ask the right questions. Look, I need you to run down to the police station and talk to the cops for me— of course you're gonna keep your mouth shut about Stewart, but tell the cops that you attempted to murder JT. I don't care what motives you make up, just do it."

"You must be crazy!"

"I'm giving you three days. That's it. If you don't do what I say, you won't live long enough to regret it."

"Are you threatening me?"

"No. I'm making you a promise. And remember, I know where you live and where you work. I know your every move. Don't fuck up. And do not tell the cops of our little chat."

I decided it was time for me to take a little

trip. I needed to get out of Pembroke Pines and go somewhere else to cool off for a while. It was a difficult decision to come to terms with, especially knowing that, with the economy the way it was, I possibly wouldn't be coming back to my two jobs. However, that was a risk worth taking, especially since my life depended on it. I'd never been there before, but I heard that Jamaica was beautiful. But what I needed, I probably wouldn't find in such a small island. Maybe I could move to Africa and do some soul searching there. I definitely needed to find myself more than anything else.

I turned on my computer, went on line and started typing. I hit the search button, then boom! Immediately the search results popped up with a wide array of travel deals. I had many options to choose from. As I researched, I noticed an ad at the top right hand corner of my computer screen. 'Great airfare deals to Cancun.' That was it! I needed to take a trip to Mexico. No telling what I'd find, or whom I'd run into while I was there. Plus, I once heard that many rich men moved to Mexico- for whatever reason. So I shifted my focus away from Africa. The lions and giraffes would just have to wait for a while. Mexico, here I come.

The Chronicles of Lexi: What a Girl Would Do to
Survive in America

CHAPTER THIRTY FOUR
NITA

"Stupid Bitch!" I hung up the phone and silently dared Sapphire to disobey me. The problem wasn't what I'd do to her if she did. The problem was what would happen to me afterwards. If she didn't do as I instructed, and I killed her, what would be my next move? What would happen to me? My fine ass had finally screwed up. And this screw up could cost me the life I'd built with Vaughnn. I think I'd taken this Lexi issue a bit too far and I'd finally bitten off a whole lot more than I could chew.

I paced the hallway mad at myself for ever hiring stupid ass Biggs, and bringing his ass here to the States so he could fuck everything up. I could have gotten the job done without his awkward, amateur ass.

All I'd asked him to do was to stalk JT, shoot him dead and return to Jamaica. Instead, he stalked JT, shot him and returned to Jamaica without ensuring that the job was done properly before he left. My cell phone rang, interrupting my thoughts.

"Hello," I answered.

"Bonita, I'm back in town."

"Biggs?"

"Yes, mon, it's me."

"Which number are you calling me from?"

"I used a pre-paid phone to call you."

"Biggs, where are you? I need to see you."

"You have another job for me?"

"Yes. I have another job for you. Wait until you hear about it. It's to die for."

CHAPTER THIRTY FIVE
VAUGHNN

Nita and I had been arrested. I'd been jailed without bail on a list of several charges that included manslaughter, money laundering and forgery. Nita was being held as my accomplice to murder. At my bail hearing, the judge, after reviewing the evidences and list of charges brought up against me by prosecutors, decided that keeping me in jail was necessary to maintain public confidence, in the administration of justice—or some shit like that. It wouldn't do me any good either, to change my good-for-nothing lawyer. It's almost as if he wanted to punk out on me now. My case was extremely serious.

Internal information had somehow been leaked, and now the Secret Service and the FBI were all over my black ass like white on rice. I'd made my mind up though. Many years ago, when I'd made the conscious decision to do the things that I'd done, I had also made up my mind to put my freedom and life at risk, in order to enjoy certain luxuries that came with my lifestyle. Was it worth it? I guess I'd have more than enough time now, to sit and figure that out. Ain't no shame in my game--well at least there wasn't. Everything was fine up until now.

As bestselling author, Agatha Christie, once said, "Where large sums of money are concerned, it is advisable to trust nobody." I wish I had clung closer to that saying. When people see you striving, even your very own become jealous of you. They begin to covet everything you possess. They lust after the things you own and the life that you live. I gave a dog a bone, and that dog turned around and bit me in the ass. Believe it or not, Stewart, my best friend and right hand man, had been biting me in the ass as well. Everything was out in the open now. I found out that he had been messing with Nita this whole time and I never even knew it. He'd managed to slide right through the hands of the law. My best friend had betrayed me and fled the country with his brothers. My lawyer told me everything. I even learnt that Lexi had gotten immunity from prosecution, in exchange for my ass. I had been the one to save Lexi, over and over and over again, yet she threw me under the bus the first chance she got. Thanks to her, I suppose the investigators had gotten enough leads to put us away for a long while.

From where I stood, things didn't look too good for me and my accomplices. The evidences supporting claims against us just seemed to pile up, more and more every day. The feds had been able to coerce many of my men into snitching on me. My men were nothing but punk bitches. All I knew was that my resentment towards Lexi Jones Miller was so strong that, if I didn't get the death penalty, she wouldn't live to see her child walk. And that was a promise.

CHAPTER THIRTY SIX
LEXI

I was two weeks away from giving birth, and I was counting down the days like a little kid at Christmas time. I actually meant that in a good way, believe it or not.   I always wanted a daughter, but I'd be having a son. I know I'll be a wonderful mother to my son. I'll do for my son everything my parents hadn't done for me. He will be a much better man than all the men that I've known.

Standing on the patio, or verandah, as they call it in Jamaica, I gently caressed my belly, while looking out at the woods across the street. It was a beautiful day. In a few hours I would be visiting JT in the hospital. I mean, what was new?   This had been the second time since reuniting with JT that he'd been struck by the enemy, and I'd have to visit him at the hospital. My heart sank when I thought about my best friend. He was still my best friend, no matter what. I totally realize now that he hadn't done anything wrong. He wasn't really cheating on me, because I wasn't really his wife. Our marriage had been nothing but a favor I'd granted him, because we were friends and that's what friends do for each other. I felt guilty for having started all this mess.

I had gone too far, and now JT was fighting for his life, because of my schemes with Stewart. But how was I supposed to know that Stewart could be so brutal, as to attempt to kill my husband? I knew that it was Stewart who'd done it. And to think that Vaughnn would have the nerve to threaten me into taking the blame for a crime I hadn't committed, in order to save his ass. He should have coerced Nita to go down for that shit, and his ass probably wouldn't be locked up right now. Making a deal with, and alerting the feds about Vaughnn's exploits was by far, the riskiest thing I had ever done, and will ever do in my entire life. What was I thinking, messing with a man like Vaughnn and his entourage? Maybe my decision to marry JT was influenced by the Almighty.

I'd been given another chance to start over, and getting married, fake or no fake, was the chance to get away from the life I'd been living in the fast lane. No way was I going to let Vaughnn screw that up. I'd now learnt one more lesson. Whatever you choose to do for others, do from the bottom of your heart. It's much more rewarding when you give and expect nothing in return. Not only is it fulfilling, it also comes back around to you seven folds. I'd been wrong for using my marriage to JT as a weapon against him.

Though he'd been doing a lot better, and continued to fight for his life, his condition remained critical. The surgeons had performed a major surgery to fix his damaged intestines and remove the first bullet. A second bullet was lodged next to his spine and remained there since it was both high risk and difficult to reach. Good thing I'd taken out a health insurance policy. The house phone rang, interrupting my thoughts.

I broke my gaze from staring at the trees outside, stepped back inside the house and moved as quickly as I could towards the phone. My heart raced as I wondered who could be calling. I desperately hoped it wasn't one of JT's doctors calling with some sort of bad news.

"Hello," I answered anxiously.

"Yes, hello. Would this happen to be JT's residence?" a deep baritone voice asked.

"Yes, I'm his wife. What's wrong?" I asked, hoping that it was nothing too serious. If I heard one more bad news, something would have to give, because I was already on the brink of madness.

"JT got married?"

"Who is this? Is JT doing alright?"

"Well, Mrs. Miller- correct?"

"Yes, I'm Mrs. Miller," I said impatiently. Whoever this was, he needed to get to the point real quick.

"My condolences to you, ma'am, I'm sorry that your husband has died."

"Shut the fuck up! JT couldn't be dead. He was doing fine last night when I left him!" Tears streamed from my eyes as I sank into a sofa and hollered.

"I beg your pardon, ma'am?"

"Check again doctor. My husband couldn't be dead! I was just with him last night," I cried as agony ripped through my veins.

"I'm sorry Miss, but I'm not a doctor. Did you say you were with JT last night?"

"Yes!" I snapped as I continued to holler. I wept and pleaded with God to bring JT back to me.

"So- JT is alive?" the caller asked.

"Is this some kind of prank?" I sniffed. I stopped crying and wondered what was going on. This wasn't making any sense.

"I apologize for not explaining myself more clearly to you, Mrs. Miller. You see, I'm calling from Jamaica. My name is Mr. Riley and I work for JT's lawyer, Mr. Freeman. A little over a week ago, we learnt that JT was dead."

"What are you talking about? JT isn't dead. Who told you he was dead?"

"You mean he's alive?"

"Yes. Who told you he was dead?"

"Thank God! That's good news. Mrs. Miller, Biggorford Thomas informed us that JT had been shot to death."

"Biggs told you that?"

"I guess that's his nickname, yes. He visited our office recently, to inquire about the documents JT had left behind before travelling to the States."

"What documents?"

"Since you're his wife, I should make you aware that JT had purchased a life insurance policy-"

"And Biggs is the beneficiary," I said, cutting him off.

"Not only that, but there's also a Will and-"

"I know of that too," I said, cutting him off again. I was puzzled.

Had JT been so careless not to have taken care of this? I remember clearly the day I'd given him the phone to make the call to Mr. Freeman.

"Biggs, as you call him, was dead certain, excuse my choice of words, that JT was dead. I've been searching high and low for some form of documentation, proving the authenticity of Tyloweschuous' passing. I found your contact information online."

"Really," I said, shocked at this new bit of information.

I wiped tears from my eyes as I questioned my sanity. I sure as hell was relieved that JT was still alive, but now I had other fishes to fry. How did Biggs know that JT had been shot? Why would he tell people that my husband was dead? Biggorford big-ass Thomas, you son-of-a-bitch!

"Mrs. Miller, are you still there?"

"Oh, I'm here," I said, clearing my throat.

"Sorry, I was just thinking. Biggs was right about my husband getting shot. We all thought he would die, but he pulled through. I forgot to call Biggs and update him. It's just that, my husband's misfortune, coupled with my pregnancy, has been very stressful on me. Plus, I lost Biggs' phone number. I wonder why he hasn't called us? He's probably upset that I didn't get back to him," I lied.

"I understand. Congratulations on your pregnancy."

"Thank you, Mr. Riley."

"Ok, I suppose I should be going now, but once things are back to normal, have your husband call our office at once, will you?"

"I sure will, umm- Mr. Riley?"

"Yes?"

"Before you hang up, I just want to say thanks."

"No problem, just doing my job. If your husband is unable to contact me himself, please feel free to follow up with me. Good luck to both you and your husband."

"Yeah, thanks again and one more thing, please."

"What's that?"

"I lost Biggs' address. Could you give it to me? I need to drop him a thank you note or something."

"Well, since you're JT's wife, I guess I could do that. Mr. Freeman will be pleased that this issue is being resolved; however, he returned to his home in Fort Lauderdale, Florida."

"Who? Mr. Freeman?"

"No, Biggs."

"So- you're saying that Biggs is here in Florida now?" I verified, wording my sentence in a way, so as not to give away the fact that I didn't know shit about Biggs.

I wrote down the address that I was given. If Mr. Riley was playing games, I'd find out soon enough.

I revved up the engine of my Z, as I neared Biggs' dwelling. If what Mr. Riley had said was true, and Biggs was here in Florida, then something was up. What the hell was he doing here, and how did he get here?

I was only three weeks away from giving birth, and the Feds were all over my ass, but I didn't give a damn. Nothing could stop me from settling my unresolved issues. Biggs had fucked with the wrong woman's husband, and I would let him pay for it.

I shook my head in disbelief. We're going through all this shit, because of Biggs' greedy ass. It was Biggs that had shot my husband. If he hadn't shot my husband, then Vaughnn wouldn't have threatened me, and I wouldn't have had a need to snitch on him. I'd still have my money in the bank, and JT wouldn't be suffering right now! I glanced over at my Prada handbag in the passenger seat. I was going to make Biggs pay, if it was the last thing on earth that I did.

I reached the Kascades Apartment Complex, in Pompano, and pulled into the parking lot. This forty five minute trip from Pembroke Pines into Pompano would be well worth it. As I parked, I suddenly noticed a convoy of police cars on the opposite end of the parking lot, along with a couple ambulances. Lights were flashing, people stood outside of their apartments gazing at the busy cops, and the firefighters seemed pre-occupied. Two men dressed in suits seemed engrossed in their discussion, as they walked outside of an apartment. They suddenly looked in my direction. I gasped when they spotted me. Why were they looking at me? There was a tap on the passenger window of my car. I looked over, and there stood Lisa Cartright, the FBI lady.

"Someone's a long way from home," she said as I rolled down the windows.

"Yeah, I know. I came to see an old friend."

"Oh," she said thoughtfully, "You mean as pregnant as you are, your friend let you journey that far to see him?"

"Yes, he doesn't know I'm coming."

"Would he happen to be Biggorford Thomas?"

"How did you- what's going on?" I rubbed my belly, and tried to control my anxiety.

"We found him dead in his apartment."

"What?" I gasped.

"Yup. He'd started working for Bonita recently. We now know who JT's shooter is. What we don't know is why he was killed. But I'm sure we'll be able to put the pieces together soon," she said, staring me dead in the eyes like she always did. I looked away from her and stared out into the distance.

"Mrs. Miller?"

"Yes, Ms. Cartright?"

"Why are you here to see Biggoford Thomas?"

EPILOGUE

I held my newborn close to me as I stepped outside into fresh air. I sighed with satisfaction as the warm summer sun soothed me. I was proud of myself. I had all rights to be proud. I kissed my son, Lexington Jr. I named him after myself. The idea was ingenious, to have given my son the first part of my name. That's right. My heart thumped with excitement as I walked towards the mailbox. I could hardly wait to mail the three letters I held in my hands.

"Your son is adorable, just adorable," Mrs. Woodstock shouted from behind the fence; her husband standing next to her smiling and waving at me.

"Thanks, Mrs. Woodstock," I replied, pleasantly this time.

Maybe I could consider inviting their nosy asses into my life. But it was just a thought. I gently shifted my son into my right arm, and held him there securely while I placed the three envelopes in the mailbox with my left arm.

The first envelope contained a letter to my Father. It was full time my daddy knew that he was now a granddad. I planned on giving him a second chance at fatherhood. I needn't keep my child away from his family, just because I hated them.

The second letter was to my mom, letting her know how much I missed her and needed her in my life. I really love my mother and I'd forgiven her mistakes. My son would also need his grandmother in his life. I had all intentions of inviting her to come and live with us.

My third letter was to my grandparents, letting them know they'd been blessed to see their third generation. How excited they will be to learn that they're now great grandparents.

As for Uncle Desmond- well he can kiss my ass.

This baby in my arms would be the miracle that would bring my shattered family back together again. I know I'm too old to be saying this but, perhaps my mom and dad will get back together- who knows? No matter how old children get, they'll always be happy to see their parents together. But if that doesn't work out, I know that things would still be alright.

I glanced over the fence as I walked back into
the house, and saw the old couple still smiling at
me. I smiled back at them and went inside.

"You're gonna spoil that child, mon," JT said,
"Give me my son."

Yeah I know you thought that Vaughnn was
the father, but bump that--I lied! Beside the
doctors, we were the only two people who knew
from the start that JT was the father of my child.
Anyway, that's none of yalls' bidniz. Like I was
saying, I put my son in JT's arms.

"Let me help you, because you are still weak,"
I told him.

"I can handle myself," He replied stubbornly.

"Ok, ok," I surrendered. "JT?"

"Yes Lexi?"

"I have a question for you."

"What's that?"

"Now that we've agreed that this is not a real
marriage, and you're free to be with whomever
you choose, who will you choose?"

"Let's see now. I'm married to you for a
green card, but we share a son. We live
together, but we've agreed to date other people.
I don't think that humans are that evolved yet to

put up with this form of arrangement. Many wouldn't understand, so I won't rush it."

"I know that, but when you do decide, do you have anyone in mind?"

"Well, if you must know," he said, then paused to heighten my curiosity, "If you must know," he jeered.

"Fool, just say it!" I demanded.

"Ok, ok. Remember when we were in Jamaica and I was at the hospital?"

"Yes," I said, eyeing him suspiciously.

"Well, remember the sexy chick that had walked in on us, and given you the fruits?"

"Who- you mean- Tanisha?"

"You got it!" he smiled wickedly.

"Why her?"

"What do you mean why her? You mean besides the fact that she's sexy and intelligent?"

"Alright, whatever," I said, "I heard that she's writing a book."

"I heard that too," he smiled, "Lexi?"

"Yes," I answered.

"What about you?"

"Who, me? Don't worry about me, I've got my man," I smiled and kissed my son's chubby cheeks.

"Are you gonna go visit him in prison?"

"Aw, hell naw you didn't!" I said busting out laughing.

"Oh, hell yes I did!" JT replied, smiling happily. Wait until I tell him that they'd killed his so-called best buddy, Biggs.

Watch out for Part II!

Part II: Teaser
JT

I stared at my cell phone, puzzled. I briefly wondered who could be calling me from a blocked number, then shook my head in disgust as I thought about Wendy.

"Hello," I answered. There was silence on the other end of the line.

"Hellooo- Wendy, I know it's you," I said, frustrated.

"This ain't no got-dang Wendy. Does this sound like Wendy to you snitch?" a gruff voice replied. My heart began to race as fear consumed me. For the past five years I'd been expecting a phone call such as this one.

"Give the phone to your wife!" the caller demanded. I stood where I was, frozen.

"Did you hear me punk? I said give the phone to your wife!"

"Wh-who is this?" I stuttered, finally finding the courage to speak.

"First name, Kharma, last name, your-worst-nightmare! How has the last five years been?"

"If y-you don't tell me who you are and wh-why you're calling, I'm going to hang up the phone and call the police."

"Call the police and I'll blow your skull to
pieces. Now, from this point forward, you're
gonna do as I say. Give the phone to your wife.
You have thirty seconds to get her on the
phone."

"JT- wait until you see the surprise I have in
store for-" Lexi's voice trailed off as she entered
the living room and saw the terrified look on my
face.

"Shhh," I whispered, as I covered the mouth
of the cell phone. I was confused as hell. I didn't
know what the hell to do next. Should I cover for
Lexi? Or should I do as I'd been told and hand
her over to the unknown caller. My family meant
the world to me. My five year old son, Lexington,
is my life.

"What's going on?" Lexi whispered.

"I think our past has come back to haunt us."

"What do you mean?"

"I think that Vaughnn is after us."

"What? But it's been five years since-"

"Somebody wants to talk to you- he said I had
thirty seconds to put you on-"

"Gimme this!" Lexi said, grabbing the phone
from my palm.

"Who is this and what do you want?" she asked.

I watched as her expression slowly mirrored mine as she listened to the caller.

"Listen to me you son-of-a-bitch! If you call this number again, I will-" Lexi paused as if she'd been interrupted by the brusque caller.
She remained silent for another minute- or two. Shit- it could have been five. Then she disconnected the call.

"What did that fool say to you, Lexi?"

"JT, I think we're being stalked."

"By whom? Why? What did he say to you?"

"He told me that soon we'll need a new sitter."

"You mean baby-sitter?"

"Yes, JT. Someone has been stalking us, he even mentioned Lexington's name- his favorite toy- favorite game-"

"I'm calling the police."

"You can't do that," Lexi said.

"Why not, Lexi? You're obviously in shock. Someone wants to harm our five year old son, and you want me to keep my mouth shut?"

"I'm trying to save our lives."

"Lexi, what did that man say to you?"

"Sit down, let me talk to you."

Acknowledgments

All praises be to God. Thank you for your guidance on this journey. Truly, I wouldn't be here today without you.

To the readers, vendors and book clubs, thanks for your support. You help to make my writing worthwhile.

Mom and Dad, I love you dearly and I admire your strength. You are truly my inspiration. Thanks for the magnificent job you have done.

Ray, I love you so much. Thanks for believing in me. You are the best brother!

Special thanks to Althia Ellis, my editor. I appreciate your hard work and dedication.

Thanks to everyone who has supported my endeavors. I'll keep up the good work just for you.

Ya girl,
Tanisha

www.ingramcontent.com/pod-product-compliance
Lightning Source LLC
Chambersburg PA
CBHW020909110726

47900CB00001B/82